I0683266

Delphi Promised

The Targon Tales

Chris Reher

Chris Reher

The Targon Tales

Sky Hunter

The Catalyst

Only Human

Rebel Alliances

Delphi Promised

Quantum Tangle

Terminus Shift

Entropy's End

also available in eBook and audio format

www.chrisreher.com

ACKNOWLEDGMENTS

Thank You to Tracy Leach, Andy Brokaw,
Dee Golberg
And Mei

Chris Reher

ONE

It took some careful maneuvering to finally free herself from a tangled bit of vegetation but, once loose, it was just a short and careful crawl across the surface of the swamp to reach her target. The massive, gray-skinned creature continued to feed contentedly, unaware of the latest parasite to climb up one of its two legs and onto its back.

Cyann tucked a rebellious strand of blue hair behind her ear and leaned forward, utterly unaware of the tension in her body or the lower lip gripped between her teeth as she crept toward the animal's humped shoulders. She figured that the two trunk-like appendages dangling from either side of its face would not be able to reach her there.

"You just hold still, beastie," she murmured, unaware of having spoken aloud.

They had determined it to be mammalian, but its skin was as hairless as a reptile's and apparently just as tough. With infinite care, she extended a small probe into its epidermis to take a sample, pleased when this didn't cause enough discomfort for her victim to start swatting the pest on its back. That tiny bit of blood and skin would provide them with endless information about this creature. Satisfied with her work, she raised herself up a little to look around the densely forested landscape.

The biped lumbered slowly through the swamp as it chewed on bulbous fungus rising above the water, only rarely using its front appendages to aid with the meal. The globes burst with a puff of spores, surrounding them in drifting clouds of orange and yellow. She secured herself a little more when her host started to move toward the rest of the small herd, eager to study their interaction. One of the others looked up and watched their approach. There was something wary about its stance and Cyann wondered if it had spotted the foreigner among them.

She smiled when it tilted its head and blinked large, intelligent eyes. Although these herbivores appeared dull and clumsy at first glance, there was something about them that made her suspect at least a rudimentary level of self-awareness – an interesting phase of any planet's evolution. The animal seemed aware of her and moved closer to inspect the strange passenger on its herd-mate's back. With ponderous care, it extended one of its appendages toward her.

A heavy hand dropped onto her shoulder and she nearly jumped out of her chair.

"Sorry!"

"Don't do that!" Cyann exclaimed. Her mental connection to the crawler probe broke when she removed the headset attached to the neural implant at her temple. She turned from her console to see Anders Devaughn, their project lead for this expedition, stand behind her bearing cups of tea. "Do you have any idea how creepy that is?"

Her boss, friend and uncle by choice grinned and looked over her head at a bank of screens displaying various angles of the research ship's marshy surroundings. "I do. That's what makes it so much fun."

"It's only fun the first few times," Cyann said, not half as annoyed as she sounded, and took a cup from his tray. She looked over to Nigel, their mission pilot and technician, bent over a workstation where he was preparing another of the silicone centipedes for deployment. "Warn me next time he sneaks up on me."

He stopped chewing his lanky blond mustache long enough to reply. "And then what would I do for fun? Ooh, tea."

"Did you get some of that fungus?" Anders asked.

"Yes," Cyann said. "And that green goo. I do think they're eggs of some kind. Amphibian, probably. Can't wait till we get below the surface of the swamp."

He regarded her thoughtfully. "Tomorrow. This is just a sampling expedition. No need to catalog the entire planet. We'll leave that to Roley's team. Bring the probe back in and then get some sleep. You look tired."

"Thanks, Uncle Anders," she said sardonically and picked up her headset. "That's something every girl likes to hear."

"I think your mother slapped me last time I said that to her." Anders dropped heavily into an empty chair beside her and scrolled through some of the data they had gathered about the planet's atmosphere and its inhabitants. "She works too much, too. But after almost thirty years around you two I still don't know when to mind my own business."

Cyann smiled at him with great fondness. A family friend rather than actually an uncle, Anders had been a part of her life since her birth and for long intervals more present than her own parents. When her interest in xenobiology had exceeded the training she was able to receive on Delphi, their home planet, she had vied for a spot on his crew aboard this science vessel and received it only after a lengthy contest. As Human as her mother, Anders understood Cyann's need to learn and discover and perhaps somehow make sense of her own peculiar origin.

She looked down at her blue fingernails, as much as her blue hair a reminder of her father's contribution to her unique status as a Human-Delphian hybrid, the only one in existence. Her clan on Delphi had accepted her and her off-worlder mother but outside that small circle she stood apart, not enough Human or Delphian to really fit anywhere. She had happily retreated into her work among newly discovered planets, far away from people who viewed outsiders with disdain and would never truly acknowledge her as one of their own.

"What is it?" Anders said, noting the darkening of her blue eyes, a sure sign among Delphians that something was bothering them.

"Tired. Like you said." She turned back to her screens and activated her neural interface to return her focus to the crawler still riding the mammal's back. "I better get the probe back before these things wander off with it."

"What'll we name them?" Anders asked.

She shrugged. "Your turn, Nigel," she called over her shoulder.

The technician rotated his cramped shoulders and then yawned hugely. "Oh, nice. I get to name the cows. You get to name the cool things with wings and teeth and loud noises." He thought a moment. "How about Cyann's Spotted Leatherbutt?"

Anders nodded and started to enter the name beside the creature's more scientific designation.

"Stop that, you two!" Cyann laughed. The quick warble of an incoming message caught her attention. "News packet is in."

She reached over to the com panel and loaded the news onto one of the screens. They caught up on developments regarding a trade agreement, an announcement of a new appointment to the Commonwealth's governing council, and disconcerting results of yet another rebel attack on Magra.

Cyann switched the report to the ship's main screen when one of the items mentioned Delphi. An asteroid of some sort was heading toward the planet. It was large enough to cause very serious damage in collision but not too large to be diverted or destroyed by Air Command technology. Remarkable, however, was that the boulder had emerged from sub-space using the same jumpsites commercial ships used to reach the Delphian sector.

"What are the odds?" Anders murmured. "Kind of

sloppy of them to let it even enter the jumpsite."

Cyann nodded. All mapped sites had at least an automated Union beacon to monitor traffic entering sub-space, mostly for the purpose of keeping track of pirates and rebels. "Must have fallen in there during someone else's transit. I think I'll skip the Low-G ball scores and get that probe back. And then I'm going to fall into my bunk for about ten hours."

She reconnected the small interface node at her temple with the ship's processors and shifted her mental focus back to her control of the crawler outside. Again taking commands directly from her brain, the probe and its small cargo of samples began to move. Her host and the rest of the herd were still grazing on the oversized mushrooms, evidently not bothered by the fog of spores they inhaled. Cyann recorded the antics of some of the juveniles before directing the crawler back toward the animal's sizable rump. It scuttled along its flank, secured to the thick hide by miniscule barbs that allowed it to cling to just about any surface.

"Crap!" she exclaimed, drawing the others' attention.

Nigel looked up at a screen. The probe had fallen off the animal and landed upside down in the mud. "Oops. Nice work, doc."

"Must have slapped me with one of its tails. Make a note that they might be ticklish around the backside. So much for having leatherbutts." Cyann maneuvered the probe, using several of its many legs to twist it. "It's caught on something."

"You're not breaking another one!" Nigel said. "These things just aren't made to stand up to your sort of abuse."

"And they're expensive," Anders added. "Can you get it loose?"

"Trying." Cyann grimaced as she worked the device. "Should have used a bug instead of the crawler. Better shoo the beasties away before one of them steps on it. Those footpads are huge."

He nodded and activated a signal to emit a low but annoying sound from the exterior of the research vessel. The animals looked up, appearing more confused than panicked, and slowly organized themselves into a tight troop that moved off into the shelter of taller vegetation.

"Hmm, no good." Cyann removed her headset. "I can't get it loose. Going to have to suit up and go get it."

"Need one more sample," Anders reminded her with a smirk. "Guess you'll have to fetch that the old fashioned way, too."

"Eh?"

"Digestion."

Cyann muttered some rather colorful language as she left the main lab space for the ship's exit area. There she stripped down to her sleeveless undershirt and tights before slipping into a hooded camouflage clean suit. It would not only shield her from the planet's as-yet unknowns but also protect this world from her own contaminants. After a short turn in the decon chamber and a check of her oxygen supply, she left the ship to step onto Cet-Norwan's moist surface.

"Damn hot out here," she said. She looked over the exterior of the ship that today was green-tinted to blend into the lush surroundings. "Seeing some condensation around the intakes," she reported. "Might want to check the coolant plugs, Nigel."

"On it," came the lazy drawl in reply. "You just go play with your pets and leave the hardware to me."

"The crawler is straight ahead by that mossy boulder," Anders said through the speaker near her ear. "Don't dawdle out there. We're nowhere near ready for contact."

"I see it. It's floating." She moved slowly to give the sensors in her boots time to react to the ground's density and alert her of any deep spots below the marshy surface. The leather-skinned herd of ruminants still huddled among some taller growth, watching her warily from the distance. "Interesting. They have their backs turned to me, but they're keeping an eye out. Juveniles in the center of the group."

"That tail swishing might be agitation," Anders said. "Keep moving. Also, I've got something approaching from your right. Might be more leatherbutts. Don't get in the middle of them." He sent another sound signal through the clearing. "And don't forget a scoop of the poop."

"Yes, yes, can't forget that, can we?" she said and reached into a bag attached to her suit to find a sample container. "Looks like some droppings over there." She turned when a nervous squawk emitted from the herd. As one, they stomped away into the green shadows of the undergrowth. "Where is everybody going?"

"Life form behind you, Cyann. Big one. Return immediately."

"Just grabbing the crawler. I don't see it."

"It floated over to your right."

"Where?" she twisted awkwardly to peer out from behind the visor of her protective suit.

"Leave it for now. We'll come back in a bit."

"There it is." She walked to the edge of the clearing where the water moved more briskly into a small stream draining from the swamp. She stepped over a few larger stones and bent to pick up the device. "Ugh. Sorry, Nigel, we lost a few legs on this one." She slipped it into her pouch and turned to retrace her steps. "Damn!"

"What?"

"Stuck on something. These boots are too big for me."

"Let's get you back on board," Anders said nervously.

Something splashed behind her. And splashed again, like something taking long strides through the marsh. Then they all heard a high-pitched shriek tear through the spore-fogged air, soon answered by another. Disconcertingly, it seemed to come from a considerable height. All of the other animals had disappeared and she suddenly felt strangely abandoned by them.

"Cyann, come on!"

She bent to pull on the boot attached to the bottom of her suit. A few trickles of sweat traced along her cheek, plastering her hair to her skin and obscuring her vision even further. So far they had not detected any overtly hostile species on this planet but what had made her leave the ship without her stunner?

She felt her heart beat somewhere high in her throat and forced herself to breathe evenly. She drew upon ancient Delphian mental disciplines to force her mind into a tranquil state of *khamal*, a level of guarded awareness that would allow her to block distractions. She felt her training and her heritage do its job to replace her panic with something a little more serene.

Another strident alarm rang through the clearing, this time from the ship. And then another, less mechanical, cry answered, followed by something crashing through the undergrowth.

"You know, uncle," she said, jerking on the boot wrenched tightly between the rocks. "I think maybe that's what's attracting things."

"Nigel's coming for you," he said, clearly close to panic. "I don't have a clear shot from here. Don't rip your suit unless you have to. Too many poisons out there."

"It's all right. I'm clear." She walked back toward the ship as quickly as the soggy ground allowed. "Whoa!" A biped had broken into the clearing to her right, looking very much like a bird but covered so densely in blue-black fluff that any wings it might have had were not visible. She was reminded of the ostrich-like birds so common on Shaddallam, a planet not far from this one. Except this one was easily five times their size and its beak bore a lining of short spikes. "Are you getting this? Avian, likely flightless."

"Dammit, Cyann!"

She broke into a trot, returning along the muddy tracks her boots had made on her way here. The splashing sound followed her, more rapidly now, and then something massive kicked at her legs to knock her down as if she was no more substantial than the marsh reeds that surrounded her. She was thrown forward, painfully aware that she had just been stepped on. When she lifted her head she saw into an open maw large enough to swallow her whole.

Soon.

"Soon?" she said.

"What?" Nigel said through her speakers. "Curl up, Cyann. Don't be such a target."

"Get up! Cyann! Move!"

"Well, which is it?" she snapped.

Out here. Out here.

Cyann froze, still sprawled in the muck. Someone was there. Someone, something had joined the mental state she had initiated through her khamal. She gasped when this something touched her thoughts, barely there, yet immensely vast. She reached out for it, unable to tear her attention away. *I hear you*, she returned.

"Cyann?" she heard Anders. "Come on!"

She stared numbly at the enormous creature looming over her and remained still. At another time she would have felt as panicked as Anders sounded but nothing could now tear her away from that frail mental contact.

The bird seemed to consider the snack placed before it and then stabbed its formidable beak into the ground beside her. She rolled away from it, aware of her complete absence of fear. Did it not see her? After churning up some of the mud with its forceful pecking, it stabbed into a deeper puddle and lifted its head again to display a shiny and wiggling creature clamped in its beak. It tipped its head back to swallow the meal and then regarded Cyann with serene disinterest. After a few moments it lifted its stilt-like legs with meticulous care and continued on its way through the swamp.

She watched it move away, only dimly aware of Nigel wading toward her, looking weirdly alien in his bulky enviro-suit.

The strange presence in her mind faded. She reached for it, tried to snatch it back before it could leave her again, but it floated away like the puffs of mushroom spores all around them.

Help me.

Nigel had reached her and pulled her up, a gun ready in his other hand.

"I'm all right. It just didn't see me," Cyann mumbled and looked around. "It's gone now," she added, but she did not mean the bird.

He ushered her back to the *Scout* where he supervised her through the decon sequence before allowing her inside and then into the med station for a quick medical scan. When she finally escaped his attentions to get a change of clothes in her cabin, Anders awaited her for another round of scolding.

"What was that about?" he said. "You should have returned to the ship at once. You should have taken a gun. What were you thinking?"

Cyann frowned. "It's not dangerous."

"We have no way of knowing that. You know better than this."

She nodded all too aware that she deserved the reprimand. "Something was out there. It spoke to me."

"What are you talking about?"

"I heard its thoughts."

"Telepathy? That bird?"

"No, not the bird." She hesitated a while, staring at nothing. "Someone out there. Reaching for me. Picking up on my khamal."

He tilted his head. "You know that isn't possible."

"Of course I know," she said more sharply than she really meant to. Whether used to heal or to share an emotion or even to communicate telepathically, the khamal mind-link used by Delphians had to be initiated by touch. Few exceptions existed and certainly not for her, who was only half Delphian or her Human mother, who was only able to engage through the use of a mechanical interface embedded in her brain. "But there was something there. It... it's familiar. Like..." she glanced at him before shifting her eyes away from his penetrating gaze. "Like before."

He exhaled forcefully and sat down beside her on her bunk, his voice more gentle. "That was a very long time ago. You were a child then. Nothing but mental echoes and imaginary friends. Isn't that what the Shantirs decided?"

"They did," she sighed. Nobody knew to what extent her hybrid brain obeyed Delphian mental disciplines and she had been both a vexation and an intellectual puzzle for several of the elder Shantirs that had taken an interest. The peculiar presence she had sometimes encountered had been dismissed as harmless manifestations of her mentors' own khamal state, somehow perceived by the precocious child. The Shantirs' Human counterparts at the Union's clinics had declared it to be the girl's desire for kinship among those who saw her as an outsider. Childhood fantasies that would dissipate with age. No one had warned her that they'd return to plague her adulthood.

"What did it say?" Anders asked cautiously.

She turned her haunted face to him. "Help me."

Anders suppressed the shiver that started low on his back and moved upward to his nape. He reached out to straighten the disheveled blue strands around her face. Her azure eyes had paled to flat and lifeless disks above dark shadows looking like bruises. "You're too tired," he said. "Working too hard."

"I'm fine, Anders. You work just as hard and so does Nigel. I can do my share."

"Well, something's not right. You've been tired and edgy and your attention wanders. That's not like you. I've been around you Delphians for all of my life and I still don't really understand how your mind works. But even I know that hearing random voices isn't part of things. I need you on your game out there. Not distracted by phantoms." He came to his feet. "We're leaving here in a few days and then you're going straight to the Shantir enclave to report this. Let them have a look inside that pretty head of yours. Get yourself some rest while you're there. You know I can't have you on my team if you're not in top shape."

She sighed. "Yes, Uncle."

He bent to kiss the top of her head. "Now, meanwhile, you're not to leave the ship by yourself and that's your boss telling you."

TWO

Being woken by the sound of shifting drives and the automatic adjustments of a ship's internal systems had long ago become a familiar way to start the day. Jovan allowed himself to rise out of his doze-like khamal and stretched his long legs. He remembered now that he was no longer aboard his own vessel, the one that had taken him far beyond the Trans-Targon sector in search of knowledge for these past eight years. For once someone else was doing the piloting. All of the jumpsites in this sector were solidly mapped and did not require a navigator of his caliber.

He sat up and, yawning, ran his hands through his thick blue hair. The bench that had cradled him since leaving his crew on Targon over ten hours ago was far more comfortable than those he was used to but his mind was already on tonight's sleep. His pale lips curved in a smile when he imagined himself wallowing in the comfort of a real bed, the windows of his room open to the smells and sounds of his home planet – he'd forgotten to check what time of year it was on Delphi but he promised himself open windows and fresh air anyway. And he would walk in the hills again to feel that wonderful cool breeze from the northern mountains.

"Shan Jovan?" a gentle voice intruded upon his idle

thoughts.

He looked up at an attendant walking down the rows of sleep lounges. Some of the other passengers now also stirred in preparation of landing.

"Shan Jovan, the captain requests that you join her in the cockpit."

"Is everything all right?"

"Yes, all is well." The young man smiled blandly and moved away down the aisle.

Jovan pulled himself up and ducked into the walkway to turn toward the service areas of the ship. He had taken a commuter trip on an Air Command sleeper, not quite as luxurious as some of the commercial passenger craft but it was faster and had allowed him to leave directly from the base on Targon for Delphi. He was not a commissioned officer but the research expedition, largely in search of new keyholes that could be turned into navigable jumpsites, had been entirely funded by the Commonwealth's military. The perks were considerable.

He knocked on the cockpit door which opened almost at once.

"Come in, let's not be formal," he was greeted.

Jovan stepped into the small space where the captain, her navigator and the com officer turned to him expectantly. All of them were Centauri, judging by their glossy black hair and eyes that carried a mild violet glow in the dim light. The captain, a broad-shouldered, crew-cut woman whose uniform threatened to come apart at the seams waved him into a vacant seat beside her.

"Come sit," she shouted without having any real need to shout. "We're honored to have you aboard our humble little ship. Rumor has it you've been to the Badlands and back."

"They're not so bad," Jovan said and took the offered seat.

"Crazy far place to travel to," she said. "Of course, me and my crew don't shuttle farther than Delphi, maybe Magra the odd time. I like that just fine."

Jovan smiled politely, thinking that he could imagine no more tedious jaunt than to ferry passengers from Targon's bleak military hub to Delphi where off-worlders weren't even allowed to leave the base.

"I hear you've been gone years now," she said.

"Eight, Delphi time."

"Well, the boys and I thought you might want to see it right away." She turned to her controls to roll the ship and grinned broadly as the blue and white ball that was Delphi slowly appeared on the ship's main view screen.

Jovan exhaled audibly. "You are so right, Captain," he said, unable to tear his gaze away from the planet. He couldn't remember if he had looked back when he left here, so eager had he been to embark on his latest assignment. He had seen many planets from a distance since earning his navigator's credential but few of them rivaled Delphi in its breathtaking beauty. Oceans and mountains, clouds and storms, ice and forests, no deserts. And dancing around it all a scattering of moons, ensuring that night never fell completely on Delphi.

"Happy to be coming home?" she said. "I'm sure not much has changed since you left."

"I'm pretty sure of that, too," he replied, liking that just fine. He had no real family on Delphi but called no other place home. Both of his parents had died early and his abilities had qualified him to move to one of the enclaves to study with the Shantirs, adding a wealth of neuroscience to his education. Had he not met Major Tychon and his Human mate, Lieutenant Colonel Nova Whiteside, he would now be part of the sect, a lifelong vocation. But instead of taking up the blue robes of the Shantir to study the mysteries of the mind and its effects on matter, he had turned to deep space on his quest for knowledge of the outside worlds. It was Nova who had made sure that he returned between assignments to complete his studies and become a full-fledged Shantir. And it was Tychon who had mentored him to become a Level Three navigator. They were his family and he felt a stab of excitement when he thought of seeing them again.

Jovan realized that he had missed something when the captain turned to him with a quizzical expression.

"Sorry, I was enraptured." He smiled with a nod to the planet.

"I was asking if you're here for the fireworks."

"What fireworks?"

"Asteroid heading this way. Small one. Got a few ships keeping an eye on it. It's on a direct course for Delphi but they want a look at it first before they divert it. Might even bounce it off Delphi. That ought to be pretty."

He nodded. "Looks like my timing is good, then."

She tilted her head. "I hope you don't mind, but I have to ask. What'll the folks think when they see you with your hair in this state?"

Jovan's hand involuntarily reached up to brush through the thick shock of blue. Although it was far from short now, he had given up the veritable mane prized by Delphian males. All of them grew their hair long, often kept in a single braid, and cutting it off was nearly unthinkable. He had not meant to go against convention when he had asked a crew mate to remove his braid. The long tresses were impossible to maintain on a voyage where personal grooming was often a luxury. In the throes of regret he had later asked a more fashion-conscious friend to shape it neatly.

He winced when he looked ahead to the disapproving looks he was sure to collect from his Shantir elders. Unshakably traditionalists, change did not come easy to Delphians and some of the notions considered fashionable on other worlds were usually met with contempt. Rarely voiced, of course, but expressed by politely ignoring the whole thing as though it never existed. He doubted he'd get away with it so easily, given that his adopted clan included a number of Humans whose forthright ways had rubbed off on the rest of them.

"I hope they won't notice," he said.

The captain gaped at him for a moment before bursting into raucous laughter. "I see you picked up a sense of humor, too, on your travels. They won't know what to make of you."

* * *

Lieutenant Colonel Nova Whiteside's sense of humor was nowhere in evidence on this day when once again Air Command's ideas of interplanetary relations did not seem to mesh very well with those of Delphi.

"Are you sure this is necessary?" She scowled at the screen. "What's so special about this one?"

"I have no idea, other than that it's extrasolar," the Centauri officer responded with a shrug. Stationed on Targon where far more pressing issues vied for her attention, she seemed quite happy to let Nova deal with this. "We're guessing it's packing something interesting. And since it came through sub-space we haven't a clue about its origin. You think you can keep everyone happy over there?"

Nova sighed. Just an hour ago word had come that the small asteroid heading for Delphi would be captured and locked into a high orbit over the planet. That meant an orbiting research station was already on its way here, there would be more ships on the ground, more security, more traffic. In other words, everything that Delphi loathed about its minimal interaction with the Commonwealth of United Planets but had learned to tolerate in exchange of trade and for protection against the Union's rebel enemies. Having what they would think of as someone else's asteroid parked in their air space was not going to please them. "How many civilians?"

"None on the ground." The Centauri's words were delayed by only a few seconds while her communication was nearly instantly relayed through the single jumpsite between here and Targon. "Couple of supply trips maybe. You'll see a few more Destroyers till they've locked it in. But we've asked everyone to stay upside. I doubt they'll be in orbit long enough to get a hankering for land."

"All right then," Nova said. If they could keep all but the military planes from landing and if no one decided to take a stroll off the base, this whole thing might go nearly unnoticed by most of Delphi's reclusive population. "I'll let the Council know," she said. "Let's hope this goes quickly."

Nova was eager to hand this assignment back to the regular base commander who was currently also on Targon. In a few more weeks she would return to her post there, busy with a batch of recruits fresh out of flight school and happily distracted while Tychon, her Delphian mate, joined Anders and their daughter Cyann on their latest research expedition.

She looked up when her Delphian aide knocked on the transparent wall of her workspace. She waved for her to enter while she signed off from Targon. "Can you believe this?" she mumbled. "One little chunk of dirt and they get all excited. The Council will no doubt think it's some clever ploy to spy on them."

"Isn't it?" The young woman grinned.

"Don't you start!" Nova slipped into her uniform jacket. "How are we doing for time?"

"Transport is here. And your boyfriend is, too."

"Finally something I want to hear." Nova went to the window overlooking the air field and the ground vehicle depot to see Tychon in conversation with one of the mechanics. A cold wind from the mountains cut mercilessly across the tarmac to whip the long strands of his blue hair around his head. He gathered his fleece-lined coat tighter and turned to look up to where she stood, as always acutely aware of her presence. The expression on his sharply profiled face did not change when he walked into the building. "The others aren't with him?"

"Who are you expecting?"

"Anders and Cyann were going to come up to welcome Jovan home." Nova ran her hands over her red hair to catch a few wayward strands and went to the door. They now felt the dull thrumming of the interstellar transport lowering its bulk onto the air field. "What a reunion, with all of us here at the same time for a change! Cyann's going to be so excited to see him."

Tychon met her in the cavernous main entrance lobby of the base where a few soldiers and civilians waited to board the transport for the return trip to Targon. She matched his brisk pace toward one of the nearby lounges. "Lieutenant Colonel," he said in greeting.

"Major," she replied just as formally. They stopped briefly to let her officially sign off duty for the day. Her promotion in ranks beyond his had been a calculated move for them, allowing her to position herself to permanently take over command of the military base on Delphi within the next few years. It promised a relatively easy transition into their eventual retirement on their clan's sprawling estate in the valley. No longer active Vanguard agents, their interest had shifted to less dangerous but no less interesting work. Nova had discovered a love for teaching and Tychon, although barely one hundred years old, had withdrawn from active duty to finally find time to join Anders on research missions.

Once they entered the lounge, Nova hurried to an observation window but saw little more than the exterior of the well-traveled commuter ship. With typical Delphian courtesy, an umbilical had been extended to keep the arrivals out of the biting wind only to delay them with tedious immigration procedures before allowing them onto the base. "Where are Anders and Cyann?" She turned back to Tychon who was shrugging out of his coat.

"He's gone to pick her up at the enclave. She stayed there overnight." He endured silently when she reached up to straighten the long hair hanging over his shoulders. When she fussed with his collar he caught her hands in his. "You left early this morning."

"Had to make up some time. So much work with the new arrivals coming in."

"Can you get away tomorrow? You're heading for Targon soon and we'll be on Cet-Norwan by the time you get back.

We'll be gone two months." His fingertips touched her chin and then brushed upward to her temple. She smiled when she felt him contact the neural interface at her temple to join his mind to hers. They did not exchange words – telepathy with a non-Delphian was painful for him and they used it only when necessary. But his soothing presence in her head had become a state of being for her; something they both enjoyed and craved. "So little time, so much to do," he added with a slow grin.

"You are referring to our guests?" She stood on her toes to kiss him negligently. "A full house again! Jovan, Cyann, Anders!"

"Yes." He dropped into a lounge and propped his feet on a nearby bench. "That's what I was referring to."

She sent him a mental touch that left no doubt that she knew exactly to what he was referring. He drew a hissing breath. "Brat," he said.

Nova glanced through the glass wall overlooking the entrance hall to see if she could get away with something a little more physical but a group of returning pilots had a clear view of whatever she might devise to torture her husband. She smiled happily when one of the tall Delphians among them angled toward the lounge.

"There he is," she said. "Oh, he's changed so much!" She watched Jovan enter the room, noting that his lanky frame had filled out but had not lost the careless grace she remembered. These past few years had aged his face, or perhaps his adventures had, but he made no effort to practice the tight-lipped restraint of his people and instead grinned broadly when Nova flung herself into his arms. She bounced up to kiss his cheek, this time caring not one bit what the travelers in the hall thought of their commanding officer in such a display. "You're home! I missed you so, Jovie. I can't believe you're here." She stepped back to admire him. "Can you possibly get any more handsome? Ty, doesn't he look like a proper explorer?"

Jovan glanced toward Tychon and made a few ineffective

attempts to smooth his well-worn leather jacket and straighten the threadbare straps of his kit bag. "Shan Tychon," he said respectfully.

Tychon had come to his feet and stared at his protégé with astonishment. "You cut your hair?"

Nova tugged on Jovan's sleeve to turn him. His blue hair was cut in a fetching way but there was no braid trailing over his back. She bit her lip before mentioning that she actually found his new look rather attractive.

Jovan turned back and put his arm around her shoulder, possibly as a defensive measure against Tychon's disapproval. "Yes. It's a long story. So! Where is Cyann?"

"On her way," Nova said with a glance at Tychon. He was still studying Jovan's coiffure, his expression unreadable. "She is going to tease you without mercy about your haircut. How was your trip?"

Jovan grinned. "The last eight years or the jaunt from Targon?"

"Don't think we haven't been studying your reports ever since you got back into com range. By now Tychon knows more about your travels than you probably remember. What wonderful things you've seen." She nudged him to sit on one of the broad lounges. "You've made him all itchy to head out with Anders in a few days. Your timing is excellent."

Tychon came to sit with them. "Just a short cataloging trip to Cet-Norwan," he said. "But we may have found a sentient species related to the ancients of Gramor and Pella."

"That would make quite a mystery," Jovan said, interested. "There's not even a keyhole linking those systems."

"How long will you be on Delphi?" Nova asked.

"A while. I had my med tests on Targon but I need to catch up at the enclave. Then I want to get some real air, some real food, some real hot baths."

"You'll stay with us, of course," Nova said. "Not that dreary enclave. The Shantirs can wait. There is a huge meal waiting for you at home and all the hot water you want."

Jovan smiled broadly. "You don't know how much I've missed that. Well, and you, of course," he added quickly. "And my little Cyann. Did she ever forgive me for leaving?"

"She got over her crush eventually," Nova smiled, remembering a time when Cyann had regarded Jovan as every handsome hero of the adventure stories she used to read. "Too busy for boys right now, I think. She's become a very accomplished biologist. Her work with Anders has drawn attention all the way to Targon. She also did a year on Aikhor as a field medic. It was time well spent."

"Until she almost got herself killed trying to patch up a bunch of rebels," Tychon added with a scowl. "She has a good heart, but I found myself vindicated for insisting on combat training for her, as much as she hated it."

Jovan laughed. "Cyann? With a gun?"

"Don't scoff," Tychon said. "She's nearly as good a shot as Nova. Ended up blasting her way out of there and escaped on a half-dead charger. Her regret was having killed the men that she just spent all that effort in healing."

Jovan shook his head. "I've missed a lot."

"You'll catch up," Nova promised. "And while we're on that subject, hand it over."

He threw a knowing glance at Tychon. "You saw that, huh?" He shifted to withdraw the gun lashed to his thigh. She took it eagerly and turned toward the light of the window to inspect it more closely. "It's yours," he added. "You'd rob me at gunpoint for it otherwise, anyway."

The men watched her expertly handle the weapon as she examined it for the new innovations he had brought back. "You're a sweet boy. How did they get this so compact?" she marveled. "This comes from Cha'el?"

"Well, that's what the smuggler said. You'll have to test it. I'd love to know where we can get more of those."

"I'll be the envy of Targon with this. I'll have to show it off for a while before we take it apart."

Jovan turned to Tychon. "Does Cyann at least still appreciate pretty baubles brought at huge expense from the

Badlands, even if Nova prefers rail guns?"

Tychon sighed dramatically. "She's her mother's daughter. If the pretty bauble you brought back comes with a caliper or a gene map, it's sure to please." He smiled when he felt Nova's touch in his mind like a playful kiss.

They turned to the door when it slid aside to bring Anders into the room. He also wore a heavy coat and clapped his arms in an effort to get warm. "Here you are. And a wise choice that is, what with it being cold enough outside to freeze the gonads off a polar daram. Right balmy in the valley compared to this."

"Hey, Anders," Nova said. "We've been worried."

"No, we haven't," Tychon said in lieu of greeting his Human brother-friend. "Where's Cyann?"

"Uh, she went to the ship for a bit. Said she had to shut down a centrifuge."

Nova frowned and glanced at Jovan. "She had to do that now?"

"Apparently," Anders said. He spread his arms and Jovan dutifully submitted to the traditional Human greeting involving embrace and full body contact that most Delphians viewed with curious amusement. Anders released him to scrutinize him through narrowed eyes. "What happened to your hair, Jovie?"

"What happened to yours!" Jovan replied, jerking his chin at Anders, whose closely cropped blond hair had turned completely white now.

"Never mind that," Tychon interrupted. "It's not like Cyann to be rude." He raised his arm to activate his com.

Anders put his hand on Tychon's wrist to stop him from calling her. "She'll be along shortly," he said. "She's... I don't know. Give her some room."

"What do you mean?" Nova said. "She was feeling better yesterday."

"Is she ill?" Jovan said.

Anders shook his head. "I don't know. Something is bothering her. Trouble concentrating. Had a close call with a native species on Cet-Norwan. Not sleeping well. And yet she refuses treatment from the Shantirs. Shan Moghen is very concerned about her." He ran his hand over the silky stubble on his head. "That voice is back. She's very disturbed by that, I think."

Nova gasped. "It's back? It's been years."

"Has it?" Tychon pondered. "You'd think she'd mention something if it had come back all of a sudden."

"Why wouldn't she?"

He shrugged. "Kids don't tell their parents everything."

"Stop it, you two," Anders said, sounding exasperated. "She is not a kid. You seem to forget that she's only half Delphian. No one knows how old she really is, compared to her peers. She's leaps ahead of people in her age group. I'm guessing she's catching up to Jovan's age now. She's got your massive streak of mischief, Nova, but she's proven a maturity that I'd not expect from a Delphian her age." His pale eyebrows drew together when he looked directly at Nova. "You should know better. But even you only see the Delphian there because that's what she looks like. Well, she's not all Delphian. And she is not a child, so stop treating her like one."

The others gaped at him in silent astonishment.

Anders seemed surprised by his own outburst. "Well, it's true," he said more calmly. "I've been working with her for years now. I see what she's capable of. But not only do we not know how old she is, we don't know how her mind works. The difference between Human and Delphian is largely cerebral and so far not even the Shantirs have figured out that synapse anomaly. Who knows what's going on in her head? If she's suffering some sort of mental aberration we need to find out, not grief her for showing up late."

Tychon nodded thoughtfully. "And we're not likely to find out if she won't talk about it or allow the Shantirs to help her."

"Isn't there anybody who might know what's going on?" Jovan said.

Anders shook his head. "Not really. I'm as close to her as anyone. She gets along with the crew, but they're just colleagues. She spends a fair bit of time with one of the younger Shantirs at the enclave. Tava, I think his name is."

Jovan made a hissing sound and sat back.

"What?" Nova asked.

"Not the most upstanding specimen ever produced by the enclave," he replied. "Although I haven't seen him in a long time, either, so who knows."

"Tell me more," Tychon said, a dangerous edge in his voice. Nova winced when she felt the change of his mood. Although he valued the Shantirs' tremendous mental abilities he barely tolerated their presence and avoided them as much as he could. He did not fault Jovan for joining their sect – it was the previous generation that had irrevocably harmed his clan, long ago. It had taken years before he had allowed them access to his only daughter so that they could study the peculiar circumstances of her birth. So far, none of them had given him reason to regret that decision.

Jovan raised his hands in a placating gesture. "Just a bit of a tosspot," he said quickly. "I would not worry."

"Yes, she's safe at the enclave," Anders hastened to reassure. "She'll come around. I told her that I won't let her crew if Shan Moghen has any doubts about her fitness. That should be enough incentive to let him take a look. But I know she's following her khamal exercises and she already seems a lot more relaxed."

Tychon's frown did not leave his face.

"I'll take a room at the enclave," Jovan offered. "Maybe I can be of help there."

"I think that'll put our minds at ease," Nova said. "But not until tomorrow. You're in desperate need of that meal I promised. Look at you! You're so thin and pale!"

Anders nudged her with an elbow. "Delphian, remember?" He grinned at Jovan. "Don't worry. She didn't prepare any of it. They've got a new cook that'll have you begging for thirds."

Jovan leaned back with a deep sigh of relief, which earned him a painful pinch to the thigh from Nova.

"There she is," Nova said, probably louder than necessary, when her daughter entered the lounge. "Hello, Cyann. Come look who fell out of the sky today."

Cyann seemed startled when all four of them came to their feet. Then the fleeting glimpse they had had of her tired face disappeared and was replaced by the beguiling smile that could turn the mood of even the most dour of Shantirs. "I'm sorry," she said. "I forgot to close up one of our experiments." She winced when she looked at Anders. "The centrifuge shut down on its own but I'm afraid the sample is spoiled. I'll start again tomorrow."

Anders shook his head at this triviality and then tilted it toward Jovan.

Cyann turned to her family's one and only liege and it seemed for a moment that she would, as had always been her custom, careen across the room and into his arms, as impulsive and affectionate as her Human mother. But instead she just smiled warmly. "Welcome home, Jovie," she said. "We have missed you."

Nova peered at the young Shantir, a little surprised by Cyann's stilted greeting. What she saw there, however, was even more surprising. She had heard his quick intake of breath when Cyann had entered the room and now he was staring at her with an expression she had not seen on his face before. Gradually, whatever it was faded behind the practiced mask of indifference that Delphians used to keep their thoughts private.

"Hello, Cy, I've missed you, too," he said.

Did you see that? Nova sent to Tychon.

He started at the small jab of pain when she did that. *See what?*

Not sure. Did these two have a fight or something before he left?

Not that I know of. Tychon studied Jovan's bland expression for a moment before returning a mental shrug. *Probably worried about her. She's not even noticed his hair.*

Not going to task him about that, are you?

He ran a long-fingered hand through his own tresses. *Suits him. Think it'll suit me?*

Don't even think about it!

Nova stepped forward and slung her arm around Cyann's waist. "Let's get home before someone notices I'm still around and starts complaining about the astronomy experiment going on over our heads." She herded them toward the door. "No doubt I'll have half the Council on my doorstep in the morning because of that asteroid."

THREE

"You are still not finding it?"

Cyann shifted her eyes from the crystal display in front of her to the Shantir seated below the curved window of the meditation room. "I try, Shan Regin."

She said nothing for a long while during which she returned her attention to the focus of her meditation. The khamal she was using was meant to reach beyond the physical boundaries of herself to help her find the source of these rare thoughts that were not her own. She breathed deeply, as always enjoying the aroma of waxed wood and the healers' herbal medicines permeating the entire communal wing of the enclave. Although she had not linked her mind to the Shantir, she felt the woman's soothing presence as much as the scents.

The Shantir nodded to another cleric that had shared the room. He rose fluidly from his mat and left them alone. "Why are you afraid?" Regin said.

"I am?" Cyann replied.

"It's what I feel from you."

"I'm afraid you won't let me rejoin the expedition."

"You would be right," Regin said dryly. She straightened an already impeccable fold of her long blue vest. "But that wasn't my point."

Cyann shrugged. "I'm not afraid of anything at the moment. Anders Devaughn is making too much of nothing. I was tired and I got distracted."

"But the voice?"

"You said yourself that I could be catching random patterns. Mental echoes from other species. Memories. Shantir meditations, even. You've always maintained that theory."

The Shantir seemed to ponder this. "Yet you feel that this voice is speaking to you. Calling to you."

"It could well have been coming from one of the natives we were studying. We don't know anything about them. I really do think that I was picking something up from them. Surely it's something we should study, no? So I need to go back there and check it out."

Regin smiled. "You are persuasive. Let me talk to the others. We'll decide tomorrow."

Cyann nodded and stretched her legs a moment before standing. The Shantir's decision had more weight than even the doctors at the Union's base clinic. Not only was the expedition to Cet-Norwan funded by Delphi's considerable scientific community, but Cyann had long ago been declared by the Clan Council as Delphian. No off-worlder ever argued with the Shantirs on the matter of Delphian mental states. And it would not occur to Anders, who had lived among them all his life, to question their authority in this. "I'll come back at noon."

She bowed respectfully and slipped out of the room and into the silent hallway. A few Shantirs and their initiates passed her. The elder Shantirs nodded, as always strangely deferential to the accident of her birth which made her the enclave's most revered mystery. She had no real idea why that would be so; both her own and her parents' genes had been studied in excruciating detail. Whatever hadn't been discovered by now would likely remain a secret, she thought. The younger Shantirs simply regarded her warily, as though she might sprout an extra nose or two. No one questioned her presence here in the publicly accessible section of the enclave.

She turned a corner at the end of the hall and hurried into one of the enclave's residential wings. The broad corridor served as a commons area, furnished with comfortable benches arranged companionably along a glass wall. It offered a pleasant view of the gardens and fields where even now some of the novices worked to prepare for the growing season. Although supported by the people to whom they dispensed healing, the sect preferred to be as self-sustaining as possible, beholden to not even the governing body of Delphi. It was no secret that it was the Council, in fact, that took much direction from their advisors within the enclave.

To her left a long row of doors running the full length of the wing led to the private rooms used by the Shantirs. Cyann quickly walked to the end and tapped on one of them. After a few moments Tava appeared and looked over her shoulder into the hall. "I did not think I would see you today," he said.

She stepped into his room. Like all of them, it was plain but comfortable, furnished in polished wood and several interesting tapestries. "I was with Shan Regin. I told you that. I'm hoping she'll let me go back out tomorrow."

He regarded her silently, without expression. It was not often that he allowed anything to show on his face and she told herself that she didn't care enough to find what he might be thinking. It was just a Delphian custom to display emotions only among closest kin and rarely meant any sort of subterfuge anyway. But the hard blue eyes in his hatchet face seemed to see a little more than she was prepared to share and she began to regret coming here today. She walked to the small balcony, little more than a platform with a low railing, overlooking the eastern mountain range.

"You know, maybe I should just get some sleep before tomorrow," she said, still looking outside. But he came to stand close behind her and she felt his hands on her shoulders.

"That isn't what you want, though, is it?" he said. His fingers brushed along her neck and then to the side of her head.

She closed her eyes and shook her head.

"You want to try again?"

"Yes," she whispered and almost at once felt his presence slip into her mind to create the khamal mind-link. His touch was as edgy and harsh as Regin's was soothing but this was what she needed. This made it work.

"Come sit," he said and turned her toward his sleeper, a neatly made-up couch along one of the walls of the narrow room. She obeyed, feeling his touch inside her head expand and take hold. Far more intrusive than the expert contact of the elder Shantirs, it felt both familiar and frightening. He eased his grip, asking for her trust and her surrender to his ministrations.

She smiled when she let her mind wander free to float weightlessly somewhere out there in the distance and yet deep inside herself. Why would anyone ever want to be anywhere else? She sighed contentedly when he took her further into this void, almost as enraptured by this as she was.

"Anything?" he whispered.

She reminded herself of the reason why she was here, why she had asked him for this most secret, most forbidden, of all khamals. As before, she began to look for the voice, casting her thoughts far beyond the confines of this planet and this solar system, somewhere out there where she believed the plaintive messages originated. "No," she said, barely audible.

He pushed her further outside herself and she allowed him to settle her into the pillows of his bed. She was only dimly aware of him now and no longer sure where she was. Or why she was here at all. She winced when the sensations he brought about seemed almost painful in their intensity. "Still not there." But perhaps something had woken. Something had noticed her. Yes! She smiled and reached out to that distant entity to lure its attentions.

"Maybe," the Shantir said, looking into her unfocused eyes. The blue-tinted corners of his lips twitched in what might have been a smile. "If you weren't just a half-breed Humanoid you'd be able to actually do this."

"Uh, what?" she said indistinctly, not sure what she had heard him utter.

"You'll never be Delphian, no matter how hard you try. You might as well make yourself useful in other ways around here." He stretched out beside her and, vaguely, she felt his hand on her waist, moving upward. "It's not bad enough that you're half Human, you're a GenMod freak like your mother. I've never understood why my esteemed Elder Brothers take you as one of their own. You're an abomination." He tugged her loose blouse from her waistband and let his hand slip around her back to touch the silky line of hair trailing along her spine, a most intimate touch among their people. "At least you're Delphian in the parts that count."

She gasped, enthralled by the grip he had on her mental state and stunned by the liberties this Shantir had taken with her body. Someone had surely spun up the room's gravity and she wondered if she was aboard the research vessel already. She was barely able to move. But why was this man here? Why was he touching her? And what was he saying? She waved her hands in some barely coordinated fashion to push him away. The distant contact she so desperately sought faded from view.

He grasped her wrists and pinned them above her head. "You just keep tripping, half-breed," he said. "I've been doing all the work so far. And taking the risk for your little jaunts. Time for you to show your gratitude." His free hand continued to move over her body, his touch far from gentle. "Just keep looking for those voices."

"Stop that," she said and tried to pull out of his grasp. She felt his teeth on her skin and stared numbly at the thick braid of hair that had fallen across her chest. "Let me go," she said, meaning their khamal, and tried to squirm out from under him.

He decided against drawing her deeper into the delirium. Not only was it dangerous, but the weak resistance she offered excited him quite unexpectedly. As was the thought that this was one of the sect's most protected secrets, daughter of Tychon, member of the House of Phera, who lay here at the mercy of his superior mind and his stronger body. Untouchable because of her birth and unreachable because none of them here at the enclave would ever meet the standards of her father's measure. That suited him just fine. He would meet Tychon's disdainful eyes with the secret knowledge that his hybrid offspring had served in his, Shantir Tava's, bed. She would not ever reveal anything he did to her because no one entered the forbidden khamal against their will. He reminded himself not to leave any marks.

* * *

"Are you having a laugh at my expense, Old Man?" Jovan could scarcely believe what Anders had just told him. He paced to the window of the library on the top floor of the Shantir enclave as if the moon from which Anders had placed this call could be seen in the sky today. But the air above them remained cold and blue and empty even of clouds.

"I'm not joking, Jovie." The excitement in Anders' voice was clear even when relayed by the utilitarian speakers in Jovan's wrist unit.

"This is what happens when I sleep all night and let you people have all the fun," Jovan said. "A moment, I'm with Shan Moghen." Jovan looked from the com unit to his mentor, the senior leader of the Shantir enclave. "That asteroid changed direction last night," he explained and nodded when the Shantir started to say something. "I know! And not just once. Then it turned into a direct trajectory to Delphi. Would have come down on the Syn'niel plateau. So they tried to deflect it and it crashed on Sola."

"Not an asteroid, I gather."

"Not even a bit." Jovan lowered his voice. "But not artificial, either. Ander says it's mainly organic, encased in minerals and crystal. Shielded somehow. Air Command's known that for a while which is why they wanted to take a look at it while it's in Delphian space. Can't get much more restricted air space than that."

"Organic? That is remarkable news, indeed," Moghen said. "Life signs?"

"We're still working on the scans," Anders voice squawked near Jovan's hand. "Now I know why we were asked to delay our trip back to Cet-Norwan. Targon didn't include a full bio-lab with the orbiter they sent."

"I've got to see this thing."

"You do. Listen, can you find Cyann? We can really use her up here but she's not answering my call. Nigel's on the base, getting the *Scout* cleared for takeoff already, so get over there. This thing is unbelievable. I'll have to figure out a way to tell Tychon we're not leaving for a few more days."

"With good reason." Jovan said. "Cyann's still downstairs with Shan Regin, I think." He glanced at Moghen for confirmation before signing off his call from Anders.

Shantir Moghen rose to his feet. "You had better get up there before the Council decides they need to put up a fence around everything until they've debated it for a few years."

Jovan laughed. "My thoughts, too."

The elder Shantir gave him a rare smile. "These years away from here have changed you, son. You have grown. Perhaps in ways your peers never can. I wonder if living among the outsiders might benefit all of them. Delphi is so small and their capacity for learning is so vast." He paused for a moment. "Even just learning how to laugh without reservation."

"Council fears that they won't return once they've left Delphi," Jovan reminded him. "Many haven't."

Moghen gazed out of the window and lifted his ancient shoulders in a shrug. "We are a civilization in decline, Jovan.

Unless we find a way to bolster our population, nothing will stop that. So what is the loss of a few more young men and women?" He seemed to realize the morbid direction his thoughts were taking. "And you returned, did you not? Perhaps someday you will return with the answers to our problem. We won't find it here."

Jovan nodded, unsure how to reply. "I'll send news back from Sola as soon as I can."

He left the Shantir and rushed with long strides to the broad stairway leading to the lower levels. "Cy," he spoke into his wrist unit. "Cyann, meet me in my room right away. I've got something fun for us to do. Hurry up." He jumped the last few risers and turned into the residential wing. Quickly, he changed out of his blue Shantir garb into a pair of scuffed leather trousers and a snug pullover. His old flight jacket was as comfortably worn as his boots. "Cyann!" he said when she had still not replied. "Where are you?"

He left his room again to look for her among the elder Shantirs with whom she was to study today. But a slammed door to his left drew his attention. When he turned he saw Cyann run toward him along the sunlit corridor.

"Hey, Cy. Didn't you hear me call?"

She stumbled and nearly fell when she reached him. He caught her before she collapsed. She stared wildly but he was certain that she wasn't seeing him at all. He felt her tremble in his arms.

"Gods, are you sick?" He half-carried her back into his room and sat her into a low armchair. Her hair and clothes were disheveled and she mouthed something he was unable to hear. "Talk to me!"

Her unseeing eyes blinked slowly when he squatted beside the chair. Her hand lifted toward him but then dropped limply back into her lap.

"Look at my hand," he said and held it up in front of her face. "Just follow it with your eyes." He spoke soothingly, allowing her to calm and finally relax back into the chair. He placed his other hand on her wrist to link their minds, hoping to discover what had disturbed her so much. He gasped and nearly recoiled from her when he found the results of her khamal with Tava. "Gods, Cyann!" he breathed, fighting the impulse to break their link. With gritted teeth he sought to bring order to her disturbed thoughts, return her to this place from wherever she had floated. He felt it affect his own state of mind and struggled to remain focused even as he acknowledged the lure of the forbidden khamal.

Slowly, he brought her back from the chaos that had taken over her mind until she became aware of him. She blinked, recognizing him, and he quickly broke their mental link, relieved to escape unscathed. He pulled up another chair and sat facing her, holding her hands in his. "Better?"

She frowned and let her eyes wander around the room, still befuddled. "Why did you wake me?" she said. "I was almost there."

"What?" he gasped. "Almost where? What are you talking about?"

"I know I almost found it. I could feel it. I know I did."

"Cyann, you almost lost your damn mind. What were you thinking?" He gestured at her disarrayed clothes. "And what were you doing?"

She looked down at herself and fingered the hem of her shirt, noticed the open fasteners and comprehension slowly came to her. "No!" she whispered. "He wanted... He tried. He..."

"Who?" Jovan grasped her arm, pained when she jerked it away. "Who did this?"

She stared at him, wide-eyed. "He was going to hurt me. He wanted to. I saw it."

"Tava." Jovan stood up. "You stay here."

Without waiting for a reply, he strode into the hall and to the Shantir's room. He straight-armed the door aside to find Tava bent over a bowl of water. The man whipped around when the irate Jovan stormed into the room.

Jovan had grasped his collar and had pushed him up

against the fragile door to his balcony before he realized that Tava's face and the front of his tunic were drenched in blood. "What did you do to her?" he snarled.

"What she wanted," Tava snapped back. "Little half-breed just didn't want to pay her dues."

Jovan kicked the door open and stepped forward to bend the Shantir over the railing. The cold air whipping past them did nothing to ease his temper.

Tava, however, was already deeply immersed in a khamal that allowed him to deal with the pain of his broken nose and Jovan's threat meant little to him. "I might not care much for the old fools' rules but you won't break your vows. I'm still a Shantir and you can't harm a hair on my head."

Jovan's eyes narrowed dangerously. "Don't try your luck. I've been gone a while." But Tava was correct and both of them knew it. To assault a fellow Shantir, for whatever reason, was a transgression that would not be forgiven. He hauled the man back inside and flung him roughly to the floor. "Talk, and make it fast."

"Or what?"

Jovan own mental processes were slowly succeeding in restoring his equilibrium. He took a deep breath and exhaled slowly. "By this time tomorrow, you will be on a shuttle away from here to minister at the Cachna mines. Don't make your life worse by having me discuss this with Shan Tychon. He's made no oaths to stop him."

Tava glared at him, knowing all too well that the ruling Shantirs' high regard for Jovan would absolutely give him the leverage to make this possible. Tava himself was only a few more indiscretions away from banishment. "She was looking to make some sort of link to whatever spook she's got in her head. No idea what that is, but she thinks it's real. So I spiked her a bit." He sat up and dabbed at his nose with a sleeve. "You probably know about that synapse aberration. Makes for an interesting little jolt if you know how to play with it. Not my fault she's not all Delphian. How was I to know it'd hit her like that?"

"Yet you didn't stop."

Tava shrugged angrily. "She didn't want to stop. I think it actually worked for her once or twice, whatever it is."

"And then you decided you want a little something more."

"Why not? She's hard to ignore." Tava struggled to his feet, keeping a wary eye on Jovan as he did so. "You and I both know she'd never tell her old man about this. And neither will you. He only needs a small excuse to tear this place to the ground. And even Phera himself won't stop him this time."

Jovan nodded, mostly to himself. After losing his son to the Shantir's machinations, Tychon would not tolerate harm to his daughter at their hands. Years of careful peacekeeping between the enclave and his clan, mostly brokered by Nova and Anders, had finally made it possible for them to begin making amends. Tava, despite the taboos he had broken, would suffer the least if his assault on Cyann became known. He looked over the bloodstains on Tava's clothes.

"She did this, in case you're wondering," Tava said. "The woman is stronger than she looks, even when she's tripping." He gingerly touched his face. "Damn GenMod broke my nose before I even got her britches off."

Jovan once again grasped Tava's shoulders and shoved him against a wall. "You are walking a very very fine line, Brother. I may be Shantir but my affinity is to Tychon's house. Don't ever forget that. I can do without the enclave. Can you?"

"You wouldn't dare! Not for that little—"

Jovan's hand closed over Tava's forehead and the Shantir found himself unable to move. Every muscle in the man's body went rigid and an icy pain stabbed from his neck to his tailbone as his nervous system reacted to Jovan's touch. Jovan observed Taha's face until it turned an interesting shade of purple before letting him fall to the floor. "Yeah, I would." He stepped over the quivering heap of strained muscle and nerves and left the room.

* * *

Cyann flinched when the door to Jovan's room opened, startling her out of the doze in which he had left her. Jovan closed the door to the hall and leaned over her to feel her face. He stared into the distance for a moment and it did not seem to her that he was checking her temperature. "Feeling better?" he asked.

She nodded. "What did you do to him?"

"Nothing. Should I have?"

She looked away and shrugged. "He hurt me."

"Because you're such a victim?"

Her eyes snapped back to him. She saw concern there, certainly, but anger as well. Why was he angry with her? "What is that supposed to mean?"

"You broke his nose. I think you're even. Now you'll tell me why you went to him in the first place. That was stupid and dangerous."

She blinked, surprised by his tone. "Don't shout at me. I know what I'm doing. He's helping me."

"You have no idea what you're doing. That khamal can obliterate your frontal lobe. There is nothing about it that'll help you."

"You're wrong! It worked... it works sometimes. It made me find the voice."

He sat down on the chair he had pulled up earlier. "Are you sure? Cy, if Regin or even Moghen can't help you, why did you think Tava could?"

"Because he's not afraid to try something more powerful. I can hear that voice when I'm upset or in pain. The opposite of their exercises. They treat me like my head's made of glass. I can handle this."

"No you can't. Even he said you're not up to it. Powerful or not, it's dangerous. And, in case you didn't notice, it has some ugly residual effects." He watched her expression for a moment. "You do know that, don't you? That's why you've been screwing up. That's why you're tired and distracted.

How long has this been going on?"

"A few weeks," she said grudgingly. She searched his face, looking for some clue to his thoughts. "You're disappointed in me."

He shook his head. "I'm worried about you, Cy. I don't want to see you in this pain. I wish..." he started to say something and then seemed to amend it before speaking again. "I wish I could help you. I really do."

She closed her eyes and leaned back into her chair. "You think I'm crazy, too? Making up imaginary friends like I used to when I was ten?"

"No, I don't," he said at once. "I think there are things we don't know about you. But butchering your brain with this nonsense isn't the way to find out."

"I have to try!"

"And look where it got you. Has this voice ever told you anything useful?"

She shook her head and looked away. "No. It just calls. It's hurt, I think. It needs me."

"And you really don't think that this might be you talking to yourself? An echo of yourself? Please at least consider that."

She grabbed his arm. "Don't tell Anders. Please. He'll never let me go back to Cet-Norwan like this."

"As well he shouldn't."

"Please, Jovie. I promise I won't go back to Tava."

"Seeing how you broke his face, I doubt very much that he's inclined to let you."

She sighed hugely. "I didn't mean for it to go this far." She leaned forward and touched his face, hoping to erase the furrows his anger and worry had painted there. Like all Delphians, male and female, he seemed chiseled from a solid piece of pale stone without a single curve to soften his features. But he had a smile that could light his eyes and transform every sharp angle into an expression of joy and tenderness. There was no smile for her now. "Thank you for looking out for me."

He reached up to cover her hand with his. For a brief moment, he seemed like a stranger to her, not the protector of her childhood, not the young man who came and went in and out of her life as his endless studies had dictated. Eight years had changed both of them. And the distance between them had left them worlds apart, even here and now.

He seemed to understand her thoughts and pulled her hand away. "That's my job, isn't it?" he said lightly and stood up. "I pledged my life to your clan, including you. And so I will beat up your assailants and stay silent to keep you employed."

"Like a big brother?" she said, smiling.

His eyes darkened and he regarded her wordlessly for a too-long moment. "I'm not your brother," he said finally.

She looked away. Of course he wasn't. He was Tychon's vassal and a Shantir as well as a top-level navigator, the sort used to span the most impossible distances through space. And here she was wasting his time with her stupid experiments. She felt a surge of embarrassment. She never wanted him to see her like this.

"Is this why you haven't wanted to join with Shan Regin?"

She nodded. "She'll be able to tell. I don't want them to know. They'd be so angry."

"Yes, they would be. Will you let me help you, then?"

She looked up. "You would do that? Aren't you leaving again?"

"I'm not leaving until I know you're done with this, Cy. That's a promise."

She smiled tentatively.

"Come," he said abruptly and held out his hand to pull her to her feet. "If you're up to it, I've got a trip to the moon for you."

"Moon? Which moon?" she said as she followed him from the room.

"Sola. The asteroid crashed and Anders wants you up there."

He was unable to answer any of her questions as they took a skimmer from the enclave to the Union air field where Nigel had already directed the ground crew to prepare the science vessel for departure. It was a short trip to this largest of Delphi's many moons and Cyann was still programming the needed equipment when Nigel announced that they were touching down on the surface.

"Point six G's," Nigel reminded them. He leaned over the cockpit controls to peer out of the thick window beside the main screen. "Is that it?" Below and ahead of them a restless assortment of awkwardly-suited researchers and Air Command personnel scurried around a fresh depression in Sola's arid ground like so many insects around a particularly tasty morsel. Instead of remaining in orbit, the research ship from Targon had been brought down to the surface. Several cruisers parked nearby and people came and went from those as well.

The moon itself was uninhabitable and valued only by poets and of course the Delphian population so used to their moons' reflected light that they had evolved with nearly no night vision at all. In deference to the Delphians among the astrophysicists, the area surrounding the site was illuminated by several light standards.

Cyann squeezed in beside him. "Not much of an impact crater. They must have brought the meteorite into the clean room already."

Jovan reached up to turn on the cabin speakers when he received a signal from the ground.

"About time!" they heard Anders excited voice. "Dock right onto the orbiter. We'll need the chip lab and a diffuser. Nigel, fire up the small dialyzer."

Cyann grinned. "You're so excitable, Uncle."

Nigel eased the *Scout* to snuggle up to the boxy Union vessel, aided by signals from below. "I wonder what has him so wound up," he said. "You'd think he'd never seen a meteorite before."

"Not an organic one," she said. "And not one with a

mind of its own."

It took a while before the three, loaded up with equipment, stepped through the *Scout*'s airlock into the larger Union ship. Cyann handed a large equipment box over to one of the ground crew and then hurried ahead of the others along the central corridor to follow the directional signs to the main lab.

"Do we know what this is?" she asked as soon as she walked into the observation room. Ring-shaped, it surrounded a large central space, separated from it by floor-to-ceiling shielded glass. She did a complete circuit, alternately looking up at the arrays of displays and monitors near the ceiling and at the irregular chunk of greenish-bronze material at the center of their attention. Several thickly-suited technicians surrounded the chest-high fragment, their air hoses tethered to the delivery system in the ceiling.

"Not yet," Anders said when she had completed her tour. His eyes were on one of the screens. "Come take a look."

She ducked in front of Jovan, who towered over her anyway, to peer at the display. It showed a magnified view of the fragment's dented surface showing a dense network of scratches and gouges.

"It's entirely natural," Anders said. "No technology. No openings that we've found. We have no idea how it managed to change direction. Or even what kind of propulsion it has."

"Anything alive in there?"

"Yes!" he said at once. "But we have no idea what it is. We don't seem to be able to scan into it very deeply."

"Now you've got me interested in this lump," she said. "What's the plan?"

"We'll see after we've analyzed the outside. Want to get some sort of idea where it came from and how old it is. I'm afraid Cet-Norwan will have to wait."

"I'm sure the Spotted Leatherbutts won't mind that one bit. Are we going to take this to Targon? Much better equipment there."

"We'll have to wait for the hazard reports. And Delphi's

permission. It's your rock."

"We're not leaving this to Targon, though?" Cyann said. "We'll be part of the team?"

"I'll be insisting on that, don't you worry." Anders tilted his head to observe her critically. "You still look a little pale. Are you up to this? Going to be some long hours."

"Try to stop me!" she grinned and then nodded toward the alien pod. "I need to get in there."

"Of course you do."

Everyone looked up, startled, when the brilliant overhead banks of lights flickered and a mildly-glowing strip running along all bulkheads changed from pale blue to orange. Jovan turned to them, a question on his face.

"Quarantine," Cyann said, more excited than disturbed by the news. "So much for taking this to Targon."

"What do you mean?"

"No one's leaving Sola until every atom here has been decontaminated," Anders supplied, equally unperturbed. "Looks like they found something unhealthy on our visitor."

"That isn't how I meant to spend the evening," Jovan said.

"You can bunk with us," Anders said absently, scanning the overhead screens for an explanation. "Plenty of room on the *Scout*. There, look." He pointed upward. "They've scraped up some really interesting extremophiles. Anaerobic bacteria and endoliths, mainly. Survived quite nicely just below the crust. And liquid water."

"Not ice? Is it melting?"

Anders shook his head. "No, we're maintaining the temps in there for now. I'm sure our tech team could use a hot cup of something by now."

"You can say that again," came a grumbling reply. "Sir."

Cyann chewed thoughtfully on her lower lip. "Do we have anything more complex than the endoliths?"

"Not on the surface. And the real mystery is what's on the inside. What brought this pebble here to begin with. What steered it."

"That's what interests me," Jovan said. "I'll leave you with your bugs and head over to astrophysics, seeing how I'm stuck here anyway." He placed his hand briefly on Cyann's shoulder. She felt his mental contact, as always amazed by the soothing skillfulness of the Shantirs compared to lesser trained Delphians. His dark blue eyes searched her face for a moment. "I'll see you in a while, Cy. To make sure Anders doesn't have you up all night counting microbes."

She smiled after him as he left them, surprised by a sudden urge to follow him as if some vacuum had been left by his passing. Had she really missed him this much over these past eight years?

"What was that about?" Anders said.

"Huh? Oh. Had a headache earlier."

He nodded. "Well, suit up and go play in there. We won't have anything to work with, though, until we get this data crunched."

FOUR

Cyann wanted to weep. Or pace around the station. Or maybe break something. It had been hours since she left Anders and the other technicians to find a bite to eat and then retire to her small cabin aboard the *Scout*. But sleep hadn't come, nor would it until she found a way to calm herself. She had tried to immerse herself into a meditative khamal in the hopes of slipping into something resembling sleep. Nothing.

This wasn't new to her. It was a nasty side effect of the forbidden khamal, the one that had no name, that left her restless and agitated. If she were on Delphi, she'd be even now finding a way to seek out Tava to ask him to ease her tension. Sometimes he complied. Sometimes he refused, perhaps out of spite. And when she wasn't on Delphi she'd be awake. And pacing. And wondering if she should go to the ship's dispensary in search of something that would help her sleep.

She sat on the edge of her bed but soon got up to pace to the window overlooking Sola's pockmarked surface. No one was out there, but she could see internal lights from two of the nearby cruisers. Bored Air Command pilots, likely, already tired of the quarantine. She picked up a comb and ran it impatiently through her tangled blue strands. The color was her father's; the stubborn resistance to any sort of order clearly her mother's.

She whirled when the door opened without warning. "What!"

Jovan stood in entrance, looking alarmed. "What are you up to?"

"Me? Nothing."

He looked around the cabin as if doubting her words. "You brought me out of a dead sleep," he said, worried. Anything able to rouse a Delphian from a sleep state was certainly cause for alarm. "What's wrong?"

"What do you mean?"

He frowned. "I don't know. I felt you, somehow. You're strung awfully tight."

"We are not in khamal," she reminded him, somewhat pointedly. "I don't know how you'd think you can feel me." She gestured for him to step inside her cabin. "I just can't sleep, that's all. Feels like bugs crawling in my head. Claustrophobia, too. That's all I need!"

"Why didn't you tell me," he said. "That's Tava's work. I can help you." He lifted his hands to her temples and she again felt the calming touch of his mind on hers, using the healing ways of the Shantir to allow her to relax. "Don't fight me. You can do this," he murmured.

She listened to his calming voice, all too aware that she was wearing only a thin, loose-fitting shirt and tights and that he stood close enough to feel the warmth of his body. Her breath caught when his hand moved to rest briefly alongside her neck.

He dropped his hands. "You should be able to sleep now," he said. "Or at least let me sleep," he added with a grin that didn't seem quite genuine.

"Um, could you..." she said. "I mean, could you not..."

"What?"

"It might help if you could, maybe, um, give it a little

more."

"You seem fine now."

She looked away. "I mean, you could, you know..."

His eyes darkened and he stepped away from her. "You want me to spike you? Is that what you're saying?"

She lifted her shoulders slowly in a half shrug. "Just a little. It'd help me sleep for sure."

"Have you lost your mind? Do you have any idea what you're asking?"

"All right, forget I asked."

He sat down on the bed and tugged on her arm until she sat beside him. "You have to get over this thing, Cy. These are just side effects. They'll go away. I'm here to help you. But I won't allow this to go on. I can't. Not as a Shantir and not as your friend."

"Or what? You'll tell Anders so he'll kick me off the team?"

Jovan sighed impatiently. "If you continue this he'll figure it out for himself. He might be Human but he's spent his entire life on Delphi. Few people know you better than he does. Do you really want him to find out that you're deliberately hurting your brain?"

"Nova and Tychon do it," she snapped.

His brow furrowed in puzzlement. "What? Why do you say that?"

"I know they do. You can tell if you pay attention. Not that they hide it very well."

He stared at her for a moment before a slow grin tugged on his lips. "Silly girl. Your parents are sneaking in a little khamal *shoi* now and then. Nothing more."

"What?" The khamal he had named was a mental connection made between Delphians during their most intimate moments. Entirely physical, it added a deeply personal and pleasurable dimension to the lovemaking of people who rarely allowed their emotions to show in public. In some circles, achieving the perfect khamal *shoi* was something of an art form.

Jovan nodded. "I noticed that long ago. Tychon's isn't exactly the most demonstrative individual and your mother is the complete opposite. So they've taken things, well, out of sight. Besides, Tychon is over a hundred years old. This khamal gets more important as you get older."

"I had no idea you could do that."

He cocked his head. "You didn't? No wonder you're so confused. Someone needs to have a word with your mentor."

She stood abruptly to pace to the window before turning around again. The mentor he referred to was the *shoi-gan*, part of the Delphian coming of age years when youths chose a more experienced partner to learn about sex. Besides discovering the complex connection between mind and body, young people were less likely to rush into choosing their mates, a lifetime and monogamous commitment. "Some mentor! I had two of them. One could barely stand to join in khamal with me and the other refused outright."

"They would hardly have offered to mentor you if they did not intend to teach you," Jovan said, baffled and annoyed that she had found such inept teachers. "No lovers, either?"

"You're not hearing me, Jovan. No one wants to touch the half-breed's mind that way. Even Tava said I was an abomination. A disgrace to Delphi."

"That excuse of a Shantir is not really the best judge of what disgrace is," Jovan said sharply.

She came to stand before him. "You show me," she said.

He looked up. "Show you what?"

"The khamal *shoi*. How it's supposed to feel."

"What? Now? Here?"

"Yes. If Nova can grope Tychon in the middle of dinner I think you can show me here in my room."

He stood up and hesitated for a moment before reaching out to, quite formally, touch the side of her head. She felt a brief sensation, utterly pleasurable, that dissipated as quickly as it had appeared.

"Nice," she smiled. "Like being kissed inside my head."

He nodded.

"But that's not what we were talking about, is it?"

"No," he said after a moment.

She closed her eyes when she felt his contact again and her breath caught when his touch seemed to reach deeper, exciting her senses without changing her mental state the way the forbidden khamal had. She shivered with delight when the sensation he created for her was precisely the feeling of gentle finger moving up along her spinal ridge.

She gasped when he abruptly broke their mental link.

"I think I better go," he said, not quite steadily.

"Why?"

"I should not have done this. This is not... appropriate."

She frowned. "Because you don't want to touch me, either."

"What? No, that isn't—"

"So you do?"

"I am not your *shoi-gan*. You're not—"

She waved her hands. "I know. I'm not Delphian and you don't like it. Tava told me that I'm like an alien in there. Just stop. I understand just fine. Messed-up synapses and voices in my head that no one can figure out but it's all *just* because I'm half Human. You are all so concerned about me, but in the end I am not Delphian. I will never be Delphian enough for anyone here."

"That isn't true!"

"Yes," she said. "It is." She went to the door but instead of showing him the way out, she stepped into the corridor. "Just don't talk to me right now."

"Cy," he called after her but she hurried through the narrow passage to the open airlock joining the *Scout* to the Union ship, not terribly concerned that she was barefooted and rather casually dressed. She did not stop until she had reached the clean room that housed the meteorite.

The space was silent except for the whirring of life support systems and a few clicks and squawks from some of the equipment. One lone technician tapped on a screen in his hand, monitoring things in what was surely utter boredom. He looked up when Cyann entered, both eyebrows raised in surprise.

"Hello," she said and quickly masked any evidence of her upset before he, with the typical and endearing Human mix of curiosity and concern, could ask her if something bothered her. "You're up late."

"Around the clock shifts so we can get it off this moon. Found some interesting crystal."

"I thought it was all organic."

"Exactly. Can't wait till we get a look inside. So far it's not giving up any secrets about what's in there, if anything. What are you doing here?"

"Wanted another look," she said although up until this moment she had not even considered doing that. She peered through the glass at the meteorite that, despite its unassuming size, carried a payload of pathogens that they had not even begun to analyze. It looked heavy, solid. She pressed her hands against the window. It seemed to be waiting.

"You might want to put on something a little more suitable for that."

"I think you might be right." She went into the decon corridor where she climbed into a clean suit. After a quick blast of treated air and a thorough scan she was allowed into the circular room housing the rock. After walking around it, she reached out and placed her flat hand onto the surface. It was deeply dented and scratched yet even through her glove it felt strangely smooth, likely from the heat it encountered when entering Sola's thin atmosphere.

"We still can't scan it?"

"Not with anything we have here. We'll figure something out when we get it to Targon."

She ran her hands over the meteorite, feeling its wounds and scars. There was something comforting in that, like stroking a pet. She thought about her encounter with Jovan just now. Why did she turn into a simpering idiot when he was around? She was, even by Delphian standards, an expert researcher and xenobiologist with a long list of accomplishments and accreditations. She had worked for her place on Anders' team – even his love for her family would not favor her for this if she hadn't earned it. And yet, when Jovan came near her, she turned back into the blue-braided little fool who once imagined him as the handsome prince of her dreams. Had she still not gotten over that stupid infatuation?

She sighed and shook her head, resolving to guard her thoughts more carefully. To have him continue to think of her as the tedious brat foisted upon him by his oath to her clan was unbearable. At least, she thought, she could try to grow a damn spine and act like an adult around him.

"It's so alone," she said quietly.

"Cyann?" The technician's voice floated through the speaker built into her suit.

"Huh?"

"What do you mean?"

"Nothing." She frowned, bewildered. Why had she said that? She watched her gloved hands sweep over the surface of the stone. But it wasn't a stone. It was organic, it was carbon and ice and water and any number of strange combinations of matter that had allowed it to reach this place. To find her.

The voice.

It was here. She felt it reaching for her, drawn to her from somewhere at some vast distance or, as the Shantirs and the doctors believed, from somewhere inside her own head. Each time she felt it had been a time of some emotional turmoil, good or bad. Breaking her leg when she was eight. Her first trip away from Delphi. Visiting the science center on Feyd with her father. Finally leaving her school to study with the Shantirs who did not scorn her for being part Human. Watching Jovan's ship leave the first time. Watching it leave the second time.

And then, over these past few years, it had found her

more frequently. It had been her secret. She was not mad, of that she was certain. Given the absence of any serious sign of dementia, thought the scientist inside her, there was no need to alarm those who cared about her or to invite more derision from those who saw her as an unlikely freak of nature. But she had found Tava who promised to help her reach farther than the other Shantirs would. And he had. Again and again, she had heard that voice, each time a little more clearly.

She touched the small control panel at her shoulder to turn off the sound system in her suit. "I hear you," she whispered.

There was no reply. Just a presence. Something was waiting. Something terribly sad. Terribly alone. She looked at the meteorite. The voice had not come from there. It was still distant, still barely there. But it knew where she was and it expected something.

She stretched her arms out over the meteorite and stepped closer as if to embrace it. Pressing her body against it, she rested her cheek on its surface, hampered by the awkward headgear of her suit. She did not hear the tech as he surely wondered what she was doing. This was a comfortable moment and she felt like, finally, she might sleep, on her feet and stretched out on this battered piece of space debris. It felt almost like she could sink into it, like a pillow.

She realized that she was, indeed, sinking into it. The surface of the meteorite gave way under the pressure of her body as if her warmth melted it. She lifted her head to see an indent where her helmet had lain. It deepened and expanded as she watched, fascinated.

The dull thud of someone banging on the observation windows roused her. The tech was waving his arms, shouting something she barely understood. She touched her control panel to re-activate the sound system.

"—the hell out of there!"

"Don't shout," she said and pulled back from the meteorite. "It's all right." She put her hand on its surface, which immediately shrank away from it, like ice melting under a flame. Some of the material flowed to the floor to form an irregular and expanding puddle. The light around her shifted when the technician escalated the hazard indicator.

"Don't you take your suit off!"

"Why would I do that?" she said. "Calm down."

"What did you do, other than make out with it?"

Two others had entered the observation ring. Seeing the new state of the meteorite, both headed for the airlock leading into the dome.

"I did nothing. I just touched it. Am I still tight?"

He checked the integrity of her suit. "You're good."

The door behind him opened again and this time Jovan rushed into the room, followed by a somewhat sleepy-looking Anders. The older man blinked in disbelief when he grasped the situation. "What have we got?" He scrubbed the short stubble on his head as he scrutinized the monitors. "Vapor samples, quick. Have we got sound recording?"

Jovan went to the window. "Cyann, are you all right?"

"Come in here," she said. She moved her fingers through the dissolving outer layer of the rock, fascinated by its texture. Neither dust nor sand, it seemed as though it was simply falling apart, losing cohesion and turning into something else.

The other technicians entered the lab, thickly suited and armed with their scanners. Unlike Cyann, they did not seem especially eager to touch the meteorite. One of them began to collect samples of the material that had fallen to the floor.

She watched her hand move deeper into the top of the rock. The clear visor of her headgear fogged and she took a moment to calm herself. The softening material easily gave way to her careful probing.

"Cyann, I'm not sure that's a good idea," Anders said.

"I know," she replied. "But I have to."

"Jovan," he called when the Shantir stepped into the ring. "Stop her. This is reckless."

Jovan leaned over the meteorite. "What is it?" he said, also deaf to Anders' plea.

"You feel it, too?"

"Yes." He looked up at the others outside the dome. "There is something in there. And I don't mean microbe."

"Feels warmer in there, but not by much," she said. "I wish I could take my gloves off." She tilted her head, concentrating on what little physical sensation her gloves afforded. But it was the touch inside her mind that guided her while assuring her that she, somehow, was doing the right thing. "Join me."

He placed his hand on her shoulder, lending her the power of his finely trained mind to enhance her perceptions. She gasped when her fingers connected with something. "I found it," she said excitedly.

"Found what," Anders wanted to know, now as enraptured as everyone else by the discovery.

"It's moving!" Cyann stroked a finger over the soft contours of what she had found. "It's alive. It's hurting. Too much gravity. Can we dial that down?"

Anders waved at someone to find the engineer to adjust the gravity fields that had been spun up to make up for Sola's weak pull. "It's communicating?"

"Yes! This is amazing." Cyann closed her eyes. "It's peculiar. Not really using language but I can feel some imagery, if that makes any sense."

Jovan reached past her to gently move more of the increasingly soft material out of the way. Deeper below the disintegrating crust a lighter, nearly translucent layer shifted easily. They both saw something dark beneath that. He leaned back to allow the overhead cameras to record what they had found.

"I think this material is some sort of nutrient matrix," Cyann said and gestured for one of the techs to take a sample from the interior. "The feeling I get is that our visitor just woke up. It's what started the decomposition of the hull. Amazing technology. If you want to call it that."

"I can see it moving," Anders marveled. "Cyann, I really have to insist that you step away. Anything that big might have teeth."

She grinned. "It also has a brain big enough to know that we mean no harm. There is nothing hostile here. It's a little frightened but I'm not really getting much panic."

Jovan nodded. "I'm getting that, too. Impatience. And curiosity." He smiled. "From both of you."

"Hah! Like you're not ready to explode if we don't get a look at it soon." She gripped his arm with her free hand when they felt a gradual shift of the vessel's gravity.

"How is it breathing?" Anders asked.

"It's not. It's absorbing what it needs from the medium it's in. But it doesn't want to stay in there. We'll need to find a way to replicate this if we want to keep it alive."

"Well, let's not get our hopes up," Anders cautioned. "We don't even know what it is."

"I wonder if we can freeze it."

Jovan sighed. "Can you two stop being scientists for a moment? It's not dead yet. And it's sentient. Let's not start dissecting it just yet."

Cyann winked at Anders. "All right, all right. Just don't get too attached to it. The odds aren't—" She jerked her hand back when the creature inside made a violent movement. They all saw the side of the melting block bulge outward. Both Cyann and Jovan stepped away. She noted that one of the technicians in the dome with them moved to a compartment near the airlock and retrieved a stunner.

The shell of this alien visitor finally gave way and a tear appeared from where Cyann's hand had broken through and then ripped downward. Something pale and shiny slid from the gap. Long limbs unfolded slowly, trembling as they moved. It gathered itself and rose, first on four limbs, and then it stood.

"Gods," Cyann whispered. "It's a Prime species."

The others all gaped in astonishment, letting the cameras, scanners and monitors do their work while they simply stared speechlessly at something that none of them, not the Delphians, nor the Humans, not the two Centauri guards summoned by the new caution level, had ever seen before.

It was only the size of a child, with thin, flattened limbs, colorless skin so translucent that the denser organs and insubstantial bones beneath it were eerily visible as dark shadows. The head was round and very flat, with small, widely-spaced eyes more round than elongated and entirely taken up by mirror-like irises. A slotted aperture in the place of a nose sat above a small triangular mouth with a peaked upper lip. Most definitely a Prime, one of the species scattered on distant worlds that had, for some reason, evolved in much the same way.

Most remarkably, the waxy skin exhibited a wonderful bioluminescence that changed colors so rapidly that it seemed to be some sort of signal. The edges of its round head, the long fingers at the ends of both hands and feet, and even the surface of its thin chest flickered in rapid waves of green and orange and yellow.

"It's holding something." Jovan said.

Indeed, the little creature's fist was closed tightly around what appeared to be a wet rag. It was gray and looked to be falling apart, like so much damp paper.

Cyann moved closer to the visitor and crouched to appear less threatening. Cautiously, she extended her hand, keeping it low and open to point at the object. The visitor looked down at it and then lifted its own hand in response. Barely daring to breathe, Cyann touched the scrap of material and smiled when she was able to gently pull it from the pale fingers. She gave it to Jovan, far more interested in the mirror eyes that had not left her own. She touched the alien's hand, careful not to trap it in her own.

Jovan tugged on the rag until it was more or less flattened out. A technician opened a transparent envelope and he slipped the artifact into it. "Looks like writing," the woman said. "Symbols. Look, those two are the same."

"Get that deconned," Anders said. "Scan it into the

system to see if we can decipher it here. Send a copy to Targon."

Jovan held the technician back to peer more closely at the writing. "Send it also to Delphi."

"You don't think we can decipher this up here? We've got some pretty smart machines."

"And we have some pretty smart coders and linguists on Delphi," Jovan said. He nodded to the tech and then turned his attention back to Cyann. "Are you getting anything from it?"

She nodded. "It's dying." The alien had wrapped those long fingers around her hand. Like its arms and legs, the digits had no joints as if, instead of bones, her body was simply supported by cartilage. "It... She knows she's dying. She knew she would before she even got here."

"What can we do?" Anders whispered.

Jovan lowered himself beside Cyann and put a hand on her shoulder in silent support. "Leave them," he said. "Just let them be."

Cyann wished that the protective suit she wore was made of something soft and comforting. The urge to embrace this individual, to comfort her, was so overwhelming that she had to fight against her instincts to tear out of the stiff fabric. "Someone pass through a towel or a blanket or something." She bit her lip when tears obscured her vision. "Oh, Jovie, she's so alone."

"Her respiration is not able to deal with any of the gas mixes we can come up with," he said to the others, his own voice unsteady. "She's barely breathing. We won't have time to figure out a stasis that'll keep her alive."

"Shh," Cyann said softly. Her gloved fingers stroked the visitor's arm. "She's aware. She's all right with it. She was sent here. She's so tired. Others are following."

"To Delphi?" Anders asked.

"To this sector. Trans-Targon, I guess. Just generally this way."

"More of these meteorites? These pods?"

"Yes. But much bigger. Asteroids. Many of them traveling together."

"Why?"

Cyann closed her eyes. "We will die. We. I don't know if she means them or us. Just 'we'. She's not using words. Jovan?"

"That's all I'm getting, too."

The stranger's coloring still shifted through its spectrum, but paler and not as rapidly. A nearby hissing sound announced the arrival of another technician and then someone handed Cyann a soft piece of cloth. She realized that it was someone's shirt. She draped it gently around the creature who allowed her to draw her close and finally take her into her arms. She was almost weightless in this gravity but Cyann felt the relief when she no longer had to stand on her own.

"She's very tired now."

"How are you doing?" Jovan said.

"I know what she knows. It isn't much."

"That's not what I meant."

Cyann shifted into a different khamal. *I'll cry later*, she sent to Jovan. "She's one of several individuals sent out in advance of a larger group," she said aloud. "She doesn't know what happened to the others. They're coming this way, partially through sub-space."

"Using our own jumpsites," Anders said.

Jovan shook his head. "Not just the open sites. They're using keyholes, too. Any breach in space."

"You mean to say that this little... person, without any technology, is able to open a keyhole, span sub-space without navigational aid or controls, and actually emerge again where intended?"

"Astrophysics is going to wet their pants," Nigel murmured.

"Yes," Cyann said. "But she was pushed here. She's not the navigator. Just some sort of advance warning."

"That a pathogen-infested asteroid field is on its way

here."

"Yes."

Jovan looked up. "See if you can reach the observatory on Delphi. We'll need the elder Asher and Leisakh. Send them what we know." He glanced at Cyann. "And wake up base command."

"Do you know how far away they are?" Anders asked. "Where? When they might get here?"

Cyann looked into the dark mirror spheres of the visitor's eyes. "There is a... a stone on the bottom of the pod. It'll have recorded the trajectory."

The alien's featureless chest fluttered rapidly and then they heard a string of language, emitted in a high-pitched gurgle. The words she spoke were not formed by her motionless face but seemed to originate in her throat. The rapid cadence flattened until it seemed that she had to push the words out with whatever breath remained.

Cyann watched helplessly as the flashes of color at the edges of the being's face faded and disappeared. The stranger raised her thin arm to place her flat and unlined hand against Cyann's faceplate. None of the Delphian aversion to displaying emotion among strangers kept a sob from escaping her lips when the little creature slipped from her mind and then lay limp in her arms.

* * *

"Cyann, they're all here now."

She looked up from her cultures when Anders' voice broke the silence of the *Scout*'s laboratory. He did not have to consult the ship's system to find her here after checking her empty cabin. Few places were as comforting to her as the well-ordered isolation of her workspace and here her troubled mind always found peace.

Their visitor's passing twenty hours ago had unleashed a torrent of activity, both here on Delphi as well as at Air Command headquarters on Targon. Data transferred, experts summoned, samples analyzed, endless calculations made to dissect every scrap of information they had obtained from the asteroid and its mysterious visitor. Both Jovan and Cyann had spent hours conveying the mental impressions and imagery they had received from the little being before they escaped for a few hours' rest.

She smiled at Anders. "I can't wait to hear what they've come up with." She glanced at the reflective surface of a cooler to check her lab smock for stains and then quickly tucked a wayward strand of hair into the loose knot at her nape. "Any news about our friend?"

"Nothing. There is no sentient anywhere in the database even remotely similar. She must have traveled a long way."

"And yet her DNA says otherwise."

He nodded. Once again, they had been stumped to find that a previously unknown species not only appeared physically similar but also shared a great deal of their genetic makeup.

Since the Centauri and their Human companions had brought interstellar travel to this sector over three hundred years ago, they had found many wondrous species, sentient or not, living in both beautiful and hostile environments. But again and again they encountered what came to be known as Prime species: highly evolved bipeds, physically alike and mentally similar in their thought processes, intellect and emotional range. These tended to be the dominant species of their respective planets – the Commonwealth Union of Planets was a partnership of these races and only a few chose to ignore the invitation to join.

"They figured that the color changes are expressive and used for communication. Barely any facial muscles. We might not be able to figure out what hers meant, given the stress."

"Anything on the language?"

"Yes, they've pretty much translated it now. She basically talked about what you and Jovan had already picked up from her telepathically. It does confirm that the pod she used originated on the asteroid she warned us about. She was definitely sent from there. The asteroid could be a habitat for her species."

"That would make her people incredibly ancient," Cyann said.

"Not necessarily. They, too, will have evolved as we did. They may not even be aware of any other existence but to travel endlessly through space. The alien's structure suggests that she developed in a low gravity environment."

"And yet they know that their arrival will harm us."

"That is the mystery here," Ander said.

They left the *Scout* for the Union science vessel where the others were waiting. She sighed inwardly when they passed the sealed doorway to the observation lab. Technicians were still at work there to expunge any trace of their visitor just as another crew was cleaning up the moon's surface contaminated by the meteoroid. The hundreds of samples they had retrieved as well as the visitor herself were now safely sealed in protective containers for future study on Targon.

Nigel was waiting for them outside the conference room, also in a fresh lab coat and, for once, neatly shaved and combed. "Enough brass in there to sink a ship," he said in greeting. "Is my breath fresh?"

"Do try to behave," Anders said.

The door slid aside and they stepped into the crescent-shaped room. Jovan and some of the Union ship's science crew lounged before a wall of video displays. He smiled when Cyann took a seat next to him, her eyes on the displays.

"You look like you finally got some rest," he said. The uncomfortable residual effects of Tava's khamal had reappeared shortly after they had finally escaped the tedious questioning by both Delphian and Union researchers. Jovan had worked patiently with her to relieve the symptoms and neither made reference to their previous moments alone. But an awkwardness seemed to hover between them now and they had soon retreated to their own cabins for long overdue sleep. "I mean," he added quickly, "you look rested. Not that you didn't look rested before. Um, good morning."

She regarded him silently for a long moment before deciding to let him off the hook. "Who's that?" She tipped her chin at one of the screens.

"The Caspian? Ceel Ptho, Targon Astrophysics. The Centauri beside him is biology – don't know his name. The one next to them is the famed Pappa Dutl, extremophile specialist and unbeaten *swaddar* player."

"That's him? I thought he'd be older. The biologist is Varon Tol, best in his field, too."

Neither of them needed the names that now appeared on the displays to know who the others were. Shan Asher The Elder and Shan Leisakh were Delphian astronomers; Shan Arivon represented the Delphian Clan Council in their jurisdiction over Sola moon. Shan Tychon, related to the ruling House of Phera through oath rather than blood, was there in Phera's name. Cyann's mother, Nova Whiteside, attended as the Air Command proxy on Delphi. The only surprising presence on these walls were two Delphian Shantirs.

Cyann smiled at her father's image when she noticed his eyes focused upon her. None of the others at this gathering, located at five different sites, seemed of interest to him. Tychon nodded, apparently unaware that his unwavering gaze made her want to fidget like she was twelve again.

"Why is your father staring at me like that," Jovan whispered beside her.

"You?" she replied without moving her lips. "He's looking at me, isn't he?"

"Let's begin," Trephan Laar, the Centauri astrophysics director, spoke from the back of the room. "We have all had a chance to review the initial findings and the recordings of the event. We all know that it is too early to report any definite conclusions but if our suspicions bear out, we may not have time for lengthy evaluation. Shan Asher will present our hypothesis regarding the origin of the alien."

Eyes shifted to the Delphian who now bent over his control board. "That's quite the surprise you found in that rock," he said. "And I'm sure the entire Targon lab is scratching their heads over how you managed to crack it open, Shan Cyann." He looked up at the screen. "Shan Whiteside informs me that you prefer that name?"

"Please," Cyann replied. Although most Delphians added, changed and removed some of their long list of names when circumstance called for it, they chose one to define them in their adulthood. Her first name had been her mother's whimsy and she had never thought to change it.

"Because it's so cute," Jovan whispered. She gave his foot a gentle kick.

The astronomer nodded. "We've been studying the asteroid's approach since it first came to our attention and then gleaned a great deal of information from the tablet found alongside the alien."

The main screen now displayed an image of a flat, sand-colored object. It bore no markings at all except for a deep groove near one edge. "We were able to scan this item, a remarkable piece of technology, although we have no concept of its manufacture. Silica fused in ways we don't understand." He glanced at Nova sitting in the same room on Delphi. "We have gifted the item to the Commonwealth who will share their findings with us."

At this point the Delphian Council representative interjected. "Which isn't possible until we are able to remove it from Sola's surface. May I ask at this point how the decontamination processes are... err... proceeding?"

Laar, as project director, replied, "Things are moving quite satisfactorily, Shan Arivon. The surface is clean now as is your research vessel, the *Scout*. Air Command has left and we are preparing to remove this ship and all remaining crew within two days."

Arivon leaned back, apparently satisfied with the answer.

Asher gazed at the Council member just long enough to make a point. "Where was I? Ah, yes. We have been able to determine the visitor's trajectory."

All eyes moved to the main screen when a star map appeared, rotating slowly to allow them to orient themselves. It was a true-scale, three-dimensional representation of Trans-Targon including all solar systems. As usual, the image then shifted into a flat and false perspective showing where the systems stood within the roadmap of navigable jumpsites. Only those systems that could be reached via a mapped breach in space now appeared, regardless of actual distance. It reduced the field of thousands of planets to a few dozen.

Cyann studied the map, awed as always by the fact that a star system at the other side of Trans-Targon could be reached within just days or weeks while a planet close enough to see at night could not be visited within their lifetimes. Or at least not until someone found a keyhole in space, a microscopic breach detectable by skilled navigators like Jovan and Tychon, which could then be expanded and mapped to allow traffic to pass through. Her eyes shifted to Jovan.

"What?" he said quietly when he felt himself scrutinized.

She shook her head and returned her attention to the display.

A red line appeared to show the journey the stranger had taken through this small part of their galaxy, tracing back from Delphi, through several jumpsites until it finally seemed to drop off the visible map, that unexplored edge that many simply called the Badlands. There was nothing particularly bad about them other than that nearly all keyholes leading out there were little-known and dangerous to traverse. It was simply the border of what they called Trans-Targon, in any direction.

"As you can see, it originated outside our sector and so we still don't know its origin. It did not spend a great deal of time in real-space. Fortunately, in that time it did not approach any known systems close enough to present a hazard."

"But you believe its ultimate destination was Delphi?" Anders spoke up, unable to contain himself any longer. "It meant to come here?"

"That is possible. We know it was able to change direction. But this is a densely populated part of Trans-Targon. The vessel will have been affected by even weak gravity wells. In fact, it is possible that gravity is what brought it here. However, some of our colleagues disagree."

He looked over to Shan Leisakh who rose to his feet to address the group. He was bent by age which was said to be over two hundred, his blue braid nearly black with age, his eyes pale disks above sunken cheeks and a beak of a nose. He moved his hand which activated a pointer on their screen as if he had outlined the trajectory with a sweep of his arm. "This path is not unfamiliar to us," he said, his voice barely above a whisper. Someone helpfully increased the volume in the meeting room. "This, and the creature's own admissions, lead us to believe that more of its kind will follow. With all the dangers that will bring to these worlds."

Jovan frowned and leaned forward as if to be sure to catch every nuance of the astronomer's speech. Most Delphians were quick to regard anything strange as a dangerous influence but Shan Leisakh, although outspoken, was not known for hyperbole.

"Some of you will be familiar with a hypothesis we have entertained for hundreds of years here on Delphi. It is the result of our own astronomical studies, the thoughts of our philosophers and our study of astrobiology over these past three hundred years of Centauri occupation." He coughed as if to draw their attention from this slip. Some of the others in the room found things to look at during the awkward pause that followed. Not everyone in this sector welcomed the Commonwealth of allied planets and Delphi, although living in peaceful cooperation with the Union, was especially reluctant to join. Leisakh's sentiments were shared by many members of Delphi's reclusive population.

Leisakh changed the display to include their entire galaxy.

"We propose this. An anomaly of some sort, perhaps even just a rogue planet or planetar, is moving around galactic center rather than a star. It's large enough for its gravity to pick up space debris along the way, some of which it loses to objects with greater gravity."

Anders nodded. "And this includes depositing extremophiles, amino acids, pathogens and whatnot on other planets. In some cases, these pieces survive. You are talking about panspermia."

"We are," Dutl, the Human astrobiologist on Targon said. "An exoplanet thrown out of its solar orbit could explain the presence of organic material. It seems that Delphi's theories may be in part validated by your visitor." He reset the star map back to its real-space representation of their sector. "The red line I'm showing you is the trajectory of the alien pod. Skipping through sub-space gaps but always following the larger orbit Shan Leisakh pointed out. Now look at the star systems I've marked in blue."

All of them noted the familiar planets he highlighted. Delphi and Targon, the nearby Myra. Further along Magra and her companion Aikhor, then Feyd, Feron, Bellac Tau, Aram and other planets on which Prime species had evolved. Even the distant Shaddallam and Callas fell within the object's path, tracing a clear line of populations whose shared ancestry had been the subject of speculation for centuries.

"This anomaly may well be what brought all of us here, to our respective planets. The origin of our shared evolution. We literally dropped from the sky." He smiled at the notion. "Albeit in our most primitive form. Scraps of DNA carried by ancient life forms."

"It's what we call the Genesis Cloud," Nigel dared to speak up.

"Indeed," Leisakh said. He fumbled behind himself until Asher guided him back into his chair. "As good a name as any, especially if it brings a debris disk with it. We, as well as some among the Caspians, estimated that it passed through here two and a half billion years ago." His thin lips stretched into a smile. "As you can imagine, we hadn't expected it to return for a little while longer. But if our alien visitor is a precursor of what's to come, we now know that it can move through sub-space. That would mean that it traveled through Trans-Targon more often than we think. It finally explains the much younger evolution of the Prime species. And now it is due to return to our small part of the galaxy far sooner than expected."

"With devastating consequences," Anders said.

"Yes," the biologist based on Targon said. "Whatever they dropped on these worlds millions of years ago found fertile ground to inhabit and evolve. Perhaps it wiped out what was already here, most certainly it changed it. But these days, few of us would welcome such radical alteration of our environment. As some of you know, there is evidence of mass extinction on several of these planets occurring at the same time."

"Do we know what new pathogens this meteorite has brought?"

Varon Tol nodded. "For the most part, much of what it carried is benign. Variations of what we already have, or things that won't affect our systems. Some of it is matter that comes to us fairly regularly from other worlds. That process is of course beneficial to all of us - it's what's made it possible for us to so easily move among planets without causing utter calamity every time we set foot on new soil."

"But?"

"This." The biologist held up a transparent cube for them to see. It seemed to contain wilted and pale greenery. "What we've discovered is a virus that, under the right conditions, can infect a vital plant protein that produces an acid. Sunlight is the right condition and we happen to have plenty of it. It's harmless in the dark, as perhaps on our asteroid, but when exposed to light that acid will create a toxin. Plants are unable to produce chlorophyll and eventually, this will prevent photosynthesis." He shook the box in his hand as if to somehow bring the pallid leaves back to life. "We're assuming the virus is dormant, biding its time in the ice and rock carried by the cloud. It took only moments under lab conditions to awaken. Our projections show that it would take only a matter of days to destroy a living plant. We're calling it the Sola virus for now."

"*Any* plant?" Anders asked, forestalling the Delphian Council member who looked clearly displeased by the pathogen's designation.

"Any plant requiring chlorophyll of any type, with the exception of those with dark-operative proteins, which is nice if you're living in a cave. For the rest of us, it means every plant on every planet with the exception of Feron, Aram, Targon, maybe K'lar. The collapse of our food-chain."

Everyone present followed his gesture toward the star map and most of them understood what he meant. Few of the planets in the path of the cloud had the means to combat a virus such as this on their own. They included primitive or hostile populations as well as rebel strongholds that would fight any effort by the Commonwealth to aid the regions they occupied. Even if these experts developed some anti-viral agent, delivering it to this vast field of worlds presented an undertaking that was beyond even the Union's means.

Cyann reached over and clasped Anders' hand. He squeezed it reassuringly, out of habit, but his expression was as worried as everyone else's.

"Elder Brother," Jovan broke the stunned silence to address Asher, the Delphian astronomer. "That a passing asteroid or exoplanet can seed life and death upon other planets is a captivating and troublesome theory. But are you proposing that the alien came here specifically to warn us of this?"

"We are," Shelyth, one of the so-far silent Shantirs, said. Her eyes were on Cyann. "Shan Cyann, we studied the video of your encounter with the being with great interest. You were deeply affected by her passing."

"I was."

"Did you feel any sort of affinity to the alien? Why would

you, as an experienced xenobiologist, become attached so quickly to a specimen?"

Cyann's brows drew together. Was Shelyth hinting that her Human nature had overtaken her ability to remain impartial? That the valued Delphian stoicism had deserted her when it was most needed? "It was a difficult moment, Shan Shelyth. The creature was in distress and I felt empathy."

"More than you would for another dying creature? Sentient or not?"

"Yes," Cyann said after a moment.

"Was there anything familiar about this individual? Something you might recognize?"

Cyann turned her head when Jovan made a subdued hissing sound. Was Shelyth referring to the voice that had haunted her throughout her life? More warnings from some immeasurable distance, perceived only by her?

On the screen, Tychon leaned forward. "Can you offer some insight into the purpose of your inquiries, Shelyth?" Everyone noticed that he had omitted the usual honorific before her name.

"No," the Shantir said abruptly. "I will do so when we have concluded our observations of the available information." Her eyes returned to Cyann.

"It was not familiar," Cyann said, aware that Jovan, Anders and her parents were also awaiting her reply with more than just polite interest. The voice had come, of course, just moments before she touched the meteorite. But it had not come from in there, of that she was certain. "There was nothing familiar there. I just wanted to comfort her. She was not a specimen. She was a sentient visitor who came a long way to deliver a message, if that's what it is. She was frightened and alone and we could do nothing to help her."

Shelyth nodded. She glanced at Moghen, apparently in silent conversation with the other Shantir. "May all of us find such comfort in our last moment."

"Indeed," Nova Whiteside said with a gentle smile for her daughter. "I think we all agree that action must be taken immediately. We will recommend that we send an expedition along the visitor's trajectory to see if we can find this cloud and determine when it will get to Trans-Targon and whether it carries the virus. I will request Air Command support along with a research ship to see if we can intercept, perhaps redirect the anomaly."

The Council member spoke up. "You propose to make this a military operation, then?"

"A Commonwealth mission," Nova replied quickly. "This affects all of us. And Targon, like it or not, has the greatest resources. No one else has the sort of mobile astrophysics lab that we'll need."

"And fire power," Moghen added.

"No one suggests destroying the anomaly if, as you believe, it is populated," Jovan said.

"But that will be an option. It always is."

"Given the possible outcome, yes," Nova said. "It will be a last resort, I assure you."

"What assurance can you offer?"

"I'll volunteer to command this venture."

Council looked to Tychon as representing the clans. "Phera concurs," Tychon said. "Let's turn this over to the Union. This is beyond Delphi's resources and jurisdiction."

Nova gave her mate a sunny smile. "Now all we need is the sort of spanner that can get us through those keyholes quicker than speedy."

He sighed. "I knew this was coming," he said. "I'm in."

She looked past him to Moghen. "Since these individuals can communicate telepathically we should take along a few Shantirs."

If Tychon had objections to this none of it showed on his face. Cyann noticed a slight darkening of his eyes and hid a grin. No doubt Nova had made sure to get his agreement before adding the Shantirs to the mission.

"I'll go, too," she said.

"Can't stop me, either," Anders added. "With Council's permission, that is."

Cyann peered at Jovan, waiting for his response. But his eyes were focused on the star map and he said nothing about joining the expedition.

FIVE

The mildness of Delphian winters, like the rest of the planet's seasons, would have brought tourism and settlement to any other world with such climate. But Delphi cared neither for tourism nor immigration and so their winters, their cool, crisp summers and the short seasons in-between remained unexplored by strangers and unblemished by outside influences.

It was rare for off-worlders to find themselves invited to places outside the Union's carefully guarded Air Command base in the foothills. But even Delphians did not enter the secret, walled gardens of the Shantir's enclave unless they themselves were members of the sect. Cyann, although a frequent visitor to the enclave, had never been out this way.

Wrapped snugly in a long, wool-lined cloak, she peered curiously from under her hood to look around the carefully groomed grounds, enchanted by the undisturbed blanket of fresh snow illuminated by Delphi's moons. Ice crystals sparkled in this light which required few of the carefully-placed lanterns to help them find their way. She walked between Anders and Nigel, who were likely also wondering what had possessed Shan Moghen to take them back here, into the enclave's most private sanctuary.

Jovan and Shantir Regin walked behind them, sharing a murmured conversation and less enraptured by the beauty of the landscape. Cyann looked up to see large rings of ice around the three overhead moons. She nearly bumped into Shan Moghen ahead of them when he slowed to ascend a few steps into a wooden pergola beside the path.

The others followed and entered the octagonal space lined with padded benches around a central, shallow brazier. Although there were no windows to stop the night air, the interior of this space was heated and welcoming. They removed their cloaks and settled into the benches.

"This place is beautiful," Cyann said. "Like a fairy tale."

Moghen smiled. "A good retreat for today's purpose, then," he said cryptically. "But chosen for its solitude. Even the enclave has too many ears." He ignited a heater under the tea urn that had been left here for them.

"You have something for us," Anders guessed. "About the alien visitor. Something important enough to delay our departure."

Moghen nodded. Nova and her team had left for Targon days ago. There they would board a well-equipped interstellar transport for their journey to the Badlands. One of Delphi's astronomers and three Shantirs complemented the lineup of experts provided by Targon. Anders Devaughn's research ship had remained on Delphi when the Shantirs asked for the delay.

"To it, then," he said. "And let's begin with the fairy tale. Tell us about the Tughan Wai, Cyann."

She looked from Moghen to Regin and then to Jovan, who seemed equally surprised by the request. "The Tughan?"

"Yes, that," Moghen confirmed and poured small cups of strong tea for his guests.

Cyann shrugged. "A cautionary tale for children. Or an old legend for those who believe such things. The Tughan Wai is a mythical construct, a god, perhaps, with powers far beyond those of the Shantirs. He is at once the destroyer of worlds and the protector of Delphi. He came into being when the Centauri arrived in Trans-Targon and began to create the Commonwealth. Delphi tried to avoid them, but when it was discovered that some of us," she gestured at Jovan, "could easily traverse keyholes and we became important to the Union, Delphi felt threatened. The Shantirs created the Tughan Wai as a shield against the invaders as well as the rebel wars that followed."

"And then?"

"The Tughan turned against them all, murdered thousands and then disappeared." Cyann's eyes fell on Anders who was watching her with rapt attention. Something worried the Human; she knew him well enough to read the tension in his shoulders and the pinched look around his eyes. She glanced at Jovan whose face remained carefully free of any expression she could read. What was he hiding? "We all know this story," she said. "It's the most basic of myths. You find it in some form or another on most worlds."

"Do you know how he murdered all those thousands?"

"The khamal *wai*. A theoretical khamal during which all knowledge is taken from the victim. I'm not too clear on that, but I think it copies engrams and neural connections – neuroscience is not my field. The Shantir using the process gains knowledge as well as personality traits, formative experiences, memories. But this intrusion kills the victim." Cyann smiled at Nigel. "We don't tell that part to the children."

"Uh, I'm glad," he said, as puzzled as she was by this strange meeting.

"A dangerous and powerful creature, wouldn't you say," Moghen said. "Carrying the knowledge and motivations of thousands of people, of many races, good and evil, inside his own, infinite brain."

"I would," she replied. "It must be very unhappy."

He raised an eyebrow. "Why do you say that?"

"I used to think that, when I was a child. To know so much and to have such power must be very lonely. Who would you talk to? Where would you go? And how could you live with yourself, knowing how you gained that knowledge."

"You didn't think it was an evil, ah, monster?"

"No," she said, staring into space. "I know what it's like to be different. How much more terrible must it be for him? Not just different, but feared, shunned." She felt Anders hand on her arm. He knew more than any of the others how it felt to be an outsider on Delphi. She met Moghen's eyes. "If he's evil you have made him so."

A long silence followed during which they let Moghen and Regin carry on whatever mental conversation was taking place between them. Cyann sipped her tea and listened to a distant wind chime, the only sound besides the gentle crackle of the embers in the brazier. She felt Jovan's tranquil presence in sharp contrast to Anders' tension. Did anything ever worry him?

Shantir Regin finally spoke aloud. "Why does your father hold such contempt for the Shantirate," she said and, with a nod to Jovan, added, "with some exceptions."

Cyann nearly spilled her tea when the uncomfortable subject was raised. "I don't think I can speak for my father..." she tried.

"Please, dear," Regin said. "Speak freely."

"His son, my half-brother Kiran, was lost during a battle with the Shri-Lan rebels because of your neglect," Cyann said in a rush. "He's blamed you for that ever since."

Regin nodded. "I suppose that is true," she said. "But not the whole story."

Anders cleared his throat. "Shan Regin, I don't know where this is going, but I have to remind you—"

Regin cut him off with a curt wave of her hand. "You are no longer a commissioned officer, Elder Brother. And none of us here are bound to Air Command rules. Be assured that this is necessary."

"What is?" Cyann said, worried now.

"We did not just lose his son. Do you really think that someone like Tychon would spend thirty years of his life carrying a grudge because someone made a mistake? Because of an accident?"

"No, I don't suppose. But it's not a subject that is talked about. Besides, the entire incident is classified. And that means just that. Neither of my parents would share classified information even with me."

Regin put her tea cup on the edge of the brazier, taking some time in making sure it would not tip off the edge, once again in conversation with Moghen. While not unusual, especially among Shantirs, excluding others in such an obvious way bordered on impoliteness. Whatever was going on in their heads was either an argument or simply extremely important.

"We are not bound to Air Command classifications," Moghen said with a look to Anders. "Tychon's son is the result of some very careful maneuvering on our part. We steered Tychon to accept a mate of our choosing, which fortunately he did, combining some very vital genetic material held by their respective clans. Once his son, Kiran, was born, we continued to work with the child's hereditary abilities to gift him with the talents of the Shantirs." He indicated Jovan, who would have received similar training as well as outright manipulation of his brain.

"You wanted him to be a Shantir?" Cyann said, absolutely certain that she did not want Moghen to continue. This sort of careful meddling was not unusual; in fact, Delphian parents routinely sought out the Shantirate to determine their child's talents and ensure that those abilities developed fully. Certainly, this revelation was no reason to hide away in a private sanctuary.

"No," Moghen said. "We made him the Tughan Wai."

Anders groaned. Jovan closed his eyes. Nigel stared, open-mouthed, his tea cup raised halfway to his lips.

Cyann groped for Anders' hand when the room seemed to lurch sideways, threatening to shake her off her bench. "What?" she gasped.

"He was the end result of hundreds of years of

experimentation. Even though we no longer really consider the Commonwealth a threat to us, the trials continued. Many failed. Until Kiran."

"Why? Who would do such a thing?"

"A misguided few," Regin said. "Please be assured that none of those involved are practicing members of the sect now. They... they have been retired."

"But you knew," Anders said. "And that is what Tychon won't forgive."

"We knew," Moghen looked at his hands as if his blue-tinted fingernails revealed some way to explain all this. "We tried to contain it. When Kiran's mother died we offered to take the boy into the enclave while Tychon continued his Air Command career. But Danaria's family interfered and so he removed the child from Delphi to a school on Feyd. That's when Kiran was taken by the rebel."

"He was six years old when he disappeared," Cyann said, barely above a whisper.

"And by that time had killed almost a thousand people. And had *become* those thousand people. He was no longer a child."

"Mentally," Anders said with an uncharacteristic edge in his voice.

Moghen nodded. "He fled the battle by taking an Air Command ship into a keyhole that we didn't even know existed. Air Command declared the boy lost to the rebel and classified the entire matter."

"If I may ask a question," Nigel said, unsure of his place in this group. "Is it true what they say about this... this Tughan?"

Regin gave him a sad smile. "Can he shake mountains and boil seas? Can he take the moons and fling them at our enemies? No. Can he destroy a mind, or a hundred? A thousand at once? Yes. Can he destroy ships in the sky? Easily. Can he affect those laws of physics you hold so dear? To a degree. He is the sum of every Shantir that ever lived. Those people whose collective knowledge he absorbed gave him insight into things we cannot even fathom."

Nigel whistled. "Damn, no wonder Tychon's pissed with you people."

Cyann looked up at Jovan. "But not you."

He shrugged. "I wasn't there."

"But you knew about this," she said. "You've known all these years and said nothing." She turned to Anders. "And you, too."

"Cyann, don't take the road Tychon chose," Regin said. "Jovan is bound to the Shantirate to keep this secret, even from you. And Anders was an officer at the time as well as a Union ambassador on Delphi."

Anders nodded. "Even Tychon's own clan assumes that Kiran is either dead or perhaps grew up among the rebels and is spanning for them. A Delphian's navigational skill is something they can't match and the only way to get a Delphian to join the rebel is to raise one of their own. That happened a few times, long ago, which is why you don't often see Delphians traveling without an armed escort."

Cyann nodded. "That's what I was led to believe."

Regin extended her hands to encompass them all. "Please don't blame Tychon and Nova for their secrecy or, for that matter, the Shantirate. Knowledge of this cannot leave this place."

Nigel frowned. "So why tell us now?"

The Shantir paused to pick up her cup which she studied for a moment as if in appreciation of the pattern painted on it. "Because the writings that the alien brought to us are Delphian."

"What?" Anders exclaimed. "We spent hours trying to decode those."

Moghen smiled. "Yet Jovan recognized them. It is a Shantir code, known only by the elders. I'm please to find that it is still unbreakable."

Jovan winked at Cyann. "Before you jump at me I have to say that I wasn't able to read it. It's that tough. I just thought some of the forms looked familiar."

"So what do they say?"

Moghen and Regin exchanged a glance. "They are fairly incomprehensible, I'm afraid. Talk about distant lands, some mathematics we don't understand, coordinates that we do know. And, most importantly, your name, Cyann."

She blinked. "My name?"

"In a way. It mentions 'Tychon's girl child' in two locations."

"Whoa," Nigel said quietly.

"I was about to say that," Anders whispered.

Cyann looked around the circle of shadowed faces before returning her gaze to Moghen. "I think it's time you presented your hypothesis, Elder Brother."

"Yes, it is," he said crisply. "Your brother, Kiran, whom we call the Tughan Wai, sent the meteorite this way, hoping to reach you. Perhaps to warn us of the arrival of the Genesis Cloud. He would have the ability to guide that pod here, even through sub-space. Because of you."

"Me?"

"We believe that Kiran is that voice you've grown up with," Regin said. "I've suspected that for a while but haven't been able to convince my brethren. Not until now. He's been trying to reach you. And he's used your connection like a homing beacon to bring the alien pod here. Not to Delphi. But to Sola moon where he knew it would do no harm to us."

"How?" Anders said. "He doesn't even know Cyann exists. He barely knew Nova when he disappeared."

Cyann nodded. "But he changed her, didn't he? It wasn't some radiation accident or classified rebel weapon that did that to her. He made her a GenMod. He made it possible for me to be born."

"That is the best likelihood. She did mention to me, just after you were born, that Kiran told her to give Tychon a daughter, if she chose. It was a confusing time for all of us. There is no other explanation for the genetic transformation that had to take place. He had as much a part of your creation as your father did."

Jovan leaned close to her. "Are you all right?" he said softly. "This is all a bit much."

She pulled away and immediately regretted that when she saw the brief flash of hurt on his face, as quickly hidden as it had appeared. She stood up and walked to the railing overlooking the snow-blanketed gardens. "All these years of wondering, thinking I might be going mad, not knowing who or what I was, and none of you thought to tell me any of this?"

"We had no way to be sure," Moghen said.

She turned back to them but her eyes were on Jovan. "What else haven't you told me?"

It seemed that he was about to speak but then, with a look to Regin, he just shrugged.

"Cyann," Regin said gently. "We knew you were special. But to us you were always just Tychon's daughter. Because of Kiran, we wanted you to have every advantage that the enclave can offer to a pupil, Shantir or not. Fully Delphian or not. You grew into an accomplished scientist, every bit as gifted as your father, in your own way, and blessed with your mother's delightful mind-set."

"And good looks," Anders tried to lighten the moment.

"Yes, you are lovely," Regin said. "But I'm not saying these things to flatter you. We had hoped that none of what happened would ever touch you, even as we watched out for any mark that Kiran might have left on you, or Shan Nova."

"Until the voice," Cyann said.

"Yes, although our main concern was that, because of your mixed parentage, you were simply susceptible to other people's mental exchanges. Or emotions. I started to keep an account of these incidences. Or at least the ones you shared with me. It seems to me that the voice comes to you when you are upset or anxious."

Cyann nodded.

"And so you went to Tava to boost your range."

Cyann's eyes narrowed when she looked to Jovan.

"He told us nothing," Moghen said. "Tava did when we... questioned him about his decision to leave the enclave."

"Told them what?" Anders said.

"It does not matter," Regin said. "The point is that Kiran seems to be able to find you at such times and perhaps that is what allowed him to send the visitor here."

Cyann returned to her seat. Jovan shifted a little to make room for her but she noted that he did not sit as close to her as before, nor did he place his arm around her shoulder again. She wished he would. She wished he'd put both of his arms around her and let her bury her face into his broad chest as he had when she was five and in need of comforting. But she wasn't five any more, she reminded herself with a glance up at his shuttered face. And maybe simple comfort wasn't enough anymore, either.

She returned her attention to the other Shantirs. "What do you want from us?" she said and then nodded toward Nigel. "Why are they here?"

"We want you to take the *Scout* and find Kiran."

"Um," Nigel raised a hand. "You're talking about your brain-sucking god monster?"

Anders scowled at him.

"Just asking. Seems to me that I just got volunteered for something pretty unpleasant."

"You did," Moghen said. "Would you prefer us to wipe your memory of this conversation so you can get out of this?"

Cyann actually felt a small grin trying to tug on her lips when she caught the light in Shantir Regin's eyes.

"What? No!"

Anders did smile. "Well, like it or not, we're under contract with Delphi, not the Union. They own our easily-breakable necks while we want jobs here. But besides that, don't tell me that you're not dying to get a look at the boy."

"No one is forcing you," Moghen amended. "But you have the skills we need and you've worked with Anders and Cyann for a few years. We don't want to bring anyone else into this." He tilted his head toward Jovan. "Shan Jovan will navigate. We know you're an accomplished pilot but some of the jumps you'll need to undertake are beyond your skills."

"How will we find him?" Jovan asked.

"We believe he sent the pod to warn us. No one else out there would know about that Shantir code. But we don't know if he's even there anymore. Let Shan Nova and her team look for the cloud and try to deal with the danger it represents to all of us. That may not be for years yet. Generations perhaps. But you must find the Tughan before we lose his trail. Go with the Union fleet and begin your search there. We hope that you, Cyann, can find him with that mental connection you seem to have and convince him to return to Delphi."

"Why?" she said. "Why do you want to find him? Is it not enough that he's chosen to exile himself? Maybe he doesn't want to be found."

"You want him back in Trans-Targon knowing what he's capable of?" Jovan added.

Regin nodded. "We have no right to ask him to return to us. But what does that voice you hear tell you, Cyann? It calls for you. It is in pain. It is asking for help. If that is Kiran, we must answer. We owe him this. But we also want to know about him. The Tughan Wai took generations to create. Our curiosity is boundless." Moghen paused for a moment before continuing. "And maybe we can ask for Kiran's forgiveness for what we did to him."

Cyann stared into the coals. "Alone. A six-year old boy. Changed forever by your misguided experiments. How terrible that must have been."

"There is another theory," Regin said carefully. "It is a remote possibility but no more far-fetched than the one we're actually considering. I can tell by Jovan's mood that it's one that bothers him, too."

Cyann turned her head to look at Jovan who seemed surprised that Regin had guessed his thoughts.

"What is that," she said to Regin.

"It's possible that Kiran did not send the pod at all. That someone else is trying to warn us. And the scrap of code they brought is simply evidence that Kiran is involved."

"What do you mean?"

"The message, although written in our own language, is difficult to decipher. It hints that the Tughan no longer thinks as we do. Nor would I expect him to. None of us can comprehend to what measure his intellect has grown. But it's also likely that he suffers from the same emotions we all share. And among them is hatred, need for revenge perhaps. For having had no choice but to leave his clan and exile himself, as Cyann said. Some of us think that he may be directing the asteroids here. That this isn't the Genesis Cloud that excites Targon's physicists but that he is simply sending the contaminant to destroy Delphi."

"That's absurd!" Cyann gasped.

"He is no longer Delphian," Jovan reminded her. "He's become too many people and few of those were ours. He has no allegiance to any of us."

She looked around the circle of faces lit only by the twitching licks of light from the coals. "You are victims of your own fairy tales," she said finally. "'The Tughan shall destroy Delphi'. Since when do the Shantirs listen to children's stories? Especially one of their own making."

"Cyann…" Anders said.

She shook her head. "Believe what you want. I've heard that voice. There is nothing hateful about it."

"It is still possible that the voice is not Kiran's at all."

Her lips formed a thin line. "Then let us find out."

"You agree to go? Not knowing what you might find?"

"Yes." She looked over to Anders, who had fallen silent and thoughtful. "Are you up for this, uncle," she said softly.

He turned his head toward her and smiled slowly. "Just try to stop me."

"Is the Council aware of this?" Cyann asked Moghen.

"Yes, they will supply the *Scout* and release as much coolant as you can store. You'll have to traverse quite a number of keyholes."

Jovan sighed. "No doubt." Although their ships' processors took care of the immense computations needed to span two points in sub-space, it took a sentient mind to direct it toward the desired exit. Such minds were found among Delphians and, in rare instances, among other species aided by pharmaceuticals. Guiding any sort of vessel through an uncharted keyhole took a toll on the navigator's body and mind, requiring hours of recovery time between jumps. The list of ships navigated by lesser trained pilots that had failed to re-emerge from sub-space was long and still growing.

"Have you informed Air Command of this?" Anders asked.

All eyes shifted to Moghen with that question.

"You're asking me if we've told Nova and Tychon," Moghen replied. "No, we have not. Let us learn what we can before we alarm them. I'm sure you can understand why."

"If you're wrong about who sent the asteroid we will have raised his hope of finding his son for nothing," Jovan said.

"And if Regin is correct with that other possibility, we don't even want him to know," Cyann said. "Because, one way or another, he must be stopped."

Nigel barked a short laugh. "How do you stop a god from destroying the world?"

Moghen took a deep breath. "He is as mortal as any of us."

"Shan Moghen," Anders said, "if you're asking us what I think you're asking..."

"I am. He could have been stopped once. He wasn't. And that decision has weighed on all of us since that day as we consider the possibilities." He shook his head. "Don't think about this now. Our best hope is that Kiran has sent the alien to warn us of the impending return of the cloud. There is no point trying to guess what's on his mind or why he doesn't simply deflect the object. Join the Union expedition and do what you can to contact him from there. We have much to learn."

"That is as far as I will keep this from Tychon," Anders said. "I see the necessity for all of this, but Tychon is my brother-friend and I can't keep something as important as his son from him. If Kiran is out there, Tychon must know."

Moghen nodded. "Agreed."

SIX

"We're coming in range of the *Repha Zi* and are now officially in the Badlands. The vast unexplored. The perilous periphery of Trans-Targon. Where there are dragons and monsters and shadows in the dark. Are ya'll excited?" Nigel strolled into the *Scout*'s main lab where Anders and Cyann were exchanging slides and lazily updating their database. Neither looked up at his announcement but Cyann waved a vague thumbs-up in his direction. He studied the scatter of tools, breakfast trays, data pads, imagers and specimen containers on the console. "Someday you're going to accidentally put a mould sample into your tea instead of sweets," he predicted.

Cyann looked around. "Maybe we should tidy up some," she said as she took the magnifier from her eye and her feet from the counter. Still in her sleep wear, she was comfortable in loose trousers and shirt and a pair of very cozy socks. "Or we can turn off the cabin cameras when we say hello."

"Sounds like a fine option," Nigel leaned over her to flip one of the overhead screens to display the cockpit video system. "They'll be in view in a few hours."

Anders started to stack samples into a case. "About time.

I think I've had my fill of cataloging pollen samples for a while. Years, probably."

"But look at the progress we've made these past few days," Cyann said, pointing to a stack of similar cases on the floor. "And it beats watching Nigel's tedious plays."

"Hey, those are all the rage on Magra. You have no appreciation for art."

"No, I have no appreciation for that Centauri actress you're slavering after," she replied. She tipped her head back to study him. "Comb your hair. You look like you just woke up."

Anders looked up to scrutinize Cyann's untidy mane. "So says the authority on fashion and personal grooming. Speaking of waking up, where is our navigator?"

"Still out, I think," Nigel said, peering into the empty tea bottle on the table. Disappointed, he flopped back onto a beat-up lounger sporting a peculiar floral pattern that he had brought aboard three years ago and refused to give up. "That last jump knocked him right over. Not that he'll admit it, but I doubt he's moved a toe since he fell into his bunk."

Cyann sat up. "I should get dressed properly. I can just see Tychon do that thing he does with his lip when he's not impressed by something."

Anders rose. "I'll get Jovan up. I've got experience with waking the dead. I mean, waking Delphians."

"Good luck with that," Nigel said. He shook his head. "I don't know how you people manage to pass out like that," he said to Cyann. "I can't get through a single sleep shift without one of you waking me with your snoring."

"I don't snore!"

"You just keep thinking that."

She grimaced and left the lab to move along the narrow corridor to her cabin. They had reduced the ship's gravity for intervals to conserve energy and she bounced lightly on her toes.

These past days had made for a tedious journey but she was used to that. They had followed Nova's small fleet out of

Targon, meeting up at some of the jump gates and then parting ways again. Nova was commanding *Repha Zi*, the Union's impressive mobile astrophysics lab equipped with some of the best long-range sensors available. Along with that came the four Air Command Eagle cruisers, heavily armed and staffed by elite Vanguard officers and pilots.

The first leg of the trip had been made using the open and charted jumpsites linking the populated areas of Trans-Targon. The quick jaunts through sub-space were expensive, using up coolant more precious than fuel, but did not require a great deal of effort on Jovan's part.

Eventually they had run out of mapped sites and had to rely on Tychon and Jovan to open keyholes, microscopic breaches in space, and expand them into traversable apertures. Using their ships' computing power along with their highly evolved mental abilities, they penetrated sub-space to determine the desired exit. Without this connection, communicated to the ship via their neural interface taps, leaving sub-space again was unlikely or, if it happened, could land them at some problematic point anywhere within their galaxy and possibly beyond.

Unfortunately, the four jumps they had taken to reach the edge of Trans-Targon's explored space meant that Jovan had spent much of the past few days asleep. But he had not neglected to continue lending his healing touch to Cyann's slow recovery and she felt better now than she had for weeks.

She bounded into her room and slipped into a slightly less wrinkled set of clothes. When she felt the slow shift of the *Scout*'s gravitational pull as Nigel adjusted it for their daytime routines, she shook her hair free and combed it into some semblance of order.

"Cyann!" Nigel called into the corridor. "Your mother wants a word."

"Don't shout, Human," she heard Jovan's grumbled complaint before the door to the ship's hygiene chamber closed.

Cyann hurried from her room into the central passage of the ship, past the hum of Jovan's decon cycle and back into the main lab.

But it was her father's image that greeted her on the large overhead screen. His attention was on something off-camera. Anders, at the main console, was also busy. As always, Tychon's hair was neatly braided, his casual clothes impeccable. Cyann fumbled with her twisted collar in an attempt to straighten it.

"Hello, Dadda."

He looked up and a smile softened his features. "Good morning, Little Blue," he said. "We'll have to sync up when you get here. We're all ready for bed." He leaned over the controls on his side of the conversation. "Here are the files, Anders."

"What have you got there?" Cyann asked.

"We've pretty much worked out the alien's language as much as we can. She didn't have time to say very much, but I think the techs did a very good job with what they had to work with. I want to know what you think, Anders."

"Ohh, wanna hear this!" Nigel said.

They waited until the files Tychon transmitted from the Union ship arrived at the *Scout* and were fed into their own system. All of them eagerly connected their neural interfaces to access the new program. "You first," Cyann nodded at Anders. "If this makes us sound like rodents I can wait."

"You're so thoughtful," he said and engaged the translator. He thought a moment before mouthing the words he meant to say to slow down the thoughts that the translator would need to calculate. Haltingly, a babble of words came over the lab's speakers, sounding eerily like the little alien.

Cyann shivered, thinking about their visitor and her last few moments on Sola. She was suddenly uneager to try the new matrix herself.

"And now for the acid test," Nigel said. He had recorded Anders' sentences and now returned them through the translator and back into Delphian, the language Anders had chosen for the experiment.

"Say joy dirty," the mechanical voice said. "Plate tidy boat."

"Huh?"

Tychon, up on the screen, sighed.

"Try another language," Nigel said.

They experimented until it seemed that a common Centauri dialect, the foundation of Union mainvoice, was the easiest to translate into the alien's language.

"Cyann is agreed to bring dirt and foul eating plates to clean on big ship"

"What? I never said that!" she protested. "You do your own cleaning."

Tychon grinned. "You try it, Cyann," he said but then turned when someone nearby caught his attention. He frowned. "Really? Are you sure?"

"What is it?" Anders said.

Tychon leaned aside, perhaps looking at another monitor. There were more voices there now, sounding excited.

Cyann turned when Jovan entered the lab, looking a little tousled but rested. He came to where they had gathered at the console. "What's going on?"

"Something happening over there," she said. "Maybe they found the keyhole. All better?"

He nodded. "You shouldn't let me sleep so long. A few hours is enough."

"Hey, Nova," Anders said.

Their mission commander had appeared on the monitor when she sat down beside Tychon who was now busy with something on the console out of sight of the camera. "Anders," she smiled, but her smile seemed harried, like a formality to be dispensed with. "Hello, Sweetie," she added with a nod to Cyann.

"Have you found something?" Jovan said.

"Yes. And it's not good. We've detected the keyhole precisely where the tablet said it would be. It's stable."

"Somehow I thought you'd be happier about that," Cyann said, puzzled by Nova's tone. Now that they had found what was essentially an entrance into Trans-Targon, they could start to probe into possible exists to look for the approaching cloud. Failing that, they would begin to plan a defence system capable of destroying the object upon arrival here.

"The planet we detected earlier is inhabited," Nova said. "Densely."

"Gods," Jovan whispered.

"We're not seeing any activity in orbit and so we've sent some probes. Sensors show a very complex ecosystem. We'll know more in a few hours. By the time you get here, for sure."

"That whole solar system will be right in the cloud's path," Cyann said.

Tychon looked up. "And we'll have barely room to move if we have to destroy the object." He nodded in Jovan's direction. "We'll start mapping the keyhole as soon as you get here. I really don't want to wait around until it comes at us from sub-space."

"Anders," Nova began and then gestured at someone off-screen. To those on the *Scout* it seemed like the entire command center of the Union vessel was in a state of guarded fretfulness. "We're going to start sending you our findings about the planet. The more eyes on this the better. If you determine the life form physiology we can concentrate on atmospheric conditions. We can't start blasting asteroids until we know how that will affect them."

"Let's hope we don't have to blast anything," Anders said. "Start sending."

"I'll see if I can get a little more wind into our sails," Jovan said. "Did anyone make breakfast?"

* * *

There was something oddly hypnotic about feeling her breath tear through her throat, her heart pound in her chest as if trying to escape from there, and the steady pace of running nowhere.

Cyann's view of the planet below was a panorama afforded by the *Repha Zi*'s generous observation window, relieving the tedium of her carefully controlled and monitored exercise routines. Her eyes were on the curving horizon, swathed so thickly in a pinkish atmosphere that no landmasses were seen from orbit.

But her thoughts were far away, couched in the deep meditative state of a khamal, following Jovan's recommendation to lose herself in the unthinking, automatic movements of her body on this treadmill while trying to cast her mind outward in the hopes of somehow, somewhere, contacting the Tughan Wai.

There was nothing. No voice calling to her from outside or within herself. No eerie feeling that she was not alone. There was no one here but the crew of this vessel, each of them palpable to her in this state of mind. Some of them asleep, some working in the labs and observatories, several aboard the Air Command cruisers docked to the main vessel. Centauri, Human, a few Caspians and several Delphians. All familiar, all belonged here.

"Are you looking for me or actually planning to exercise?" she said and slowed the treadmill to a fast pace.

Anders Devaughn walked past her to look out over the planet. "I'm losing my touch," he said. "You caught me this time. You're up late."

"As are you. How are things coming along?" she asked, meaning Tychon and Jovan's efforts to find their way through the keyhole located within this solar system. Patiently, they had mapped several possible exits, using the trajectory demonstrated by the alien's capsule and the astronomer's predictions of the anomaly's orbit. Soon, they would use one of the cruisers to launch through the breach in the hopes of detecting the approaching object on the other side.

"Slowly." He shrugged. "And here?"

She shook her head. None of her efforts, or Jovan's attempts at helping her reach farther outside herself, had brought results. Just as well that they had not yet told the others about the Shantirs' suspicions about Kiran, she thought. "Still working on it," she assured Anders. "I'm learning a lot from Jovan."

"Oh? Shantir secrets?"

"I wish! He's making sure I mind my own business." She stopped the exerciser. It was nearly time to find Jovan for one of the healing treatments that had become so important to her. The crawling, anxious, restless mental state she still felt at times was beginning to nag at her and she ached for the relief Jovan was able to offer.

"I'm going to spend some time with Tychon and Nova," Anders said. "Why don't you join us for a bit, since you're up anyway?"

"Ah, thanks, but I think I'll just spin through decon and then get some sleep."

"Sure? Nova and I are going to drink wine so that you and your father can frown at us and act superior, seeing how you don't indulge in such pollution."

She glanced at him sharply. "What do you mean by that?"

"Well, you know. Nothing more sober than a Delphian."

"You make that sound like an accusation." Was he hinting at something? Did he know?

He seemed bewildered. "Just joking, Cy. You're awfully tense for someone just off the treadmill. Is everything all right?"

"Yes, why?"

"You seem a little... strained. Are you sure your exercises with Jovan aren't taxing you too much?"

"I'm fine, Anders. Tell them I said good night."

He nodded but didn't seem convinced. "See you in the morning."

She watched him leave, already regretting her sharp words. She debated catching up with him in the hall outside to take him up on his offer. Certainly, her parents would welcome some time with their daughter. All of them had careers that rarely saw them in the same place for very long and she missed them.

But Jovan would be looking for her and that thought was enough to make her hurry to the *Scout* moored safely to the Union ship to get cleaned up. He would relieve that itchy craving inside her head but it was also his calm, powerful presence, focused on her alone, that she craved more with each passing day.

He was not yet aboard the *Scout* when she got there and still hadn't arrived by the time she had changed her clothes and returned to the ship's common area. Surely, he and Tychon had concluded their day's work by now. She resisted the urge to call over to the observatory to find out if they were still there. Instead, she tidied up a little, mostly by pacing around and moving things from one place to another. After a while of this she called up something to read but soon got tired of it. When she tried to concentrate on some work nothing seemed to fit into her brain and the images on the screen blurred and hurt her eyes. Where was he?

She paced from one end of the ship to the other and back again, beginning to feel a little panicked. His treatments of the residual effects of the brutally damaging khamal induced by Shantir Tava on Delphi had become a vital part of her day. She wondered if she was becoming dependent on that, too, now. She cursed silently, angry for bringing all of this upon herself.

How could he be so inconsiderate as to leave her waiting like this?

More than an hour later she heard the soft hiss of the airlock door opening. She rushed to the entrance, hoping that it wasn't Nigel or Anders returning for the night. With relief, she saw Jovan stoop through the door.

"There you are!" she said. "I've been worried."

"About what? It's not like you can get lost up here."

"Well, I mean... I thought you might have decided to stay over there tonight."

"I thought about it," he said. "Damn tired. Your father is a slave driver."

Her smile faded. "You thought about it? I was waiting for you."

He walked past her into the main lab. "Were you? Sorry."

"I'd think you'd notice. I'm not in... not feeling so good. I was hoping you could... We could work together a little."

"Need your fix, Little Blue?" he said. "Maybe it's time you got over this. You don't need me anymore. You can do this yourself."

"What? No, I can't."

"You can. And you will. I'm too tired, Cyann. My brain went to sleep two hours ago. You're just going to have to deal with it." He bent over the console that linked the *Scout* to the Union ship's astrophysics lab.

She gripped his arm. "Please, Jovie. I feel terrible. I won't be able to sleep."

"You'll be fine," he promised and pulled away. "You're in no danger now. This isn't easy for me, either, you know."

"What is?"

"Maintaining that khamal with you. It's exhausting."

"Why didn't you say that before?"

He shrugged absently, his eyes on an overhead screen. "Because you needed it. You don't anymore."

"It's difficult because I'm not all Delphian, is that what you're saying?"

Jovan frowned and paused as if considering her question. "I suppose."

Stunned, she searched his bland, closed-off expression and saw nothing there but fatigue. "You... you don't like it? Joining with me? You never said so."

"I know how touchy you are about being half Human."

"Touchy?" she whispered.

"Something else you'll have to get over. You are what you are. Maybe it's time to admit that and get on with it. Live your life and quit looking for approval from Delphi."

She stared at him, speechless.

He pointed at his head. "So your brain works a little differently. So what? You're short for a Delphian. And you have a few freckles. Why do you worry about stupid things?"

She touched her face. He knew quite well that the pale sprinkle of blue pigment across her nose, a gift from her unapologetically red-haired mother, had bothered her since she was very small. He had comforted her more than once when the teasing of other children had brought her to tears.

Those tears now threatened to spill and she bit her lip, angry and hurt by his words, unable to fight through the distracting haze that he refused to remedy. "Don't talk like that," she said, more angry yet when her voice sounded pleading even to her own ears.

"All right, I won't," he said and turned to the door. "Need to get some sleep anyway."

"Jovan!"

He sighed. "I'm not talking to you if you're going to snivel like that."

She ground her teeth, almost painfully. "Yes, I've had enough of you, too," she said, furious now. "I don't know why you're being a jerk, but I don't like it. Go get your beauty sleep, if that's so important to you. Don't let my mental problems keep you up a moment longer."

"They probably will," he said, still without any expression she could read. When had he ever seemed so utterly blank to her? "Another reason for you to finally shake this nonsense. You're distracting me all day long." He gestured at the screen monitoring the keyhole. "We have work to do, so get your head together and do your damn share!"

She saw that his hands had balled into fists. The blue eyes had turned dark and foreboding. What had she done to deserve his ire? His contempt? She had always been so sure of his concern for her welfare and respect for her family that she did not think him capable of anything but unquestioning, unconditional loyalty. Seeing an end to his patience was a painful blow. But what right did she have to burden him with her demands? He had returned to find her still occupied with microbes and test tubes, living safely at home, beset with emotional issues that he no doubt found tedious and distasteful. And he'd finally had enough. She felt his disappointment in her like a cold draft in the room.

Hear me.

Cyann froze and her eyes widened in surprise when these words entered her thoughts.

Help me.

"I'm here," she whispered.

Jovan stepped closer to her. "What is it?"

She shook her head, all of her attention on the weak signal from somewhere out there, that tenuous touch on her mind that threatened to slip away at any moment. "Kiran," she said finally. "Kiran? Is that you?"

Jovan gripped her arm even as he leaned over to slap at some of the controls on the lab's console to connect his neural interface to the ship. She slumped against him when he drew her close and then she felt him inside her mind, lending her the strength and power of his abilities. "Don't let him go, Cy," he said urgently.

"Kiran," she said again, barely aware when Jovan lowered her onto Nigel's threadbare lounger, still wrapped in his embrace.

Pain. Don't pain.

"Are you hurt?" she asked.

You. You hurt.

"No," she said, smiling through tears of joy now. "I'm fine. Are... are you Kiran?"

A pause. *Yes?* came a somewhat uncertain reply.

"Where are you? How can we find you?"

Silence.

"I'm losing him, Jovan," she said.

He looked up at the screen. "Hang on a little longer," he said, sounding strained.

"Talk to me. Where are you?"

Here?

Cyann fought a wave of dizziness, knowing it was

affecting Jovan as well. "Can you find us?"

No. You find. You come. You. You.

"I will come."

You and you. You you come.

"Jovan?" she said. "You want Jovan to come, too?"

Jovan. You name?

She smiled. "Cyann."

They sensed a fleeting moment of amusement when she said her name.

Come soon. Hurry. Dead soon.

"Who, Kiran? Who's dying?"

All.

Both Jovan and Cyann collapsed back into the sprung couch cushions when the fragile contact with Kiran dissolved and the tension that had held their bodies rigid left them. She allowed Jovan to maintain their mental link to once again use his Shantir training to heal and soothe. He stroked her hair as he did so, perhaps without realizing it, and she remained in his embrace to listen to the steady beat of his heart under her cheek.

"You did that on purpose," she said finally.

"Yes. I'm sorry." He kissed the top of her head. "Forgive me?"

She sat up, slowly, but allowed him to keep an arm around her shoulder. "You hoped I'd get upset enough to catch his attention. Clever."

He smiled tiredly. "I didn't want to hurt you. But nothing else was working."

"Did you mean any of that?"

He thought a moment. "Yes, I suppose I did. Some of it. You don't need me to heal you. You can do that yourself. You're not sick or weak and you don't need a personal Shantir to hold your hand. You're stronger than you think." He leaned forward and kissed her nose. "And I adore your freckles. I always have."

She sighed. "But you don't like to join with me."

"When did I say that?"

"You said it bothers you. It's a strain."

He grinned. "I'm a Shantir, Cy. I can join a tree if I had to, strain or not. There is nothing you can do to keep me out of your head. I love it in there."

"You do?"

"I always have." He brushed his fingers across her cheek. "It just about killed me talking to you like that."

The sound of the *Scout*'s airlock startled both of them. Moments later Anders came into the room.

"Did it work? It worked, didn't it?" He rushed to the lab console and called up the program Jovan had been running. "Have we found our exit?"

"I think so," Jovan said, his eyes still on Cyann. "I'm not touching those numbers till the morning. We're both ready to pass out."

Cyann glowered at Anders with narrowed eyes. "You were in on this?"

"It was his idea," Jovan said. "I'd never come up with anything so heinous."

"You're welcome," Anders said. "Took a lot of arguing for me to talk him into it, so you can blame me entirely. So? Is it Kiran? Were the Shantirs right?"

Cyann nodded. "Yes, it's him. I'm sure of it."

Anders exhaled a soft whistle. "Amazing. So who's going to explain all this to Tychon?"

* * *

For a man whose long-lost son had suddenly appeared in the far reaches of their galactic sector, Tychon took the news remarkably well.

He had listened without interruption as Cyann and Jovan explained the Shantirs' suspicions about Kiran's whereabouts. There was little more than a raised eyebrow when he heard about Cyann's recent contact. It was Nova who paced in agitation, who scolded everyone including the absent Shantir Moghen for keeping secrets, and who obviously worried about Tychon's reaction to all of this.

But her mate simply reclined silently in his lounger, waiting until the others had finished their story and then looked over the proposed coordinates that Jovan had gleaned during their contact with Kiran. He pursed his lips and hummed to himself before lifting the thin display screen in his hand. "You're sure about this exit?"

Jovan nodded. "As sure as I can be without processors crunching the numbers. That is where that... signal came from."

"The voice." Tychon's eyes shifted to Cyann. "Looks like you were right all along that someone's trying to reach you."

"How is this even possible?" she said. "How can he find me so far away? And without contact? Without touching me."

"I've seen it done," Nova said, looking to Tychon. "Once."

Tychon nodded. "Yes, it's possible. And we don't know what distance was involved. Given what we know about the Tughan, he can span anything. It would be simple for him to jump all over Trans-Targon without anyone knowing about it. If he's alive and able to travel, he could even have been back on Delphi."

"But now he's left the sector," Jovan said. "And he's calling for help."

"Why would this Tughan need anyone's help?" Nigel said. "If he's got such a big Shantir brain, I mean."

"He still needs a ship to get around, doesn't he?" Cyann asked. "He could simply be stuck out there without coolant. Reason enough to send someone else to warn us about the asteroid."

"Maybe he's not such an awful lad," Nigel said.

"He's no lad," Tychon said. "Physically, he'd be middle-thirty now. But he was already far older than that when he left us." He stared off into the distance for a moment before continuing. "We have no way to know what he's like now. What he's become. Or what he wants."

"So let's find out," Cyann said. "We know where to exit

the keyhole. Let's just go look."

"Just like that?" Jovan smiled at her.

"Yeah."

"Let's not get too excited about this," Nova sat down beside Tychon and took the screen from him. "Well, okay, I'm excited, too, but we don't know for sure that Kiran is anywhere near the cloud. And the cloud is our priority. We can't leave here until we know its position and when we can expect it to get here."

"You don't think these things are related?" Jovan asked.

"I do, but I also think it's likely that he's lost somewhere. This is the Tughan. If he was worried about an asteroid he'd just deflect it. Believe me, he can. The most likely possibility is that he's on a planet out there. Or some satellite from which he sent the alien to warn us. We can't go chasing after him unless we're sure that we're not about to be pummeled by meteoroids coming from elsewhere."

"So what do you suggest?" Cyann said. "We have to go to him. I promised we would."

"Without knowing what's waiting for you on the other side of the breach?"

"It's what we do," Anders said. "Jovan's jumped without a safety net dozens of times, am I right?"

"Well..." Jovan said. "You're not supposed to say that out loud in front of the Colonel."

"And we've taken the *Scout* into some barely mapped regions. It's why it's called *Scout*. There is a chance in a million that we'll find anything of interest in any point in space and I don't even remember the last time we had to use our weapons. We're explorers. So let's go explore."

Nova looked undecided.

"He could be hurt," Cyann said. "If he's so powerful, why doesn't he just come over here? Something is keeping him. We have to help."

"We do," Jovan said firmly. "If for no other reason than to get the voices out of Cy's head."

"I will stay here," Tychon said to Nova. "Let them make

the jump and take a look around. Then report back here. We have to start probing exits anyway to find where the cloud is coming from. Might as well start there."

"You don't want to go?" Anders said, surprised.

"Our mission is the cloud. If that means finding Kiran in the process, then I'll be very happy. If not, we've still got a problem right here. Taking both spanners into the breach is not something we should risk."

"I could stay here," Jovan offered.

Tychon smiled. "You belong on the *Scout*, Explorer. We're just a couple of old soldiers getting ready to blast rocks out of the sky. That's our job."

"Speak for yourself, you," Nova elbowed him lightly. "Old soldiers, indeed!"

"So it's decided?" Cyann said eagerly. "We can go?"

"You'll take two of the Eagles with you," Nova said. "And let me be clear. You're to have a look around. If the cloud is approaching from there, gather what data you can. Mostly, we need to know how much time we have before it gets here and if it's actually as dangerous as we think. If it is, return here and we'll take this ship through. I'd rather deal with this thing outside of Trans-Targon if we have a choice." She turned to Cyann to make her next point. "Only after you've got what we need about the cloud will you go looking for clues about Kiran. If we're in a first contact situation you're to return here before making any moves in that direction. I want nothing but 'yessir' on that."

"Yes, ma'am," Anders said with a wink. He came to his feet and stood by the door to the hallway. "Let's get busy. Nigel, get an inventory on our coolant situation. Cyann, get the lab ready. Set up a separate database that we can ship back to Targon. I want to suck up as much information about that sector as we can grab."

The others filed out of the room but Tychon remained seated and put his hand on Cyann's arm until they were alone. "Are you prepared for this, Little Blue?" he said. "This could be a dangerous jump."

She looked up into his serene, much-loved face to see the blue eyes scrutinize her intently. "Yes," she said at once. "I need to do this."

"I'm sorry that we didn't tell you more about Kiran. Nova wanted to. I wanted to. But other than breaking any number of rules, what would it have accomplished?"

She shrugged. "He's my brother. I would have liked to have known the truth about him."

He picked up a loose strand of her hair and pushed it behind her ear. "Your brother is gone. He disappeared before our eyes in more ways than one. Don't forget that. He is the Tughan Wai and we know nothing about him."

"He is your son!" she objected. "And he needs us."

"He's killed nearly a thousand people," he reminded her. "Many of those died only because he wanted them to. And he's become those people. Soldiers, rebels, geniuses, monsters, healers and murderers. Who knows how many he's taken since then? We have no way to know which of those have shaped him into whatever he is now. You need to stay objective, no matter who you think he is."

She nodded. "What if we do find a monster?"

"Jovan will know what to do. I won't ask anything of you that will hurt you."

"And what if we find your son?"

"If you find Kiran, we will bring him home."

.

SEVEN

Usually, there never seemed to be enough time to run through the hundreds of items on the pre-launch checklist before a scheduled takeoff. So often, Anders had to harangue his crew to get the last of the supplies on board, flight plans approved and laid in, ground services signed off, equipment checked, pre-flight completed – all before the *Scout* finally rose above the Chalyss valley and headed into space.

This time it felt like she was the only one ready to go and she ached to feel the ship power up beneath her feet already. Cyann sat rigidly at the com console in the *Scout*'s cockpit, working with Anders in the main lab to sync their systems with the Union ship. But most of this was done. Now she wanted to get on the way, to see what lay beyond this keyhole only a few minutes and countless light years away.

The cockpit lights had been lowered and even the overhead screens were muted to allow Jovan to prepare for his leap through the breach. The Delphian lay motionless on his couch, already communicating with the ship's processors via his neural interface to calculate their way through sub-space.

A slight shudder moved through the *Scout* when first one,

then the other Eagle connected to a docking port on either side. The Union ship slipped from the overhead screen when Jovan rotated the *Scout* away from there to give them room to maneuver. Cyann adjusted an external camera to keep it in sight. There was something assuring about its cumbersome bulk, orbiting over the oblivious planet below, prepared to protect it from whatever would come through the breach.

Her mother's image appeared beside the main view screen. "The cruisers are docked. Let's hope you won't need them."

"Don't worry so, Colonel," Cyann said. The small, heavily armored Eagles were primarily ships of war, often deployed in battle alongside Air Command's fighter planes but with far greater range and arsenal. More agile than the *Scout*, these two would add firepower should their exit lead them into unfriendly territory. "I'm more worried that we're leaving you short of cover."

"Have you seen the pistols this bucket is carrying? I made sure we got properly outfitted before we left Targon."

"I'm sure you did," Cyann grinned. Nova was no fonder of warfare than any of them, but weapons of any kind had always held her fascination. Along with the physicists and geologists sent along on this mission, her expertise would ensure that, if left with no other option, no organic debris made it past her guns alive.

Nigel stepped into the cockpit. "All systems green," he announced and took his seat in the co-pilot's couch. He would take over to stabilize the ship when they emerged from sub-space when Jovan would likely be in no condition to do so. "Anders is going to ride this out in the lab. Ready, Jovan?"

"Ready."

Nigel began to power up the ship's propulsion systems, like Jovan now connected to the machine by his neural interface. A low whine emitted from the lower level of the ship. Slowly, the *Scout* and its two hitchhikers pulled away from the *Repha Zi* and headed toward the keyhole, gaining speed with every second that passed.

Cyann turned back to Nova's image on the screen. "We're off. See you in a day or two." She shut the com down and secured herself into her seat. The *Scout* handled most jumps with ease but this was a long one and she had landed on her head more than once before.

The *Scout* sped toward the microscopic breach in space, ramping up its forward motion even as Nigel began to feed its energy into the slowly expanding aperture. "Full negative, compensating for the birds," he said for her benefit, moving no more than Jovan did as his commands were relayed directly from his interface to the ship's systems. Cyann watched, fascinated, as the indicators on the console in front of them responded to his mental signals without delay. "Jovan?"

"Almost," Jovan replied, focused entirely on the ship's processors probing far ahead, deep inside the fissure, seeking the exit that Kiran had promised. "Taking a while."

"Can't slow now," Nigel reminded him. "Converters are full up."

"I don't see it. It should be there. I know those numbers are right."

Cyann studied the screens. They would be at their entry coordinates in moments. The new gate was already large enough to allow the ship's passage and soon the energy flow would make it impossible to swerve away. To enter without a mapped exit would leave them stranded in sub-space. None of those lost in the breach had ever returned to describe the experience.

"Go or no-go?" Nigel said, a nervous edge roughening his voice. "Not going to hold this much longer."

"Cyann," Jovan snapped.

She leaned forward and gripped the hand he extended. Instantly, she felt the mental contact not only to him but also to the ship. It was as if he was no longer contained by the familiar boundaries of *Jovan*, but had become part of the tremendous processes needed to penetrate into sub-space.

Was this what deep-space navigation felt like? She was part of something so infinite and untethered that she nearly pulled her hand out of his grasp, afraid to look deeper into the mind and machines that made this all possible.

His grip tightened painfully and she remained linked despite her fear, contributing her small Delphian talents to help him find their way to the correct exit. Together, they directed the processors to override the usual protocols to give preference to Kiran's supposed location.

"Got it," he exhaled forcefully but did not release her hand.

Cyann squeezed her eyes shut when the *Scout* shot forward into the breach and her world disappeared. Her mind rebelled at the sudden loss of every one of her senses, leaving it to grapple with the absolute *nothing* that had removed her reality. Nearly overpowering vertigo felt like the inside of her head was perhaps on its way elsewhere and she realized that she had never taken a jump this deep and this long.

It was over within seconds. Cyann dared to open her eyes to see Nigel leaning over the cockpit console to visually check the commands his brain fed into the navigational controls faster than his hands ever could. He was mumbling to himself about coordinates and trajectories and a possible coolant backwash – things he always mumbled about after every jump. The *Scout* was jarred when first one and then the other Eagle disengaged from their ports to start scanning the vicinity as far as their sensors ranged. Except for a brief, coded blip to report a successful traverse, they would maintain radio silence.

She became aware that Jovan's hand still lay limply in her own, disturbingly cold. She unbuckled her restraints to move around his bench. "Jovie?"

He lay with his eyes closed and she had to put her hand on his chest to assure herself that he was even breathing. His face seemed younger, somehow, without the hard blue of his eyes seeming to pierce far beyond what most people saw. He did see more, of course, as a result of his training and his breeding, but at this moment he seemed almost like someone who needed the healing he so freely dispensed to others.

"He still with us?" Nigel said.

She looked up, startled, and pulled her hand back. But Jovan reached for it again and held it in his. "He is," he said faintly. "Or he will be." A long silence followed and Cyann did not dare to move as he found his way back from wherever the tremendous mental strain of the jump had taken him.

"Cyann!" Anders' excited voice reached them through an overhead speaker. Jovan winced.

"All is well," she reported.

"Get over here!"

Jovan squeezed her hand. "Go," he said. He opened his eyes and smiled at her. "He sounds like he's ready to bust a vein."

Impulsively, she bent and kissed his cheek. "Sleep, Jovie. Nigel will make you a big dinner when you get up."

"Hey! And who's gonna make my dinner?" Nigel said.

She grinned and left the cockpit to hurry through the narrow corridor and into the lab space. A sudden deadening of the air around her informed her that the area had been sealed as much as possible from the electromagnetic interference of the ship's processors and engines. "The *Scout*'s fine," she said, stepping into the main lab. "Nigel didn't shout about things as much as he usually does, even. I think he has to admit that Jovan knows what he's doing."

"Yes, yes, look at this!"

Cyann came to the bank of screens arrayed along the bulkhead. Some were scrolling long rows of data confirming the information pouring into their information system. Others had started to return real-world imagery of their location via the powerful telescopes mounted fore and aft. Still more scanned radiation and space debris for useful bits.

She frowned, a little disappointed. "Nothing much out here." She switched one of the sensors to display more details. "A binary star. No satellites. Not even a single exoplanet. Nearest star system a hundred and twenty light years. One big empty."

He nudged her and pointed at another screen. "Except for the mother of all asteroids coming right at us."

"What?" She squinted at the data displayed in front of her. "Oops. You're right. But those numbers look off. Any chance at a visual?"

"I hope so, shortly. Definitely something odd going on with this fellow."

She sat down at the console. "Slow, though. Definitely not going anywhere fast without jumping through sub-space."

He nodded, ruffling the short white hair on his head into a spiky mess. "How much time do we have?"

"Not much! Twenty-five hours," she said, meaning the *Scout*'s usual time increments which were similar to Delphi's. "So much for it taking years to get here. Oh, got a sketch."

He looked up when she switched an overhead display. A graphic representation of the asteroid appeared there, showing a few large central pieces surrounded by a mass of smaller, irregular drifts of space debris. "I guess we were right to call it a cloud," he said. "Big pile of rubble."

Cyann frowned. "Is that correct? Look at the size of it!"

Anders leaned closer. She raised both eyebrows when a muttered string of curses escaped his lips, not something he usually did in front of his brother-friend's daughter.

"What's got Uncle Anders' wobbly cheeks shaking like that?"

Cyann turned briefly when Nigel sauntered into the lab. "Our visitor," she said.

Nigel looked up. "Shit."

They stared, awed, as the *Scout*'s programs extrapolated how the object would appear from various angles. Nothing they had brought with them would more than fragment the smaller companion pieces; perhaps crack the more massive objects. They would simply spread out the hail of meteors over a broader range, still large enough to survive atmospheric entry in large numbers. Some of the virologists' proposals to simply blanket the asteroid with an anti-viral agent if one could be found in time suddenly seemed utterly absurd.

"When?" Nigel said, coughed, and said it again when the first attempt at the word didn't quite make it.

"Not enough time to go back home and get us a bigger pistol," Cyann said. "It'll get to Trans-Targon; that is certain."

"We better get back there," Anders said. "Send the Eagles back to civilization to get something in place that'll take this thing out before it gets too far into the sector."

"We can't leave right now," Cyann reminded him. "The leap to get us here took all Jovan has. There isn't any way he can jump us back now."

Anders looked up at Nigel who nodded. "Rough ride," he confirmed and flung himself into his dilapidated couch. "The processors are going to take a while to cool, too. This gap's a bitch to span."

Cyann chewed on her bottom lip. "We're making assumptions here. How do we know this thing is even what you call the Genesis Cloud, Nigel? That's still just a theory. It's an asteroid heading for Trans-Targon, that much we know. But we still don't know if it's the same stuff that came to Delphi. We haven't found Kiran. He could have sent his message from somewhere else. The alien pod could have picked up that virus along the way." She put her hand on Anders' arm. "Let's pretend we're astrobiologists and check this thing out."

He smiled wanly. "You're right," he said. "Let's see what we can squeeze out of the sensors until Jovan comes around."

"Five or six hours should be enough," Cyann said. "After that he's just being lazy. Once we're back we can leave this problem to the experts. If there's a way to neutralize this thing they'll find it." She returned her attention to the overhead image of the asteroid, still rendered as a wireframe based on sensor readings. She added some false color. "Not a lot of craters," she said. "Could even have an atmosphere of sorts."

"Surely it would lose that in sub-space?"

She nodded. "Definitely some gravity. Those larger pieces of the cloud aren't budging in relation to the main bodies. It probably sloughs off the smaller bits when it gets too close to other gravity wells."

"That whole end is blurred. Sensors aren't even getting to the surface," Anders said. He turned to Nigel. "Care to lend us your brain, young man?"

Nigel sighed and moved from his lounger to the console. "I doubt there's anything we can figure out that Nova's people can't." He looked over the data. "Whatever is going on at that end is interfering with the *Scout*'s feelers. Could be an energy field of some sort."

"How so?"

"Well, something's causing it to open keyholes. Can't do that without an awful lot of energy." He scratched his head. "Could be a big chunk of negative mass."

"Then you'd hardly have an asteroid following around in its wake," Cyann said.

"Could, if the keyholes are what's attracting the mass. Things would get really contrary to expectations."

She nodded, looking up at the display. Her eyes narrowed. "What's that?"

"Hmm?"

She tapped the screen to zoom into the image. "On the side of that big chunk."

"Can you get closer?"

She pulled the display up a little more. "Doesn't look natural."

Nigel whistled. "My my, what have we here?"

"Transfer it to the hologram," Anders said.

They shifted to the table-top emitters where soon a three-dimensional model of the asteroid field displayed. One side of it continued to show blurred and incomplete but the area Cyann had pointed out came into view when she rotated the projection as far as their sensors had been able to draw it. Along one side, four perfectly round domes rose above the surface. Shallow, wider than they were tall, their shape and placement left little doubt that these were not natural formations.

"Looks like your Shantirs were right," Nigel said. "Someone's at home over there."

"Or was, at some point," Anders amended.

"Given the size of the main body, those things are pretty massive," Cyann said. She used a pointer to feed a measurement back to the display program. The segment lit up in green. "You could fit a whole town in one of those."

"And that's just the parts we can see. There could be sub-surface areas, too."

Nigel nudged Anders. "I say we take a closer look."

Cyann looked up at Anders, immediately taken by Nigel's suggestion. Their mission boss, no less curious but far more restrained by procedure, seemed undecided. Her experience told her that he was only moments away from making a protocol-inspired decision.

"It would only take a few hours to get there," she pressed. "Nova didn't say we had to stay by the keyhole. We'll get better readings if we can get to the side of whatever's messing up the pointy end." She gripped his arm. "And we could get some real-vid."

Anders grinned. "True, and it'll take just as long to get the sample probes back. I'm dying to find out who's on that rock." He walked to the main console and tapped into their com system. "Vanguard Twelve, come in."

"V12," came the reply. "Standing by."

"I take it you've picked up the asteroid?"

"Affirmative, *Scout*."

"We're going to move in for a closer look."

"Sir?"

"Some readings aren't clear and we may have detected

habitation."

"Sentient, sir?"

Anders glanced at Cyann. "Uncertain. We've not picked up any sort of radio transmission or power source. We can't return just yet, anyway. Our schedule won't be affected."

"Understood, sir."

"V5?" Anders said, addressing the other Vanguard team.

"Sounds a whole lot more fun than hovering around here, sir."

"Prepare to depart. Maximum sweep configuration. Radio silence, all sensors active. Let's not alarm anyone."

"Yay," Cyann said when he had cut their connection to their Air Command escort.

Nigel pumped a fist into the air and left the lab for his cockpit.

"I'll monitor the scans," Anders said. "I'd like you to get some rest and see if you can pick up anything from Kiran. Something makes me think he's on that asteroid." He smiled. "Jovan isn't around to annoy you, but I guess that's not going to work a second time. Try your best."

* * *

But there was nothing out there for her and Cyann's attempts at attaining the correct sort of khamal simply threatened to send her off into a deep snooze. Likely, Jovan was aware of her efforts but the voice she sought remained silent.

Frustrated and just a little bit grumpy, she left her cabin after hours of fruitless meditation to return to the lab. She was surprised to see Jovan there with Anders, perched atop a wheeled stool pulled up to the monitors. She was even more surprised when she quickly smoothed her tousled hair and found herself worrying about the state of her wrinkled shirt.

"No luck?" Jovan said when she had taken a chair beside Anders.

She shook her head. "Not a thing. Did you hear all the news?"

"Yes. It was interesting to find that I've been kidnapped in my sleep and whisked away into the great unknown."

"Not so unknown. There's nothing out here but chunks of asteroid. You don't approve?"

He shrugged. "Seems like an interesting idea. As long as you don't plan to land. We're not authorized for first contact. There is much we don't know."

"Any indication yet that they'll see us coming?"

"Not really," Anders said. "Still no noise from there. But you don't build a habitat on an asteroid by growing wings to get there. If they hitched a ride they must have had some very advanced methods."

She looked up at the screen. "Maybe they're all gone. Dead."

"Oh, we have real-vid now," Anders said excitedly. He switched the display. She now saw a number of irregular shapes, dull brown and bronze, worn smooth over time and accompanied by hundreds of smaller rocks inside a cloud of what might be thousands. The light of the star in this sector threw harsh shadows over the uneven surfaces.

"Looks a lot like our alien's pod," she said. "Same composition?"

"In parts. Try not to hug it. Don't want it melting on us."

Jovan laughed at that although Cyann furrowed her brow. "Not funny."

"Yes, it is," Anders said. "We've taken a little detour to approach from the side where we've seen those domes. I don't want to risk running into whatever is jamming our sensors at the front end. Look." He zoomed into a small section of the asteroid until the round objects on its side because visible. "Most definitely made by something sentient."

"Makes me wish we'd brought along a few more of the experts," Cyann said. "Look at that raised edge all around the domes. It's almost like they built a roof over a crater. What are those bubbles around them?"

"More structures, we think. There are few straight angles

to be found. We have detected an atmosphere of sorts, but it's still a good idea to build down and not up. A good meteor shower would do all sorts of damage."

"Have we been able to look inside?"

"Not really. No more than we were able to look inside the rock on Sola back home. Sensors think these cores might be ice, at least the bigger pieces. So there's your source of water, if these folks are, indeed, a Prime species. There is ice on the surface, too, under a layer of debris. Cold there."

"Oxygen?"

"Not much on the surface, but it's venting from the domes, along with waste gases. Point five gravity. Spectrometers aren't all in agreement, but I'm afraid that this is, indeed, our Genesis Cloud. The composition is almost identical to the shell of the alien's pod. We'd need samples to get at the endoliths, though. We won't find the virus from here."

She turned to him. "You're not thinking of visiting, are you?"

"If this were my expedition I might give that a thought. After all, I feel sort of invited. But I think our Air Command escort would place us all under arrest for even thinking that."

"With good reason." Jovan stood up and stretched his long limbs. "We should start heading back to the keyhole. I'll be ready to jump us back. We know what we need to know about this thing."

"No we don't," Cyann said.

"Huh?"

"We still don't know what Kiran expects from us. And surely you're not saying that we should seriously think about destroying this thing until we know who's living there."

"Cy, we cannot let it get into Trans-Targon. That's not even a question. We know where it is, we know when it'll get there. Now we have to stop it and we only have hours, not months or years, to figure that out." He looked to Anders. "Am I the only one who's worried about that?"

"Maybe we can offload these people somehow," she said.

"We should try to make contact. We can't just blast them out of the sky."

"Offload them? How? Where? There could be thousands of them. How else could you sustain a civilization on a rock like that? We don't even have the means to keep them in quarantine."

"There must be a way to divert it. Maybe the *Repha*'s retro boosters—"

"Look at the size of it!" He waved a hand at the screen. "It has its own gravity! Atmosphere! We don't have anything that'll do more than nudge it a bit."

"Well, that might be enough to veer it away from the keyhole."

"It's not going from keyhole to keyhole by accident. It's being drawn there. You'd have to move it a huge distance to get it off course."

"You don't know that for sure. And what if Kiran is on there? There's got to be a way to get to him."

"You would risk all of Trans-Targon for a 'what if?'"

Anders came to stand between them, perhaps fearing that their argument would turn physical at any moment. "I get nervous when I see Delphians raise their voices," he said. "I agree that we need to head back and hand this over to our commander. She and Tychon have dealt with more hostiles than any of us."

"These aren't rebels," Cyann said. "They're not hostile. These are people who have no idea that we're planning to murder them."

"To save billions," Jovan said.

"So maybe it's our time to get revisited by them. That's how we got here in the first place, isn't it? They're part of our evolution."

"That's a theory, nothing more. You're being un-reasonable."

"And you're being Delphian!"

GetOutGetOutGetOutGetOutGetOut!

Cyann gasped. "Kiran!"

"What is he saying?"

"We have to leave here," she said. "He's so scared. Angry and scared. He can't stop it."

"Stop what?" Anders said.

Jovan dove for the com console. "Bug out. Back to the keyhole. Vanguard take defensive positions. Bug out. Bug out."

GoGoGoGo. Away. GetOutGetOutGetOut!

"V5 under attack," they heard over the speaker. "Taking damage but I don't know how. Systems are going down."

The asteroid slid from their real-vid screen as Nigel rolled the ship. The maneuver was painfully slow. Something made the *Scout* shudder and the lights flickered overhead. Some of their screens went offline when Nigel rerouted power.

"Nigel," Anders shouted. "Get us the hell out of here."

"Could use a hand up here, Jovan," Nigel replied. "Shit! V5 just completely fell apart. What the hell are they using?"

Anders and Cyann went into the corridor and started to pull open bins and cabinets to retrieve portable air supplies and weather gear, the lightweight protective suits used in hostile environments and even short space walks. Another shudder went through the ship.

"Get tactical," Jovan said when they arrived with their loads in the cockpit. "See if you can show them we have a few arrows in our quiver." He glanced at Cyann. "Guess they're hostile, after all."

Anders manned the station while Cyann slipped into her coveralls and then quickly helped Nigel with his. Once Nigel had returned to his bench Jovan also dressed. "Talk to them, Cyann," he said. "See if you can reach Kiran."

"He's gone again. And you're not likely to get me any more angry than earlier."

"Didn't do that on purpose that time," he said and pointed at the com console. "Talk to them anyway."

She sat down and switched their programs to include the translation matrix developed by Targon's linguists. "Hello," she said awkwardly. "Please stand down. Err, stop hurting us.

We mean no harm. No danger. We want to visit. Want to help."

Anders nodded. "Yes, keep it simple."

"Please stop hurting," she said again. "We are damaged."

Nigel cursed. "Give it up, Cy. They just took out the other Eagle."

"Anders," Jovan said. His attention was focused on the helm where he and Nigel were plugged into their sensors to anticipate incoming waves of energy from the asteroid. "It's coming uphill of the dome by those big spikes."

Cyann looked up at their display that was now again showing the asteroid field. Anders directed the *Scout*'s limited armament at the dome and released a warning volley.

"Didn't even scorch the thing," Nigel said. "We've got four missiles on board. I suggest today is a good day to use them up."

Anders fired at the same moment when another shot from the surface strafed the *Scout*, turning it aside. His shot went wild and did little more than add a fresh crater. He cursed and loaded another. Cyann cried out when the overhead lights dimmed and a row of warning signals glared from the console.

"That's propulsion," Nigel said. "And aft shields."

"Land on the asteroid," Cyann said.

"Are you crazy?"

"What choice do we have?"

"Do it," Jovan said, his eyes on Cyann. "Take us down."

Nigel shook his head but turned the ship into a wide approach onto the asteroid. "You're all crazy. Damn Delphians. I knew you'd be the end of me yet."

Anders opened a compartment and withdrew a selection of guns, com units and emergency kits which they stowed into their suits. "Should never have left the keyhole," he mumbled.

"Should have stayed in bed this morning," Nigel added. "Looks like they stopped shooting. Hang on to something. Going vertical but for all I know this floating piece of pestilence is going to fall apart when we touch it."

"Don't talk about my ship like that," Anders said with a half-hearted grin.

The *Scout* lurched sideways and all of them felt the grip of gravity. Jovan compensated quickly, but a second lurch followed. Anders was thrown from his seat and slid across the floor to the cockpit door. A final thump and the ship came to rest.

"Uncle!" Cyann leaped from her chair and rushed to Anders, disoriented by the lighter gravity and the tilt of the ship on uneven ground.

He groaned. "I think I broke something."

"Lie still," she said. "I'll get the kit."

Nigel conferred with Jovan over the *Scout*'s systems. "Life support is all right," Nigel said. "The shields will reset. Maybe. Lost the exterior com array. Manual controls are fried. Something's blown the coolant relays. We're not going to get far without crossdrives, so forget about jumping home."

"Repairable?"

"We might be able to launch by rolling off this thing with the thrusters but that'll just have us floating in space."

"Which will just make us a target. Unless we can get out of their sight."

"True. But for all we know they have those weapons all around this rock." He consulted with another display. "Can't send a distress call without the long-range but I think we have the juice to send a message packet back to the keyhole. The Colonel is bound to come looking for us. She'll find it when she gets through."

"Send a few of them in case they get caught up in that energy field. You might want to mention that they don't like visitors here. And that our xenologist isn't in the best shape for interplanetary diplomacies." Jovan turned to Cyann and Anders. "What's the damage?"

She consulted her scanners. "Concussion. Two broken ribs. You're kinda fragile, Anders."

"What I am is sixty-two years old. You try flying across a room into a metal wall and see how you feel afterwards."

"Cognitive function okay," she reported with a grin.

Jovan scanned the vicinity with the external cameras. "I don't see anybody out there. We're not too far from those domes."

"No one's shooting at us now. I consider that a plus." Nigel checked his sidearm. "Why would they just start firing without making contact?"

"Because we were sneaking up on them?" Cyann said. She moved aside when Jovan came over to check Anders' broken bones. "Then again, with guns like that you'd think they'd have the know-how to send a warning or something."

"But maybe not the interest," Nigel said. "I still don't even know how they did it. And the Eagles! Best pilots in the fleet and they went down like someone swatted them out of the air."

Jovan leaned over Anders. "A lot of pain?"

"Yeah," Anders said around shallow gasps for air.

The Shantir touched the neural interface at Anders' temple to reach the Human's brain. Anders, like most operators of precision tools and all pilots, had long ago opted for the embedded device. The implant also enabled Delphians to more easily touch the minds of non-Delphians although few outsiders were granted the experience. Healers used it to help their patients use their own abilities to relieve nearly all ailments. Anders closed his eyes when Jovan guided him to gradually release the endorphins he needed to deal with the pain and to calm his breathing. "Try to keep breathing as deeply as you can," Jovan advised.

"You need to lie down," Cyann said. "Nova will come for us soon, I'm sure."

Anders coughed. "I've spent twenty years in Air Command and I've known Nova for longer than that. It'll be a day or so before she'll worry because she knows Cyann and I are nosy. When she does start to worry she may send another Eagle through, but not without a lot of deliberation.

It would mean sending Tychon along those half-assed coordinates you got from Kiran because he's the only one over there that can handle them. That will leave them without a Level Three spanner on the Trans-Targon side. The only other option is to send an Eagle back to Targon to request backup. So forget about them charging to our rescue before this pile of pebbles is at the keyhole."

"You think she'll wait that long?" Nigel said. "With Cyann out here? And you?"

"Didn't say she'd be happy about it. But she's Air Command. And Tychon will remind her of that."

Jovan sighed. "Now you know why I'm a civilian. We need to find out more about these aliens. Whoever they are."

"We're about to," Nigel said. "Will you look at that."

The video system showing the exterior of the ship had picked up movement in the distance and automatically focused on that. Soon they distinguished a dozen or more shapes moving toward the *Scout*, walking upright and very cautiously. In the harsh shadows cast by the asteroid's outcroppings, the flicker of their bioluminescence appeared like a sea of colored lights in the dark.

Nigel tugged the tactical console from its resting position.

"Don't shoot at them," Cyann said.

"They shot at us!"

"She's right," Anders said. "Help me up, Cy."

Jovan and Cyann scooped Anders carefully off the floor and propped him up near the main console. He studied the shapes carefully. "Definitely the same species as our alien visitor."

"Taller though," she said. "And the colors move differently."

"Related to emotion, I think," he said. "Make sure to capture that."

Jovan regarded them in utter bafflement. "I think we've left the expedition, folks. Let's figure out a way to not get killed before we ask them for DNA samples."

"Does everyone have the translator loaded?" Cyann

pointed to the data sleeve on her forearm. "We couldn't be in a worse contact situation, so let's try to mind our manners." She looked meaningfully at Nigel. The others responded by tucking the translator's receiver behind their ears.

"Look." Anders peered more closely at the monitor. "They're wearing some sort of breathing mask or filter."

"Yes," Jovan said. "This atmosphere isn't healthy for them, either."

"That would mean they didn't evolve on this rock," Cyann said. "I suppose they're not the ancient ancestors we're looking for."

"No, but the asteroid still might be," Ander said. "We'll need soil and air samples."

"Mostly, we need to find out if our Sola virus is here."

"Beaker-heads, both of you." Jovan shook his head, half amused and half exasperated. "Zoom in a bit."

Nigel adjusted their view. The taller strangers moved with a peculiar head-nodding that none of them had seen before on a Prime species. Their legs and arms were thin and long, hinting at protracted exposure to this gravity. Like their alien guest on Sola, their circular, flat heads were hairless and, like the rest of their visible bodies, pale and waxy. Eerily, their translucent skin clearly showed the darker areas of brain and trachea. Most of their bodies were covered in loose layers of coarse cloth without pattern or fit.

"See any weapons?" Nigel said.

"Nothing I can identify." Jovan pointed at the screen. "The shorter ones in the back look more like the one that came to Delphi."

Cyann focused the ship's camera on the individual at the front and brought the image as close as possible. "Kinda look like Nebdanese, if you squint."

The delegation from the dome came to a halt at some distance from the ship. They stood in a loose semi-circle and now several of them raised their hands away from their body.

"Is that a greeting?" Nigel said.

"Empty hands. Showing us that they're not armed, maybe."

"That's nice of them, seeing how they just shot us out of the sky."

Cyann opened her kit. "This is your field, uncle. Let me give you something to help you breathe."

He nodded and grimaced when she administered a drug.

"How's the pain?"

"I won't be going dancing for a while." Anders leaned forward with a groan and activated their external speakers. "Hello," he said and added various versions of the greeting.

The beings outside reacted by turning and bending toward each other. The ship's sensors were not able to pick up more than a low murmuring muffled by the masks they wore. The strange bioluminescence flickering beneath their skin intensified.

"We are not an enemy," he continued. Cyann winced when his measured, calm voice relayed in a tinny drone lacking any sort of expression. Then again, she thought, who knew what expression these people responded to. "We are injured. Please. Do not use weapons."

They waited silently while more conversation took place outside. At last one of the aliens took a few steps forward. "Hello also," the overhead speaker conveyed. "We have no weapon."

"Like hell you don't," Nigel murmured which earned him a sharp cuff from Cyann.

"You have no enemies here," the alien continued. "You can visit."

"Someone shot at us," Anders said into the microphone. "Two ships were lost. Broken. Five... people are dead."

"Regrettable. Sad. We have no weapon. Energy flux there. Dangerous." The alien pointed a long arm toward and to the left of the domes, the leading end of the asteroid field. "But safe there." It now pointed past them, into the opposite direction. "Better to stay far and scan for danger before landing."

"He's got a point," Jovan said.

"How do you know it's a he?" Nigel asked. "Are we going to believe that?"

"I'm not sure that we have a choice. And we haven't detected any sort of weapon."

"Come visit," the voice from outside said again. "No harm. We want to meet, to see."

"Do you think they even realize that we crashed?" Cyann said. "He seems to think we're here for first contact or something."

"Possible," Anders said. "Or the translator could be confusing some of the vocabulary. It'll improve itself as we continue talking."

"I'd love to take a look," Cyann said. "They don't seem to mean harm. Neither did the alien back on Sola."

"Or maybe they'll cook us for dinner," Nigel said. "I think I'll stay right here."

"This isn't the first contact you've been through, Nigel." Anders said. "We've never been threatened by sentients."

"We've never been shot at before, either," he said. "Unless you count rebels."

"We have little choice but to make friends with these folks. If this asteroid takes a jump through sub-space I would not want to ride along on its back in the *Scout*. Those domes look a whole lot safer."

"We gain nothing by sitting around out here," Cyann said.

"We're safe in here. Maybe Anders is wrong. Maybe Nova will come looking for us sooner."

"In that case, update that signal to let them know to approach from the back end," Jovan said. "If there are natural discharges of radiation, they may be attracted by the ships' energy field, even the shields."

"We should find out more about that." Cyann gestured at some of their other monitors. "Right now, it's showing absolutely no reason for those at all. Things are as calm as when we got here."

"Are you getting anything from Kiran, Cy?" Jovan asked.

"Nothing. It doesn't even seem like he's here. I thought I'd maybe feel some sort of presence. Or that you could."

"I'm not even getting anything from these individuals," he said. "Something's blocking me. What's the weather out there?"

"Chilly," Nigel said. "Tolerable. Pressure is a bit light but also tolerable. Radiation tolerable. A lot of UV from that star. The energy source at the front of the cloud is moving outward in flares. Still, keep your monitors ticking. But this is definitely Prime species accommodations, if not the best I've seen. Ever."

"Well, let's take a look," Anders said. "Nigel, you'll stay on the *Scout*. Try to get the shields reset. I like the idea of having this place as a bit of a fortress if need be." He winked at Cyann. "Remember that swarm on Torren, Cy?"

"I've never seen you run so fast."

"Make sure to lock up as soon as we're out, Nigel, and monitor all media," Anders continued his instructions. "We'll need sealed suits out there. Keep the guns handy but not in hand. Touch nothing and no one. We need to find out how many of them there are. Maybe they can be removed, like Cyann suggested earlier. Let's not forget why we're here. Samples, DNA if we can get some." Anders rose from his chair only to immediately collapse back into it.

"Uncle?"

"Big headache," he said.

"Maybe you should stay here, too," Cyann said. "I'm worried about that concussion."

"Just a bump on the head," Anders said. "The Shantir would have noticed if I'd done any damage."

"Hmm, yes, but I think Cyann's right," Jovan said. "You hit that wall pretty hard. We'll go and have a look around. Maybe convince one of them to visit us here to negotiate a ride in their habitat if things don't improve for us here."

Anders started to object but after a few moments just nodded. "You're right, of course. I'm feeling a bit dizzy." He returned his attention to the microphone and those waiting outside. "We will visit. We will come to you for a short while to meet with you."

Cyann and Jovan went to the airlock followed by a steady stream of instructions from Anders in the cockpit. "We'll send out some crawlers to get samples. You two be sure to remember protocol. Listen and learn and don't volunteer anything until we know more about them. They may not even be aware that they are bringing pathogens to Trans-Targon. Don't alarm them with tales of Air Command guns pointed at them."

Before she lowered her visor, Jovan reached out to touch Cyann's cheek. "Let's be careful out there," he said as they linked their minds in a telepathic khamal. It was not an easy connection and it would require concentration to maintain, but she felt grateful for his assuring presence. He looked up at the unseen speakers in the airlock's ceiling. "Got it, Anders. Protocol. Right. We'll be polite."

"I'll try to poke a hole in whatever's messing with the sensors," Nigel said while running the decontamination sequence. "If you get a chance, see if they can spare a couple of recoiler gaskets, will you?"

"They don't even have shoes," Cyann reminded him.

"Think they'll want to trade for my spare boots? Just come back in one piece. Please."

EIGHT

By the time they were cautiously walking down the *Scout*'s exit ramp, the beings had come around to this side of the ship. Cyann lagged behind Jovan to record the meeting via the camera attached to her hood. She shivered but their suits reacted quickly to the frigid temperature and their visors adjusted to the lower light levels out here.

Jovan raised his arms much like their hosts had done earlier. "Thank you for the... visit," he said. "What will we call you?"

"We are Jur," an individual wearing a broad band around his neck stepped forward. "You came from far. No one lives here."

"Yes, through a gate. We believe that is how you came to this empty sector, too."

"Gate. The dead place. You fell through the dead."

"Sub-space. Yes."

"We go there."

"We know. Why do you go there?"

The Jur stood aside and, with an eloquent gesture, directed them to join his people on a walk to the nearest of the domes. "Bad air outside here. Inside safest."

Cyann turned her head to scan the others in the group. The rough fabric that covered their gangly bodies in broad wraps seemed to be made of some sort of natural fiber. It looked uncomfortable against their smooth skin, like something braided with rough rope. Their long-toed feet were bare despite the cold and it seemed only the air out here bothered them. *What do you make of their coloring?* she sent to Jovan.

I don't think we can assume things but, by our standards, some of the others seemed a little excited when I mentioned sub-space. The colors changed more quickly.

She bent to adjust her boot while taking a clearer video shot at one of the Jur's bare legs. They, like, the rest of their bodies seemed strangely flattened, formed around jointless bands of cartilage that supported them in place of bone. And yet, these people moved stiffly as if walking or gesturing took some effort.

They began the short trek toward the dome. The Delphians bounced unsteadily in the light gravity but soon moved with more confidence. The Jur walked with a rolling gait that would have been graceful except for the head bobbing that accompanied their movement. There were smaller ones, walking apart and behind the others, who seemed to require less nodding. Unlike the taller Jur leading the way, they were dressed in little more than rags. Nothing more was said, by any of them, until they reached the habitat.

Cyann glanced down at a display panel near her chin when she surreptitiously touched the wall of the dome. *Silica,* she sent. *Mixed with the same organic compounds as the pod on Sola.*

Any idea how they shield it? Jovan replied as he stooped through a narrow door that had opened for them.

Nothing that the sensors aren't picking up.

When the gate closed behind them Cyann felt uncomfortably like remaining outside would have been a better choice. Something hissed as gases were exchanged and then the Jur removed their somewhat primitive-looking respirators.

"We won't need the hoods," Cyann checked the conditions outside their sealed suits. "There is more oxygen here than outside but still a bit thin. I'm not seeing anything unrecognizable in the filters. Anders?"

Aboard the *Scout*, Anders and Nigel scrutinized the information that her system had sifted from the environment. "Yes, you should keep the air but I'm not too worried about anything flying around in there. To be on the safe side, don't eat anything and keep your gloves on. Better yet, don't touch anything."

"Yes, Uncle Anders." She removed her hood and shook out her hair before fitting the thin tube of the oxygen booster under her nose. While generally annoying after a while, she was glad for the device today. The air inside the dome carried a peculiar chemical odor. She was reminded of a mildewed refrigeration unit.

The Jur with the neckband leaned toward her, bending from the waist. His eyes moved over her face and she fought an impulse to pull back. Instead, she busied herself with attaching her protective hood to her belt, as Jovan was doing.

"You are much like us," the Jur said. "And like the other."

"You've met people like us before?"

"One." He raised a long-fingered hand as if he wanted to touch her hair but then dropped it again. "Blue strings on its head."

Kiran! she sent to Jovan. "You've met someone with blue hair... head strings before?"

"Yes," the Jur said. He ran a hand over the metal wall of the airlock. "It helped build much of this."

Jovan followed a seam in the construction upward. "This lock is from a plane, I think. Salvage?"

"Salvage," the Jur repeated. His unmovable face did not convey the question but a brief flash of orange across his cheek seemed to indicate confusion.

"Made of pieces of old or broken ships."

"Yes."

The interior door to the airlock opened now and they were ushered inside. The other Jur wandered away as if the strangers were no longer of interest to them. A narrow passage extended left and right and, although the door they had passed was made of metal, these walls were of a murky, translucent material that resembled glass still embedded with unfused grains of silica. A vague light source came from the other side of these partitions and they could see figures move behind them like shadows. Like the dome itself, the walls and door openings were rounded. In the distance, more of the slender, translucent people peered around corners or flitted across open spaces.

"Is he still here?" Cyann said. "The man with the blue strings."

"No. Dead. So sad. Come this way."

Cyann threw a puzzled glance to Jovan. He shrugged and nodded for her to follow their host. *Not what I expected to hear. We know he's either lying or unaware. Did his color pattern change?*

Not even a bit. Nor his expression. Not that they have any.

Jovan ran his gloved hand along the wall. "How do you produce your oxygen?"

The Jur turned briefly. "Repeat."

"Air. How do you make air. For breathing."

"Ice. Below."

"We didn't detect a power source," Jovan pressed. "How do you remove the hydrogen?"

"Your words don't fit. Air is air and we breathe it." He tapped his chest. "In here." He pointed at Cyann's nose. "Through there."

Humor? Jovan asked.

Not sure but I the translator is picking things up a little better now.

They stepped through a low, arched doorway into a round room connected to another and another after that, like so many bubbles randomly attached to each other. A geometric pattern in the glass-like walls hinted at the manufacture of these enclosures.

"Like someone blew air through a straw into soapy

water," Cyann said. "Probably injected something to fuse and melt these spaces. The rock must be very porous. Look how shiny those walls are."

"That would take a lot of power," Jovan said. "Why are you here?" he asked the Jur. "On this asteroid?"

"Asteroid." More orange flashes across the pale cheek.

"This rock. The place that floats through space."

The Jur observed Jovan for a moment and then turned his flat countenance to Cyann. "Your home is like this?"

"I think he likes you better," Jovan muttered, using a Delphian dialect that was not programmed into their translator.

Cyann stifled a grin, unsure of how facial movements would be perceived. "Not like this, Jur, but similar. We would like to know more about you. How you came here."

The Jur waved them through another doorway. Now they stood on a wide terrace of sorts. The roof of the dome arched high above them and, as they stepped out onto the platform, a vast central pit gaped below. Cyann and Jovan moved closer to the unguarded edge to peer into the depths. More terraces overlooked this well, perhaps carved out of a crater, and they saw movement on the open lower levels as the Jur people bustled about whatever activity kept them busy. A low, thrumming sound rose up from the depths.

"There must be hundreds of Jur," Cyann said. "Thousands." *So much for offloading them.*

"Yes, many," the Jur said and she could swear that the translator picked up a hint of pride. "We have many breeders. Too many."

"Why do you say that?"

"Soon there will not be enough food. We will pass the dead space and find a new home."

"Home? Your plan is to colonize... to live there?"

"Yes. Blue visitor told of many many planets there. And one will be new home."

"Why did you leave your home?" Cyann asked. She sent a mental nudge to Jovan when she noticed a new band of brilliant color flicker along the sides of the Jur's face. He nodded, having seen that, too.

"Wars. Enemies came from the other planet." The Jur raised his hands and described something orbiting around something else. "We have one sun, two planets. They had many planes and weapons and we had few. They destroyed much. Our people were dying and we had nowhere to go. To hide from the invaders. The blue visitor helped us. He said this... asteroid? This asteroid will take us where our ships cannot. We came here."

"Your ships can't go into the dead space?" Jovan asked.

"No. Only to the other planet."

"Where is your home? How long have you traveled?"

"We have lived on this asteroid for fourteen *arut*."

That was helpful, Cyann sent to Jovan.

Aren't you up on your arut conversions? he returned.

"You need to go through the dead place to find a new home," Jovan said. "Because there is nothing here that you can reach in time, before your food runs out."

"Correct. We have no ships now. Parts needed to build this. Blue visitor showed us how."

"Well, that must be the power source," Cyann said. "Or parts of your technology being used to create power from the asteroid's resources."

"Maybe. I do not go below there. We have engineers. Builders."

Just then one of the smaller Jur came out onto the platform overlooking the pit. It walked purposefully toward them, thin arms stretched up. The colors on this one flashed green and blue and it wore only a scrap of cloth wrapped around shapeless hips.

"Hello, little one," Cyann smiled when it stopped to look up at her.

The Jur who had toured them through the dome stalked toward them and with a quick swat shoved the new arrival over the edge of the terrace. Stunned, they watched it tumble some distance before landing on a lower level where it bounced and rolled until it came to a stop. After a moment or two, it gathered itself and disappeared into a domed tunnel.

"Why did you do that?" Cyann exclaimed.

The Jur made some vague gesture. "He is not allowed here. Must not bother visitors."

She glared at him, ready with her retort when she felt Jovan send a note of caution, like a hand placed on her arm.

He's probably fine. They don't have bones to break.

It would still hurt to fall like that!

"What is your function here?" Jovan asked their host.

He seemed to ponder that question for a while. "Guide. I guide other Jur. To prepare us to leave here."

"Some sort of leader, I guess," Anders said, startling Cyann who had forgotten that he and Nigel were following their progress via their com systems. "Or overseer, guard even."

The Jur turned back to the door into the hallway. "Come see drops." He stalked away, apparently certain that they would follow.

"You know," Cyann said after turning off her translator. "This place is starting to feel creepy."

"I have to agree," Jovan said. "Why is there no one else up here? Is no one curious?"

"Maybe some sort of hive mentality," Anders said. "Or an oppressive governance. Obviously the smaller ones have been told to stay away. Are you getting any telepathy among them?"

"Nothing," Jovan said. "If they're communicating that way I can't feel it. I'm not even getting mood or physical presence. I should at least be able to tell how many there are, roughly."

"Nigel," Cyann said. "Are you finding anything unusual?"

"Nothing you aren't. But your signals faded a bit when you were closer to that pit. Anything below you is pretty much shielded from the sensors. And I still can't cut through the plasma interference from the front end of this rock."

"We'll keep trying," Anders said. "But see if you can get some sort of headcount anyway."

They followed the Jur through another series of bubble-like spaces. Movement behind some of the walls made it clear that others were nearby, perhaps watching or following. But apparently only their guide was interested or permitted to interact with the strangers. All of them had visited places where off-worlders were rare or even unheard of. Never had they been met with so much indifference.

"It's like they don't care if we're here or not," Cyann said. "They know what guns are, obviously, but they haven't asked us to remove ours. Barely even looked at the ship. No curiosity, no fear, nothing."

"I know a few Delphians like that," Nigel quipped. "You're about to reach the end of the dome. There is a tunnel of sorts coming up."

The Jur was waiting for them not far ahead at a round metallic opening leading steeply upward. It was darker in there and they followed with some trepidation. But they soon exited again into another dome, this one much more vast and without a central pit. It enclosed a single open space. Fading light from the nearby star penetrated the murky substance that formed the roof and emitted from several Jur that barely looked up when the strangers entered.

"Doesn't this look familiar," Cyann said.

Most of the floor space here was taken up with clusters of pods looking exactly like the one that had come to Delphi's moon. Jur moved among them, wielding tools and scoops of a muddy-looking substance, perhaps repairing these or building more. Each pod was open at the top, showing a nearly liquid interior.

Their guide Jur waved both arms to encompass the collection. "These are the drops. Do not touch."

"There must be hundreds of these," Jovan said. He turned to the Jur. "Very many here."

"Yes. And many more in the other places."

Jovan exhaled audibly. "You will use these to leave the

asteroid?"

"Yes. Drop to new planet. Gravity will help us get there. Very dangerous. Some will die. Sad. But we have only this way."

"Do you know which planet?" Cyann said.

"You have many planets," he said. "One will fit. One will be home. We will keep looking."

"He's got no idea," Cyann said in Delphian. "At the speed of this asteroid, it could be generations before they find a hospitable location. Trans-Targon must be some sort of paradise for them."

"I wonder if they even know that this asteroid is going to poison the entire sector," Anders added.

"Jur," Jovan addressed their host. "There are dangers after the dead space. Dangerous planets. Bad air. Much gravity. Enemies maybe. Like on your home world, they may be hostile and fight."

"We know," the Jur said and again nothing in the blank expression hinted at his thoughts. "We are stronger now. Blue visitor showed us. Enemies are nothing. You are nothing. Your planes died. You can die, too."

"Gods," Cyann whispered.

"You do have weapons, then?" Jovan asked.

"No. We must find a new home. Nothing matters."

"Told you, didn't I?" Nigel's voice reached them from the *Scout*'s cockpit. "We're going to be dinner any minute now."

"I don't think they care about us being here at all," Cyann said. "He really seems to believe that they will defeat us. That we can't harm them. We can't stop them. Their survival is all that matters."

"I agree," Anders said. "Although he did mention a food shortage."

"This is not the time for jokes," Nigel grumbled.

"Words don't fit," the Jur interrupted when the translator crackled in protest over the unknown language.

"We need to regroup before we tell them anything," Jovan said. "Let's see if we can politely find our way out of here."

Cyann took an experimental step back toward the tunnel to the main dome. "We thank you for showing us your home. It is impressive. We will return to our ship."

"Why."

"To... join our people. One of them is injured. We must help him and then we must rest."

"He is broken? Sad. Broken Jur can't help the journey. They go outside."

"Outside? Why?"

"So they end faster. Very sad. But necessary. Injured Jur cannot help the Jur."

Cyann frowned. "You put them outside to die?"

"Yes. Cold there. And the air is wrong. So sad."

"You don't have healers? Medicines?"

"Your words don't fit," the Jur said. "Rest here. The doors are closed."

Nigel swore.

"Can you open them?"

"No. It's time for the turn. The star is soon that way." He pointed to his feet. "Cold outside." The Jur gestured toward the tunnel. "Rest there. Come." He led the way back into the habitat and then turned into another hive of bubble rooms that seemed to go on forever. At times, the ground either dropped or rose, perhaps following the asteroid's natural contours. A few other Jur crossed their path but quickly hurried into other directions.

Cyann indulged her curiosity and peeked into some of the side rooms opening off the main passage to see what looked like nests on the ground; three or four round bowls stuffed with the same material that clothed the Jur. Apparently the lack of solid bones allowed them to remain comfortably curled in a small space. Like in those "drops", she thought and shuddered when she imagined a hail of them falling on places like Callas or Nebdan or even Delphi. There was nothing else. No furniture, nothing decorative, not even discarded clothing.

At last, their guide stopped and gestured for them to enter one of these rooms. "Blue visitor space."

"Look!" Cyann exclaimed. She had discovered a box on the floor, the sort of plastic container found on any ship or Union base. The markings on the broken lid displayed Air Command symbols. She crouched beside it. "Union issue," she said. Carefully, she pulled out a few pieces of clothing and held them up to show Jovan and the camera at her shoulder. "These are also from Trans-Targon, I'm sure. Might even be from Magra or Pelion."

"Belonging to Kiran, you think?" Anders asked.

"I cannot imagine anyone else with blue strings on his head flying an Air Command plane all the way out here." The plain shirt she unfolded was of a size that might fit Jovan and she realized that, for some odd reason, she had expected it to be child size. "Guess he grew up, too," she said, oddly affected by the find. She briefly touched it to her face. The discovery of a comb tucked in among the clothes made her smile. "I guess *he* didn't cut his braid off."

Jovan grinned back and ran a hand through his hair. "No snips in there?"

"No, just clothes." She looked up at the Jur guide standing motionless by the entrance. "You said the blue visitor is dead?"

"It went outside."

"When?"

"Long ago. I will ask," he replied. "You will rest here." Before they had time to reply, he turned and vanished down along the curved passage.

Jovan watched him depart. "There goes the warden."

"Lying warden," Anders said. "If Cy is sure that Kiran's the one that's been talking to her."

"I am." Cyann exchanged a worried look with Jovan. "You sound terrible, Anders. Get Nigel to scan you to make sure those ribs aren't poking a lung. Don't move around."

"I'm all right. Headache's bad, though."

"We really need to get back to the ship, Jovan. You

should take another look at his head."

"That Jur might be right about the temps outside," Jovan said. "If we've rotated away from the sun, this gear might not be enough. We'd need the space suits."

"Nigel," Cyann tapped her microphone. "What's the weather out there?"

"Cold, yes," came the reply. "But you can make it if you hurry. We've got frost kits."

"I don't see why they wouldn't allow us to leave. They don't know what we can tolerate. Let's just find the door and see if it opens. Or just shoot the damn thing."

Jovan shook his head. "Let's not risk hostilities. Don't forget that, if the others don't find us, this rock is the only thing that'll get us out of here and back into Trans-Targon. When that keyhole opens, they need to be in a mood to let us ride it out in here."

"I'm less and less interested in asking these people for help and more and more convinced that we have to get off this rock," Cyann said. "I say we take our chances on Nova."

"Something worries me a bit," Nigel said. "It's possible that the Jur might want us to stick around for when we get to Trans-Targon. We'd be valuable to help them negotiate, if need be, maybe even as hostages."

"Then we're probably safe here for a while," Jovan said. "Let's wait it out and see if they'll open that door for us. How much time before we're facing the sun again, Nigel?"

"Hmm, let's see." Nigel hummed to himself for a while. "'bout four hours from now."

"That's not bad," Cyann said. "Can you get Anders comfortable? I'm worried about that headache." She waited for some sort of peevish comment from Anders but there was only silence. "And make sure he stays still."

"Will do," Nigel said. "I'll check back with you if anything changes. You do the same."

Cyann twisted the clothing Kiran had left behind in her hands, watching Jovan return to the doorway to look out into the hall. The silence of the dome was a little unnerving.

They had seen dozens of Jur in the distance but now it seemed as if they were all alone. No one spoke, no one was moving about - or if they were, they did so silently. There was nothing relaxing about this overwhelming stillness accompanied only by a dull drone from somewhere below.

Jovan turned to peer at her and then came to sit on the ground beside her. "Are you cold?"

She nodded.

He turned his com unit to *receive* only and then reached over to switch hers as well. "How are you feeling? You seem a little... edgy."

She shrugged. "Frightened, mostly. Worried about Anders. I guess I could use a bit of your Shantir magic, if you're offering."

"I am."

She closed her eyes when he reached out to take her face into both of his hands. Gradually, she felt herself relax and able to push away the nagging mental itch that had crept back over these past few hours.

"I'm sorry that I barked at you earlier today, on the ship," he said. "I have no right to do that. You were only thinking of these people. How we can avoid harming them. I should not have disparaged you for that. It was callous of me."

She opened her eyes to find him watching her intently. "I suppose you were right. We have a big problem if they get to Trans-Targon. That's clear now. And there isn't anything we can do to stop it." She grasped his hands. "I've never been in a spot like this before. I'm scared, Jovie. Really, truly scared."

"So am I."

She gave him a weak smile. "You are? You don't get scared. That's not what you're trained for."

He did not reply for a moment and then switched to the khamal that still existed between them. *What I'm not trained for is hiding from you.* His thumb stroked her cheek. *And what I'm scared of is not having the chance to show you.*

She felt something urgent beneath the words he was sending. That polite distance he had always maintained suddenly did not seem as if it was born of obligation. He had sworn allegiance to her clan which made him a servant in name and had made her safety his duty. But now, with their minds firmly linked, she realized that indifference was not what he felt for her. "Show me," she whispered.

He leaned down and even before his lips touched hers she felt the full, undisguised measure of his need. The remote affection he usually displayed for her was driven aside by a passion that she had not ever suspected to find in him. She returned his kiss, ignoring the uncomfortable breathing tubes across their lips, aware of nothing but his touch on her mind and the arms that held her. How often had she imagined this moment, when he would sail away with her on a cloud of bliss adrift on a summer's breeze? She missed the cloud and breezes no more than she noticed the hard floor inside this bubble of gritty glass on an asteroid heading for annihilation.

I wish... she thought and let her mind reach out for him, wanting to touch all of him, right here, right now. Jovan pulled away when another moment of this would likely overstep any remaining propriety in this alien place. She reveled in his comforting embrace, blocking out everything that wasn't part of this moment.

Why have you never told me? she sent.

He shrugged slowly. *Because I thought it would go away. That you'd find your mate. I thought I could just keep pretending and hiding.*

But why?

You deserve better than me. I don't even have a home. I don't belong anywhere. Your father—

My father? she sent a mental exclamation that made him flinch. "This is about Tychon? You're worried because you're a Shantir? That he wouldn't approve of you lusting after his daughter?"

"Uh, yes. I suppose. And it is... inappropriate. I am pledged to his service, even if that is just a title. He took me into his clan. He made it possible for me to study navigation. This seems... disrespectful."

"I suppose it is. He will stomp and frown and then Nova

will sort him out." She kissed him softly. "Is that why you left? The last time?"

He nodded. "You got to me. It was flattering and amusing when you were younger. Tychon shipped me off to Feron. But when I got back from there I realized that it wasn't so funny anymore. You'd suddenly grown up and I hadn't even noticed. When you chose your first *shoi-gan* I just wanted to be gone. I couldn't stand to see you with someone else, even just a mentor. So I left for the Badlands tour. And now I come home and nothing's changed. You're all I want and I'm not pretending it's otherwise. I can't be around you unless you're with me." He smiled wistfully. "When you badgered me into that khamal *shoi* on Sola I thought I was going to lose my mind! I decided then to tell you this. Maybe find the perfect moment on Delphi to sweep you off your feet and see if you still wanted me, I guess. "

She smiled and brushed her fingers over his lips. "Things didn't quite happen the way you envisioned."

"No, they didn't. But I need you to know. Now. In case I don't get that chance again."

"Shh, let's pretend we're not lost in the Badlands." She reached up to smooth his furrowed brow. "Should have listened to me years ago."

"You were a child years ago." He grinned. "And so was I. Tychon would certainly have had none of it. I could almost hear him grumble." He sent her a mental impression of the elder Delphian, exaggerated in playful detail. "Son, you're barely fifty years old. Grow your braid a little longer before you come courting my only daughter."

Cyann stifled her laughter. "And then you go and cut it off."

His smile faded when he bent to kiss her, gently, taking his time until, suddenly, he froze.

"What is it?" she said when he looked over her shoulder to the door. She turned. "Uh, hello."

One of the smaller Jur stood in the opening, regarding them silently.

How long has that one been standing there?

Jovan flipped on his translator. "Please visit," he said, copying some of the Jur guide's words.

"Come with me," the Jur said, using perfectly understandable Delphian. "Hurry."

"What the..." Cyann pulled out of Jovan's embrace and came to her feet. This one was considerably smaller than their guide and dressed in what were little more than rags. Something about the Jur's presence, as amorphous and formless as the others, seemed feminine. "Why? Can you open that door for us?"

"Not allowed. My name is Tik. Come with me." Her speech was high-pitched and accompanied by a melodious trilling deep in her throat.

"This is about Kiran," Cyann guessed. "You were sent by him."

"Yes."

"Anders," Jovan said into his microphone. "Are you there?"

It took a few moments but Nigel's voice finally reached them. "Anders went to lie down. He's feeling woozy. Might upchuck, too."

Jovan crouched before the little Jur. "Will we be able to return to the ship soon? Are we prisoners?"

"I don't know. Come with me." The Jur's luminous colors flickered red and purple, seemingly in agitation.

"Nigel, we may have made contact with Kiran. Going to check it out. Get Anders to stay still and run another scan. Check for bruises or bleeding around his brain. We'll return to the ship as soon as we're able."

"How do you know they'll let you?" Nigel said. "So far they haven't been too generous with the facts."

"Neither have we," Cyann replied. "But this one speaks Delphian."

"Come!" the Jur said and this time the urgency in her voice was clear. "Hurry." She stepped into the passage.

Jovan and Cyann followed her through a series of empty

bubble spaces that by now seemed almost familiar. But soon the spaces narrowed and became darker. Some of the walls were unevenly formed, even crumbled in places. The Jur led them on a steady downward path, taking countless turns and ducking through more of the narrow tunnels.

"Nigel, are you tracking us?" Jovan said.

"You're circling but moving downward. Signal is fading, though."

"Fading?"

"Yeah, you're entering that blurred area I noticed before. I can't scan into it. Not precisely shielded. Just a lot of interference. Something's in this rock that our sensors can't get through."

Cyann halted to peer through a gap in the wall. A vast hollow area lay beyond, filled with row upon row of stone walls of some sort. The air was humid here and warmer than above. Thick mats of purplish-brown growth draped over the stone rows, dripping with water. A number of Jur were moving among these, carrying bundles of the fibrous material away into the side passages. "Look. Food source maybe."

Jovan peered over her shoulder. "Algae? Looks like seaweed."

"The color is a lot like the stuff they're wearing."

"Come," Tik said. She reached up to tug on Jovan's hand. "Don't let them see you. They may tell the guides."

The trio continued onward, still moving lower into the hollowed crater. When Jovan tried again he was no longer able to reach Nigel. Worse, the khamal he shared with Cyann was also fading. *Can you feel me? I'm barely able to maintain the link.*

I don't like this.

Tik stopped near another opening into a narrow tunnel made of metal. "You will slide a bit but you won't fall. Lie down in there." She seemed to notice their great reluctance to squeeze their larger bodies into the chute. "It's safe. The guides don't come this way. Only some of the engineers sometimes."

Cyann sighed. "We're putting a lot of faith into you, Little One."

"Tik," the Jur corrected.

These people have no sense of humor, Cyann sent to Jovan.

He grinned. *I'll go first.*

Stop treating me like a baby. You've lost that privilege now. She shifted her air tank from her back and followed the Jur's direction to enter the tunnel feet first by grasping a chipped ledge above the entrance. Sliding awkwardly and hampered by her loose coveralls, she began to regret her impulse to prove her toughness to Jovan. The walls of the tunnel were cold enough to engage her suit's temperature controls. "Gods, we're either very close to the ice core or that little alien has taken us outside the asteroid."

"I was trying not to think that," he replied from somewhere above her.

Cyann exhaled a tense breath when the tunnel ended only a short distance below her and she was able to wriggle out of the space and onto relatively solid ground.

"Yes, we were outside the big rock," Tik said. "Three of these conduits connect to the... bean."

"Bean?"

"Shaped like that. I think you call it bean."

Cyann looked around. Again, this chamber was rounded, if not as spherical as the hollowed spaces on the main asteroid. "Why is this here? That big rock is massive."

"The ice is here. We live here to bring it to the domes. For air and water. They give us food for it."

"So that's your job?"

"It was. Now I tend to Kiran. Come." She slipped into a side passage and they hurried to keep up, barely able to squeeze through the cleft. Now more of her people passed them but this time they stopped to study them and did not duck out of sight at their approach. They were all of Tik's size, perhaps chosen for the work in these small spaces because of it.

I think social status goes by size here, Cyann sent to Jovan but felt only blankness there now. She turned and saw by his expression that he had no luck, either. Then the mental connection between them severed entirely and she no longer felt his presence inside her head.

"At least we know now why you're having such trouble holding on to Kiran's thoughts."

She nodded. "I wonder what he's doing down here."

"Hiding," Tik said. She turned a corner into a larger space. Several of her kindred turned upon their arrival and Cyann had a peculiar impression of guards at the door. Ahead of them another opening led into a more brightly lit hollow. Tik stopped them. "He said to tell you it's all right. That you won't like this. I don't know why. But he is not like you. He is not..." she stopped to grapple with something but her unmovable face revealed nothing. "He's not still."

"Why is he hiding?"

"Because they think he's dead. They will kill him if they knew he was here. Then all is lost." She paused again. "Maybe it is already."

Cyann actually shivered, so much more because of the Jur's hopeless words than the cold that was creeping into her suit despite its well-designed technology. "Let me see him," she whispered.

Tik took Cyann's wrist and tugged her along. The space they now entered was larger than any they had traversed on this asteroid piece and illuminated by lamps that they actually recognized. Still, it took a moment to discern the tall, slender shape pressed into a natural curve in the rock wall.

Impossibly thin, not due to starvation but through long exposure to reduced gravity, the Delphian stared back at them as if they were figures come alive out of a story book. He was dressed in a collection of rags combined with some of the Jur's rough cloth and, like them, barefoot in spite of the cold. The blue hair hung in unheeded strands to his waist. The pale Delphian skin showed a blue hue usually seen only on the very ill or old among their people. He seemed accustomed to the air here and breathed without a respirator.

She took a step closer. "Kiran?"

He regarded her silently.

She glanced at Jovan. "It's me, Cyann," she said, feeling silly for stating the obvious, but there was nothing in his expression to show them how he felt about this meeting. "We've come for you."

He stepped away from the wall. She gasped when his face moved out of the shadows. The gaunt features were so very much like Tychon's that no doubt remained of who they had found here among these strange people. His pale blue eyes moved from her to Jovan and then back again. "Cyann," he said as if tasting the word.

She dared not breathe when he raised a blue-nailed hand to touch her face, barely making contact with her skin. "Cyann," he repeated after a while, whispering. "You came. You heard me. I've been trying for so long."

She smiled. "Of course I came. I've been hearing you always. I didn't know it was you."

"Such a difficult link," he said. "But I felt your pain. That's when I found my way to you. You're so beautiful," he marveled.

She raised her arms to embrace him, moving carefully until he did the same. She winced when she felt the slight body that, although he was far taller than she, seemed without substance. "I can't believe we found you."

"Yes." He looked at Jovan. "Got any food?"

Cyann blinked and stepped back. "Huh?"

Kiran turned abruptly to walk to the far end of the space only to turn around and stride back again. "Food. Sweets would be nice. The stuff we have to eat here is terrible! Terrible!"

Jovan dug an emergency kit from one of his pockets. Cyann watched him, startled by the oddity of the moment. "You've missed much, then," she stammered.

"Yes! These people don't even smile! Smile for me, Cyann. Someone please smile!" He stared at them as if expecting some sort of magic trick. "Or sneer. A good sneer would be fine, too. Anything but these blank faces."

Jovan handed a few ration packets to Kiran. "That one is sweet, sort of," he said.

Kiran wandered off again, peeling the top from the package. "That's your mate, little sister? A Delphian, huh?" He came back with a mouth full of whatever he had chosen. "Humans not good?" He pointed at Jovan. "Where's your hair, Delphi?"

"What's happened to you?" Cyann said, stunned.

He laughed harshly. "Trying to save your asses, I am," he said. "So where's Tychon?"

Jovan turned to Tik. "What's wrong with him?"

Tik did not reply. She went to where Kiran stood now facing away from them, mumbling into his food. She reached up to touch him, like a child asking to be lifted into a grown-up's arms. He looked down at her and said something. When she replied he nodded and patted her head.

Kiran turned back to them. "Spent years on this rock," he said. "Years! That can make a man a little..." he gestured vaguely. "Eccentric! So Tychon did not come?"

"No," Cyann said. "He is guarding the keyhole. Do you know what's happened?"

"Of course I know. Twenty years to bring them there and it's all for nothing. I failed. I failed! Should have killed me when they could, back there on Shaddallam. Now we're all dead. It's too late. You're too late. Where's Tychon? We need Tychon if this is going to work." He drummed his fingers on his chest and looked very thoughtful for a moment. Then his eyes wandered back to Cyann and he smiled broadly. "Isn't she beautiful?" he said, taking her arm to turn her toward Jovan. "I made her, you know? Switched things around a bit for Nova. And here she is, pretty baby." He leaned conspiratorially closer to Jovan. "I ought to lecture on this. Much easier to muck about mommy's DNA than try to alter things later." He jerked his head toward Tik.

Jovan nodded. "We suspected that's what happened."

"Suspect? Suspect they did!" Kiran threw his hands up and paced away from them. Cyann saw a ladder of thin scars on his forearms, too deliberate to be anything but the result of lonely hours spent in battle with his own tortured mind.

"Jovan, can you do anything for him?" she said, close to tears. This was the mighty Tughan Wai? This was the boy whose loss had haunted not just Tychon but most of Delphi's Shantirate for all these years?

Kiran's eyes snapped to Jovan. "You're a Shantir? The ones that made *me*? And all you can do is suspect? Brilliant! I don't think I ever thanked you. I'll have to remember to do that." He shook his head. "Shantir with a gun. Why do you need a gun, Shantir?"

"Please, Kiran," Cyann said. "He might be able to help you."

"No, Little Blue," Kiran said. He tapped his forehead. "No, no, no. Dangerous. Tughan is very dangerous. Mustn't touch."

Jovan took a deep breath and stepped forward before Kiran had a chance to react. He gripped a frail arm in one hand and placed the other along the side of Kiran's head. The two men stood in silence until Jovan's hand began to shake as if he had to strain to keep it on Kiran. Or as if he was trying and unable to tear it away. He groaned.

"Jovie!" Cyann braced a foot against a nearby wall and shoved him away from Kiran. She overestimated the asteroid's gravity and he slammed into the opposite wall and then fell to the floor. She rushed to him.

"You didn't mean that I'm sure," Kiran said.

"What did you do to him?"

"Answered some questions," Kiran returned his attention to his food.

"Jovan?" She helped him sit up. "Are you all right?"

He nodded, breathing in harsh gasps.

"What happened? What did you see?"

"The Shantirs were right. The Tughan cannot be contained by one person. He's... he's taken too many. He's become too many."

Kiran came to crouch beside them. "He means I've gone crazy, I think. Do you have any more of this?"

Numbly, Cyann reached for her own emergency pack and handed it to him.

"The Jur guide was also right," Jovan said, running a hand over his eyes. "There was a huge destruction on their world. Kiran helped them escape and create these habitats here. He knew the asteroid was heading for Trans-Targon."

Kiran shook his head. "Genesis Cloud," he corrected.

"You knew?"

"Yes. Wasn't poisoned then, though. Would have sailed through without bothering anyone much. As long as you don't do something stupid like fly into the plasma spikes!" He laughed. "So it makes a fine space ship, doesn't it? The Jur don't have the mental to span sub-space. I hoped they would make it to Katra Four. There is a moon there that'll fit them nicely. Is this thornberry? From Magra?"

She peered at the package in his hand. "Yes. You meant to save them? By bringing them to Trans-Targon?"

"Nothing for them out here." He rose to show the berry paste to Tik.

"He didn't mean to stay with them," Jovan said. "The asteroid will get there on its own. The design of those drop pods is workable."

"Of course it is," Kiran said. "Designed by Air Command's finest engineers. I ate two of them. Engineers, not pods." He reflected on this. "No, three, I think. They weren't happy about it."

"Ate?"

"Absorbed their mental processes, memories, knowledge," Jovan said. "What the Tughan was designed to do."

"Wasn't designed to kill, though, was it?" Kiran said."Was it!"

"No."

"Did, though. And now everyone is sorry."

"Yes," Cyann said impatiently. "Everyone is sorry. But it can't be undone. Can we get back to the asteroid?"

"We *are* on the asteroid," Kiran said with a disquieting giggle. "Floating right into that keyhole. Nothing Nova can do. Nothing Tychon can do. It'll kill everybody." He sat on the floor against a wall and rested his elbows on his knees. "You tell her. I'm very busy."

"His plan was to help them settle here and drift into Trans-Targon. They've already made two jumps without much damage. But the asteroid's trajectory hasn't come by any useful planets. So Trans-Targon is their best chance. He figured that someone there would understand what was happening and assist them."

"She knows that part! Tell her about the comet."

"Yes. The asteroid passed through a comet tail a few years ago. Some of the dust and ice impacted and the virus mutated in the atmosphere outside, living on those extremophiles we found in the pod. They don't affect the Jur's food source, grown below the surface."

"But they will in Trans-Targon," Cyann said.

"The most densely populated sector I've encountered," Kiran said. "And I've been traveling out here since I was but a lad."

"Kiran came back a while ago to see how the Jur were doing. They are suffering on this rock but they're surviving. Barely. When he realized what happened with the comet he decided to stay and change the asteroid field's trajectory away from Trans-Targon."

"And that didn't work?"

"He never got to try. The Jur got angry when he told them of his plan. They can think of nothing but reaching Trans-Targon, the promised new home world. Even if that means bringing harm to other worlds. They destroyed his ship so that he could not use his abilities to divert the asteroid field away from the keyhole. He tried to convince some of the others. The... non-guides. Workers. Breeders. When the guides tried to kill him he fled into the lower levels." Jovan gestured at Tik. "He made some friends."

"Can't do it from here," Kiran explained. "Too much wrong energy here for me, for the Shantir. Trapped, like you are now. All lost."

"So that's when you started to call for help? To send those messages to me?"

"Yes, but you didn't hear. Tried for years! Bad energy gets in the way and voices are lost in the dark. Sub-space really complicates things. You have no idea! You were there sometimes. But so far away and you didn't hear."

"Until I went to Tava," she said. "That khamal amplified things. That's how you found your way to Delphi. To send the pod."

Jovan nodded. "I think so, too. What you were getting wasn't any withdrawal or residual effect. I was wrong about that. It was Kiran trying to reach you."

"Very bad for the brain," Kiran muttered. "Sorry about that. Had to try. Had to. Had to."

"And then you were able to steer the Jur in the pod to me. To let her tell us what's going on out there. But how can we help you? What can we do that the Tughan can't?"

Kiran looked at Tik. He got up and paced. He went to the entrance and peered outside. Paced some more. "Only one way now," he said. He slapped his head with both hands. "Noise! Can't do it by myself. Not now. Not here. But he can. He must."

"Who?"

"The Shantir," Kiran said impatiently. "That one right there. And Tychon. And you."

She frowned. "Tychon isn't here. He can't help us. They won't get here in time."

"I know."

"So what's your plan? Will you stop pacing?"

"Have to exercise. Look at my arms! This is what happens when the gravity spinner spins its last and you can't get a new plane. And then you get stuck here. Bad for the body. Very bad."

"Kiran," she said evenly after taking a deep breath to keep from snapping at him. "What do you intend to do?"

"What I said. Divert the cloud. Bring everyone here and do it together." He faced a wall to draw his fingers over the uneven surface. If there was some design he painted there, they did not see it. "Tughan lost its mind so I can't do this by myself. I need Jovan and Tychon for this. And Little Blue." He half turned to them. "Are there any other Shantirs with you?"

"Three. On Nova's ship."

"Good. Use them, too."

"How? And if we divert it, what about the Jur? They'll be stuck out here."

"Yes, two years plus, as Delphi tells time. Another keyhole awaits. But they did not believe me. They wanted to kill me when I tried to tell the others about it. Just two more years and no one gets hurt. But they wouldn't listen." He glanced at Tik and whispered. "In case you didn't notice, they're hard to talk to sometimes. Very single-minded."

Tik made a fluttering gesture with her hands.

"She's laughing at me," Kiran translated. "Anyway, you let me worry about the math, Cy. But it'll take all of you to do this. You have to get them here." His last comment was directed at Jovan. "That bit might be a little difficult."

Jovan scratched his head. "Indeed. Did anyone mention to you that our ship crashed? We barely have cruising speed, if we even manage to break away from the asteroid."

"Yes, that's a problem," Kiran said. "You have to use one of the pods."

"What?"

"Out of the question," Cyann exclaimed. "Have you lost your mind?"

"Yes, I have. I thought we had established that. But I'm still the Tughan and, given the proper tools, such as a dangerously fluctuating energy field dragging a pile of rubble through space, I am still very much functional. Mostly. We put the Shantir in a pod and throw him into the keyhole.

He's caught by your people on the other side and brings them back here."

"Is that all," Jovan said. "For a moment I thought you were going to propose something utterly lunatic."

Cyann frowned at him. "That is a huge risk to take."

"So is waiting around to see if Nova will come to our rescue before this thing starts feeding its energy into that keyhole."

"Yes." Kiran walked to the back of the room where a bed-shaped nest of rags had been piled. "I'm tired. Leave me alone now. Wait for the good energy and then we launch the Shantir."

"And then what?" Cyann said, ignoring his request as he curled up on his bed. "Let's imagine that, for whatever bizarre reason, Jovan survives this and gets Tychon back here. Then what?"

He turned his shoulders to look back at them. "You're going to shove your ship off the asteroid, Tychon will pick you up, I'll direct our khamal to use the energy field to divert the cloud."

"How's this even possible?"

"It's possible if you try to remember for a moment that I am the damn Tughan Wai. I steered a damn pod to Delphi through damn sub-space! Try doing that without brain damage. If you keep me steady I can do this, too."

"Is it going to hurt you?"

"Yes."

"But—"

"Go away! Tell Uncle Anders I love him. I remember him teaching me how to write. Tik will come for you at the next turn. She can't be outside in the cold. They don't feel the cold. They just drop dead after a while. The plasma charges will be at their best then, too."

Cyann stared at Jovan, speechless.

"Go!" Kiran shouted.

Tik rushed to them. "Yes, go now," she said. "This is upsetting him. He'll be fine by the turn. I'll take you back."

"Take you back," Kiran muttered. "Back on track. Pe Khoja says hello, Cy. Tell her that. Kiran didn't kill them. Kiran is sleeping now. Never coming back. Never!"

Cyann felt tears burn in her eyes. She stood undecided, looking at Kiran's broad but emaciated back. "Oh, Jovan..." she said, unwilling to leave this place. She ached to go to Kiran, to hold him until, somehow, his madness passed.

"Come on. Let's do as he says."

"Yes!" Kiran shouted. "Do as he says! Do as he says! Listen to the Shantir. They always know best, don't they? They can even turn babies into monsters!"

Tik was now pushing them toward the door. "Come, let him sleep."

Cyann saw little through the tears that blurred her vision when the Jur led them back to the conduit to the main habitat. Some of her people passed them, moving toward Kiran's room and Cyann was somewhat comforted that he was not alone.

She crouched down and touched Tik's shapeless arm. "Thank you for looking after him," she said. "Did he... did he get sick here or did he come to you like this?"

The Jur considered a while. "He was not like you when I met him. Not *still* like you. Not calm. But he saved us and he built this and showed us how to survive here. He touched my head and taught me your language. He gave names to us and told us stories about Trans-Targon. But his mind pain got worse here. His thoughts come in strange ways. The shouting. The laughing. He has many regrets. There are... people in his head. The ones he killed. Not all of them are kind, I think. They torment him, especially in sleep." She made some small, trembling motion with her hands at her side and her bands of color shifted to a deep violet. "He cannot be like this! He will help you, if he can. Then he will die. He wants to leave the voices."

Cyann looked up at Jovan. "He must be in such pain. Did you see no way to help him?"

He hugged her briefly when she stood up again. "There is

nothing I can do here. By myself. I can't even tell what's wrong with him. If there is help for him it will take a long time. There is much... damage."

She sighed. "So much depends on him, and he's barely coherent. It's probably safer if you stayed out of his mind entirely. This could affect you in a bad way."

He started to say something but then just nodded. "Come, let's get back to the dome."

A noise from above drew their attention and then two of Tik's companions slid from the chute into their midst. They warbled something to Tik but were already done and gone by the time the Delphians had reached for their translators.

Tik stood silently for a moment, moving her hands in some peculiar fashion around her head. She looked oddly thoughtful doing that, but Cyann wasn't sure why she assumed that. Finally, Tik spoke. "The guides are looking for you."

"Oops, we better get back here," Cyann said.

"No," Tik said. "They are angry now. You did wrong."

"We'll just tell them that we went for a walk. He didn't say we had to stay in that room."

Jovan nudged her. "Yes, he did. He said to rest there."

"So? That doesn't mean..." She considered. "You're right. They seem to be a little yes-no in their thinking, don't they? This or that. Right or wrong." She turned to Tik. "What will they do?"

"Put me outside," Tik's color band shifted to a purple that was almost black. "Maybe hurt you. Come this way."

NINE

Cyann had begun to worry long before the Jur guide stepped into their path. They had made their way back to the main asteroid and below the dome. Likely now several levels below where their original host had left them, they moved through series of domed spaces, most of them low enough to force them to stoop. Tik had hurried them along, navigating this warren with ease. Several times she motioned them into recesses or side passages while other Jur moved past them. Eventually they moved up a level and that's when one of the taller Jur barred their way, head bobbing and colors flashing in agitation.

"Visitors," he said. "Stop here."

Cyann pulled Tik to stand behind her and activated the translator. "We are now returning to our ship. Thank you for the visit, Jur. We must go to our ship now. And eat our food. Jur food is not good for us."

"It is cold outside," the Jur said. "Dangerous. So sad. Stay here."

Jovan took a step closer to the guide and raised his gun as if to inspect it. "I think we'll just hurry before we get too cold."

The Jur's color bands shifted into a blue spectrum when he saw the pistol. "I will find your guide."

"You do that," Jovan said. "We'll wait right in there."

"Yes, wait." The Jur gestured toward Cyann but clearly meant Tik cowering behind her. "She comes with me to the guide."

"Well," Jovan said. "No."

The Jur stared at him for a long moment, perhaps unaccustomed to being disobeyed. He moved around Cyann and grasped Tik's arm.

"I'm done with this." Jovan leveled his pistol and shot the Jur. Tik slapped both hands over her mouth to cover a scream when the guide crumpled to the ground.

"Gods!" Cyann exclaimed. She had read about Jovan's travels and heard stories about the things his crew had encountered but to actually see him use his gun startled her. She shook herself out of the moment of surprise and bent over the fallen Jur. "What setting did you use? I can't even tell if he's dead or not."

"It's not set to kill. Let's keep moving. I'd like to get back to the ship before they've got the entire population looking for us. I think we need to assume that these Jur brains do not work like ours." Jovan picked the oddly stiff body up and folded him neatly into a gap in the wall.

"Tik seems to think like we do," Cyann pointed out.

"Yes, but she was touched by Kiran. Who knows what he did to her. Wouldn't be the first time he's altered someone. And he's obviously tampered with his own systems to be able to breathe this air." He squatted beside the frightened Jur. "Tik? Let's go, all right? He won't hurt you. We need to keep moving."

She stared at him round-eyed before slipping past him to continue along the hall. They followed her into ever more narrow passages that soon no longer showed much evidence of being manufactured. Raw stone tunnels led into several directions and they had the impression that they were climbing through a densely packed and fantastically large clump of gravel. In places it looked like individual boulders had been removed to widen passages that now slanted upward. Soon they had become so narrow that it took considerable maneuvering to squeeze their bodies through the gaps.

"Getting colder," Cyann shivered. "We must be close to the surface." She helped Jovan push through a fissure in the rock, careful to adjust his air pack as he moved on.

"Yes," Tik said from somewhere ahead of them. Cyann turned to illuminate the space with the small lamp attached to the chest of her suit. Tik's ghostly shape flashed shades of yellow in the dark. "Up this way."

They entered a slightly larger space to see a jagged shaft lead upwards from here. The lazily spinning fan bolted into the opening appeared to be salvage. Tik climbed up along the wall by inserting her boneless limbs into the stone crevices. Nimbly, she began to unfasten some pegs that held the fan to the shaft. Her waxen skin seemed unaccustomed to the chore and soon a clear liquid dripped from her cut fingers.

"Wait," Jovan said. He dug into his kit pocket to find a small hand tool. One of the attachments was a set of pincers. "Try this."

She took the device from him and cooed over it for a moment before getting back to the task at hand. Soon Jovan was able to lift the fan out of its position in the ceiling. "You can keep that," he said with a smile.

Tik made a pleased gurgling sound. "We are not allowed... things," she said and carefully placed the tool under a nearby stone. "I will hide it here for next time."

"You come this way a lot?" Cyann asked.

"Yes. When Jur are sent outside we bring them back through here. Sometimes Kiran can fix them." She pointed up. "You will fit. It's very cold outside."

"Nigel," Jovan opened his com unit. "*Scout*, come in."

"Jovan," came the reply a few moments later. "How was the nap?"

"Enlightening. Can you get a fix on us?"

There was a brief pause. "Yeah. How did you get over there? You're at the edge of the dome, looks almost like you're outside. Something venting above you. Waste gases from the dome, I'm guessing. Don't breathe too deeply."

"How far from the ship and can we make it there?"

"Hmm, I'd run. Crank the suits up to max. The *Scout* is just beyond a small rise to your left. You should see the array though."

"How's Anders?" Cyann said as she adjusted Jovan's temperature controls.

"Staying still, finally. We sent the crawlers outside and found the virus all over the place. So now he's resting. Still got a big headache with that concussion."

"All right," Jovan said to her. "We're going to climb up this shaft and make a run for it. I think I ripped my suit but I have the feeling Nigel will make us take a bath anyway."

"You bet your blue fur on that," came Nigel's unhurried drawl.

Cyann bounced around the small space in an effort to raise her body temperature while her suit warmed up. Given the shortage of gravity, it did little but bring an amused smile to Jovan's face.

"You're laughing at me?" she said.

"Yeah. I have a better idea." He grasped her collar to pull her close.

"Ooh, yes, body heat," she smiled.

He kissed her, a little awkwardly around the thin oxygen tubes running across their upper lips but there was no obstruction to his touch on her mind. She gasped when he used a delicious combination of the khamal *shoi* and more conventional Shantir manipulations of her core temperature until soon they were both quite ready to tear out of their bulky suits.

"Stop," he breathed. "Or this is going to end up really weirdly."

She pulled her visored hood over her head and smiled down at Tik who was staring up at them with orange flashes of confusion. "We're going now. You will come to the ship when it's time to go?"

"Just before the turn. No one will be outside then."

Cyann nodded and reached up to grasp the stone edge of the shaft above them. The climb was easy and there were enough spaces in the rock for hand and footholds. Jovan, behind her, cursed once or twice when his larger frame threatened to get stuck in the narrow space but soon they tumbled out of a gap in the rubble to find themselves outside.

"Run!"

They raced across the space between the dome and the waiting *Scout*, leaping over boulders and ditches with almost comical ease. Despite their increased core temperature, she soon felt the bite of the asteroid's frigid atmosphere cut through her suit as if it wasn't even there. A red warning strip helpfully appeared on the inside of her visor to inform her that the current conditions were less than optimal. She pushed on, feeling her fingers and cheeks grow numb, and leaped after Jovan over the rocky outcropping barring their way until, finally, the ship came into view.

The *Scout* sat at a precarious angle; clearly part of the landing structure was damaged. But its main door opened smoothly and soon they were inside, heavily blasted by the strong formula Nigel had cooked up to decontaminate them.

"Leave your suits in the lock. I don't even want them in here."

They peeled out of their coveralls and, after another, entirely gratuitous blast of decon, gratefully removed the air tubes from under their noses. Cyann rubbed her lip, happy to be back aboard their ship. It felt a little like coming home. She submitted blissfully to a vigorous arm rubbing by Jovan, less in need of having her arms warmed and more so of just having him touch her. Eventually, Nigel declared them clean and allowed into the ship.

Cyann rushed to the *Scout*'s small med lab where Anders rested on the single gurney, a respirator over his face. She added some compounds to the gas mixture to allow him to breathe more deeply. The scanner showed damage caused by the splintered ends of the broken bones but they had not punctured his lung. Jovan added his skills to help him manage the pain in his head and ease the bruising of his concussion.

Gradually, Anders responded to the treatment. "Oh, Cyann, did I nod off?" He smiled but his breathing came in ragged gasps. "I don't feel so good. Time to go home now, I think. Is there any tea?"

"Soon, Uncle," she said. "I'm going to give you another shot. Just give it a moment."

"Did you find Kiran?"

"Yes! He says hello. He remembers you well. He sends his love."

"He was such a bright boy," Anders said. "A head full of blue curls and nothing but mischief on his mind. Hmm, actually, that might have been you. Things are a little blurry. I think maybe I'm getting too old for these jaunts into nowhere. Remind me to retire when we get back home."

"Don't talk," Cyann said. "Just rest, all right?"

They turned to scrutinizing their own systems for hostile organisms but it seemed that Nigel's decontamination concoction had done its job.

"You're also very pretty on the inside," Jovan said in low murmur when he reached around her to run a scanner along her back.

She caressed his cheek and then ran her fingers over his neck with an alluring gaze deep into his dark blue eyes. He winced when the sampler in her hand pieced his skin and removed a blood specimen.

"That is pure mischief," he said, rubbing his neck.

"I'm not sure why we're bothering. We're going back out there."

"You're what?" Cyann and Jovan turned from the medical displays to see Anders regard them curiously. "Back to the dome?"

Cyann stepped away from Jovan and leaned out into the corridor. "Nigel, can you come in here, please? If you got that tea made."

"At your service, Mistress," he called back to her. Indeed, he soon entered with a tray of tea, juice, and bowls of a thick stew they called Chunky Gunk outside of earshot of those who supplied the *Scout* with quick-prep food portions.

"There is no one outside now," he reported. "Guess our hosts haven't figured out that you're back here by now."

"They can't go outside in these temperatures," Cyann said. "We should be fine for a while."

While they ate, Jovan and Cyann took turns in telling them about Kiran and his plan to divert the cloud. By Anders' and Nigel's stunned expressions, it was clear that their hopes for success did not exactly surpass their own. Cyann noticed that Jovan did not dwell on Kiran's mental state other than to call his legendary Tughan abilities hampered by conditions here on the asteroid. In a way, she supposed, that was true.

"Is this the part where you tell us you're kidding?" Nigel said when they had finished.

Cyann sipped her tea, savoring its sweet warmth. "Nope. Kiran is as convinced as our guide Jur that Nova isn't going to be able to neutralize the asteroid. I am inclined to believe him. We can't let this thing get to the Trans-Targon. They're probably only beginning to worry about us. They don't even know how close it is to the keyhole. For all they know, it's not going to arrive for years yet. How much time do we have?"

Nigel consulted a screen on his data sleeve. "To the keyhole? About twelve hours."

"Our best chance is to go back and bring them here," Jovan said. "And since the *Scout* isn't going to get us very far, one of those pods might do it. I'm guessing that Kiran's going to use those energy emissions to launch it."

Nigel sighed. "Mother told me not to get mixed up with Delphians. But did I listen? No, I said, going to get a job on

Delphi! Pure science and none of that Union resource exploration drudgery. See where that got me? Beyond the Badlands without crossdrives." He shook his head in wonder. "We've got a few hours before sunrise. You two get some rest. I'll stay up here with Anders."

"I'm fine," Anders protested. "No need to play nursemaid."

"That's not Cyann's diagnosis, Old Man, so you'll just have to endure my presence at least until you've shaken off that headache."

Cyann bent to kiss Anders' forehead before leaving the small med service. Jovan walked behind her but when he moved past her at the door to her room she snatched a corner of his shirt and pulled him inside.

"Where are you going?"

He smiled. "You said you were tired."

"I lied," she said, suddenly very unsure of herself. Or of him, standing here in her cabin. The things he had told her in the dome had seemed so wonderful and uncomplicated but now she had no idea what to say. "Jovie..."

He reached out to shut the door to the corridor and pulled her close to erase every doubt from her mind with his kiss. She responded to his touch, holding nothing back when she felt the length of his body press against hers.

He lifted the hem of her shirt and pulled it over her head before drawing her close again. His kiss grew more demanding and then she felt the firm touch of his mind on hers, more intimate than the hands on her body.

She gasped when the khamal *shoi* he had initiated strengthened the link between them until she was unsure of exactly where his being met hers. His lips trailed to her throat and then his mental touch conveyed the sensation of his fingers moving slowly over the sensitive ridge along her spine. He followed this immediately by actually touching her that way, forcing a moan from her lips. She felt his smile on the skin of her neck when he repeated this, again and again until her knees threatened to collapse under her and she was no longer sure which touch was real and which was in her mind.

Tentatively, she tried for herself what he had shown her, touching his mind this way, pleased when he arched his back with a moan. "Gods, Cy..."

She pulled him to her narrow bunk and it took only moments for them to discard their clothes to continue this wonderful new way he taught her, exchanging both mental and physical touch, using fingers and lips, thoughts and words in rhythmic waves of pleasure until both of them reached a matchless plateau of ecstasy from which they leaped together.

She sprawled over him, gasping for breath, unable to speak for a long time after the last shudder subsided. "What..," she managed, "was that?"

"Ancient Shantir secret," he said breathlessly, equally thrilled by what they had shared.

She looked up. "We... umm, we didn't even..."

He grinned. "Guess we'll have to practice some more to get there."

"Lots of practice!"

"Oh, yes, I think so." He glanced at the time display near her door. "Later."

"I've waited so long for this," she said, watching her fingers stroke his face. "I... I was right to wait for this. For you."

"Are you sure?"

She raised herself up. "I've been sure since around the time I first noticed these," she said.

He admired the view for a moment. "I'm serious. You're not yet thirty."

"I'm also not all Delphian. Do I seem like a little girl to you?" But she knew what he was asking. Simply taking a lover was not on his mind. Both of them had their choice on Delphi, where browsing among them was accepted and expected long before choosing a life mate. But they had, for all of his absences, shared all of her life together and to simply end up in bed was just not enough for either of them.

She leaned down to kiss him slowly. "I'm sure," she said.

* * *

Sunrise. "There she is," Jovan said when a movement outside their ship alerted their sensors. He looked up at the cockpit's main screen showing the little Jur hiding behind an outcropping, unaware of the thermographic scanner that found her there. "She's awfully cold, though. I wonder how much they can tolerate."

Cyann came to stand behind him and ran her fingers through his hair. It had suddenly become very difficult *not* to touch him. "Where? Oh, I see her. I guess it's time to go." She was also suddenly very much against what they were about to attempt.

"Is there no chance of talking you out of this spectacular and suicidal jaunt through what we know to be a ridiculously long jump?" Nigel said behind them, voicing her thoughts.

He entered with a suit he had altered for the journey. Since Jovan would not fit into one of the alien pods with a full space suit, Nigel had made some improvement to temperature and pressure controls as well as the air supply conduits. He held it up for their inspection. "I even picked your favorite color."

Jovan stood up. "You don't know my favorite color."

Nigel winked at Cyann. "Yeah, I do."

She busied herself with climbing into her own suit, wondering how much noise had made it past her cabin door these past few hours. "Keep us on your scanners and let us know if you think they're onto us."

They stepped into the airlock and soon ducked around the *Scout* to where Tik was waiting for them. She gestured for them to follow her and slipped around the steep outcropping that sheltered the domes. They moved quickly, able to take broad leaps over obstacles and trenches, until they had skirted the crater. Tik motioned to them to keep low when they crossed an open area until they reached the edge of one of the domes.

As soon as they arrived, a narrow slit opened in the wall and a dark shape rolled toward them. It was one of the pods, now tumbling more quickly as several of Tik's people pushed it out of the dome. They all looked very much alike, dressed in rough rags and wearing poorly-fitted respirators that had seen too much use. "Here's your plane, Shantir," Kiran ducked out of the shadows. "Just need a little fuel now." He gestured to Cyann. "Come, help, it's too heavy for the little people. Too heavy for me, now that I think of it. Can't roll it up the hill."

"Where are we taking this?"

"Up there," Kiran said without pointing in any particular direction and strode away from them on his stilt-like legs. His companions, with the exception of Tik, disappeared back into the dome.

Cyann and Jovan grappled with the pod, able to lift it up between them, and awkwardly stumbled after Kiran. By the time they had made it halfway up the hill he had chosen, both were out of breath and feeling the strain of carrying the pod despite the asteroid's weak gravity.

"Come look!" Kiran called. "Very pretty up here."

They struggled onward, cursing and gasping, slipping on the rough terrain until, finally, they were able to set the pod down without fear of it rolling back down the hill.

"What if they see us up here?" Cyann said.

Kiran turned back to look down at the domes. "They have no windows. Try to be observant. Look!" He waved for them to come up the last few steps to the crest.

Jovan and Cyann joined him and saw a massive, lifeless expanse of weathered hills, tall outcroppings showing more recent erosion, and deep furrows and grooves worn into the surface. Above them and all around drifted the cloud of companion fragments, obscuring the endless canopy of millions of stars.

Cyann glanced at Jovan. "Umm, nice asteroid..."

"You can't see that?" Kiran said, pointing toward the far

end of the rock.

"See what?"

Jovan looked down at his data array. "He's looking at the energy field. It's still just showing up as plasma interference on our scanners."

"It's not interference." Kiran reached out to them and briefly touched their heads. Both of them flinched in surprise but when they looked again to the horizon they saw a corona of green, white and blue bands of color streaming through space. "Pretty, huh?"

"So there are particles? Not just radiation?"

"No, it's radiation. Tiny little anomaly at the front of the asteroid, pulling us. Making energy backwards. Very busy with that."

"How tiny?"

Kiran held up his thumb and forefinger to describe a small space. "Keyholes call to it, attract it. Pretty sure this cloud used to be a planet. Before it met the little anomaly. Boom! Now it's just along for the ride. You have to go now."

Jovan was still staring up into space, seeing the shifting display of light through Kiran's eyes. At times, a flare shot out to whip violently into a new direction. "This is what brought down the ships?"

"Yes. Your pilots are not agile." Kiran leaned over the pod and folded the top of it outward. "All aboard!"

Cyann grasped Jovan's arm. "This is scaring me."

"Yes, me too," he admitted and tapped the visor of his hood. "This is awkward. I'd really like to kiss you goodbye before I cast off into the unknown."

She smiled and touched his arm, sending a gentle touch from her mind to his. "I'd like that, but you don't have to."

He grunted briefly when she added a mischievous tweak to the end of her mental caress. "You learn quickly."

"All right, all right," Kiran said impatiently. "My turn."

Jovan stepped away from Cyann and faced her brother.

"What do you mean?" she said, puzzled.

"No kisses for the Shantir, but a hug will do," Kiran said.

"I'm going to have to link with Kiran," Jovan said. "With... with the Tughan."

"What?" she gasped. "No!"

"Did you think he can just hop into that keyhole by himself?" Kiran said. "Sure he can, sure he can, but he won't get out. Needs to do the math. Needs to find the exit."

Cyann watched fearfully as Kiran placed his hands on either side of Jovan's head. Jovan took a stumbling step forward, nearly knocking Kiran over, but then grasped the edge of the pod to steady himself. "Let's do this," he said through gritted teeth. He turned back to Cyann and then looked down at Tik. "Get back to the *Scout* before the sun comes up, in case some of those guides decide to go outside to look for us. Try to keep Kiran calm. He's making my head spin already."

"I will try," Tik said. "Maybe he can sleep until you get to the dead place."

"Won't take long to get there," Kiran said, watching Jovan fold his limbs into the cramped space. "You'll see. No time for leisure cruise."

"I hope not. My feet are falling asleep already."

Cyann rearranged his air supply in front of him and tested the connections. He gripped her hand and their eyes met briefly before she moved away to let Kiran close the pod.

"Heat will seal exterior like fifty layers of graphene," Kiran said proudly. "See that black thread in the lining? When you want to get out, put that hand on the thread, and the other hand on this one here. See it? I made that myself. Releases catalyst to dissolve the exterior. Nothing else will, so don't lose your hands anywhere. I guess you could use a foot, but you're not flexible. Too many joints. Not like the Jur. They bend."

"Kiran," Jovan said, irritated.

Kiran laughed and folded the top of the vessel. "Time for the show!" He stepped back and shoved the pod with his bare foot.

Cyann cried out when it tipped over and then began to roll down the far side of the hill. "What are you doing!"

"Watch, little sister," Kiran raised his hands and a wide, undulating stream shot toward them from the energy field in shades of blue and white. Tik made a squeaking noise and threw herself to the ground. But the flare angled sharply toward the tumbling pod and, under Kiran's direction, enveloped it completely before whiplashing back again to the far end of the asteroid, leaving nothing behind.

"You were serious," Cyann said. "You really just threw him."

"Did you think I was hiding rockets out here? Too slow. Too slow. Time is wasting."

"Is that how you're going to get the Jur off this asteroid?" she said, still looking into the distance, where, somewhere, Jovan was hurtling toward an invisible fracture in space.

"No. They don't have to go that far. Just enough to escape the gravity." He bounced a few times to demonstrate what he meant by gravity. "They can do that themselves."

Cyann looked back to the domes. "How?"

He bent to put Tik back onto her feet. "I showed them how. Had to build a machine, though, to capture the flares. Not easy to do but once you know what to look for, it's one two three."

"Kiran," Cyann said slowly, fighting a very definite need to panic. "These Jur have the technology to affect this energy?"

"Yes." He looked into the distance. "I can see your plane from here. I used the Jur planes to build the machine. Crossdrive would be better, but I only had mine."

"Stop talking for a minute." Cyann tapped her data unit after making sure that her translator was offline. "Nigel, see if you can scan this side of the domes to see if you can pick up any sort of technology that's not made of glass and whatever this stuff here is. Mechanical parts, electronics even. Not a power source." She frowned at Kiran. "We've found our power source."

"Can't scan very deep," Nigel replied.

"It'll be near the surface, but maybe on one of the other fragments. It might even just look like junk if it's not turned on."

"It's not junk," Kiran said.

She took his hand. "Kiran, listen. Has it not occurred to you that they might be using your machine as a weapon? That they shot us down on purpose? And that they might shoot Jovan down when they get back here?"

He frowned at her. Glanced at Tik. Then back at Cyann. "That is not the purpose of its design. Its intended use is for the transport of refugees from asteroid surface to destination planet. Proceed when in range."

"Kiran, where is this machine?" she asked gently, remembering that the only thing that kept Jovan on target right now was the Tughan's limited attention span.

He sat on the ground and drew his knees up. "My fault. See? I try to help and everyone is hurt. I break everything." He looked up at her and she saw tears on his face. "Dadda is going to be angry if the Shantir doesn't get home. He'll go away again and leave me."

Cyann crouched down beside him. "Kiran? Please don't cry. Come, show me where the machine is. This isn't your fault. You didn't know. No one is angry." She stroked his stringy hair, wondering if she was seeing the six-year old Kiran, buried by the sheer mental weight of the adults he had killed. Had he ever had the chance to grow up? She pulled him close. "Shh, come now. We need your help."

He sat stiffly in her embrace and did not reply. Cyann looked up at Tik who stood helplessly nearby, flashing violet ripples.

"You know," Cyann said. "I want to see your machine. It must be amazing. Tik wants to see it, too. Won't you show us how it works?"

"It works fine, I'm sure," he snapped.

"But is it pretty?"

He turned his head. "It's a focusing aperture using

negative energy. It's beyond simple, once you figure out the containment issue. How pretty can something like that be?" He scrambled to his feet. "Come, I'll show you."

Tik and Cyann raced after him as his long strides set a quick pace down the hill. "Nigel, I think we've got it. Just keep an eye on life forms around us."

"I see you," came his reply. "That little one is with you? If so, there are four larger ones ahead of you and to the right, a fair distance. No idea if anyone's below you. I suspect tunnels. Whatever this stuff is made of, we need to get us some of that."

"From what I've seen, the asteroid material is fused by the energy emissions to make things." She briefly shook her head, reminding herself to stop playing the explorer and focus on their situation. "I think Kiran is rubbing off on me. Let's worry about this stuff some other damn day."

Cyann scooped Tik up from the ground to gain some speed. Not sure where the Jur liked to bend, she seated her into the crook of her arm like a child. The small creature made an unclear sound but then grasped a fold of Cyann's coveralls and looked around, apparently pleased with her new vantage point.

Kiran had sprinted some distance ahead, now on level ground behind the smallest of the domes. Cyann thought it might be the one they had toured with their guide Jur. They reached a row of five flat metal structures, each no higher than her knees and several paces across. Beside each a small pedestal stood ready to receive an occupied pod. Kiran knelt beside the first and pulled on some latches. "In here. Look."

Cyann put the Jur down and came to help Kiran with the bolts. Three of them slid aside with a squeal. She braced herself and worked her fingers under the lid. It was likely not something she could have accomplished on Delphi, but here the sheet of metal lifted with ease and she was able to flip it aside.

"See?" Kiran said. "Want me to show you how it works?"

"No, that's okay." Cyann leaned over the device sunk into

a pit. Nothing about it looked even remotely familiar, but a set of controls flashing on its side seemed to indicate that it was in working order. "Does it look like they've tampered with it since you built it?"

He peered into the pit and reached down to tap at the controls. "No. Settings still rhyme." He frowned. "Things still add up... um."

"I got it. Let's check the others." Cyann moved to the next box and then the one after that until all five lids were tipped back. Kiran dutifully checked the mechanisms, mumbling to himself.

"This, look. This!" he said excitedly. He ran his hand over the aperture. "New protocol. Double output. More! Clever Jur."

"Does this have a power source? Fuel?"

"No, just the starter module has a little juice," he said as if she were especially simple-minded. "We have that!" He gestured in the direction of the energy field.

She nodded. "Move back."

"Why do you have that gun?"

Just then Tik began to emit a high-pitched wail. She ran at Kiran and pummeled him with her little hands to get his attention. They looked around to see what had upset her.

"Was there an alarm on these boxes?" Cyann said.

"Umm, I don't remember."

Several Jur had come outside the central dome and now moved quickly toward them, heads nodding and arms waving. Even from here, Cyann saw that their coloring had turned an angry purple. They were saying something but she had no interest in finding out what that might be.

"Going to break your machine now, all right?" She did not wait for Kiran to answer before she fired at the connectors and what she assumed to be the main control unit of the device. For good measure, she also shot the aperture fixed to the housing.

Kiran stared, eyebrows raised. "Uh, all right."

She moved to the next one.

"No!" Kiran yelled. "No no no no. Don't break those, Silly Blue. The Jur need those to leave the asteroid."

Cyann cursed. "How long would it take them to recode these?"

"How would I know? They should have told me."

"Come on," she bent to grab Tik again and took his hand. "To the ship. Hurry."

They raced in long, loping strides around the dome and the edge of the crater to where she hoped the *Scout* waited. She scanned the ragged skyline to find one of the peaks she knew to be near the ship. "Nigel," she shouted into her com unit. "Got trouble."

"I see it. More coming at you from around this side of the dome. Veer to your left, into that gully."

She followed his direction. Kiran, long used to this gravity, huffed behind her, dragging on her arm as he started to fall behind. "Come on, Kiran," she pleaded. "Just a bit farther."

A sharp pain tore along her arm and she nearly missed her step. She looked down to see that her suit was torn, but not burned. "They have guns?" She pushed him behind a rock wall and put Tik on the ground. Carefully, she peered around the stone to look for their pursuers.

"Slingshots, sort of. Very powerful."

"Why do they need slingshots!" Cyann fired a few rounds, startling the Jur into hiding as well.

"Sport," he said. "Fun sport, actually. With targets. But sometimes they hunt, too."

She sent a few blasts into the rocks. "There is nothing to hunt out here," she said, unwilling to take a closer look at her wounded arm.

"There is when they send out the extra Jur," he said, nodding in Tik's direction. "The small ones they don't need any more. Broken ones. Old breeders."

Cyann stared at him in disbelief. "And you want to save these people?" She ducked when another of their missiles splintered a chunk of asteroid above them.

"These are good people. Were good people. Don't be mean." He peered around a corner and pointed across the valley that housed the crater. "The guides live there, in that bubble. See it? They're the misery here. They changed the Jur ways." He shook his head. "I should not have brought them here. Better off on their home world."

Tik raised both hands to nudge him. "Home world is dead, too," she reminded him.

Cyann continued to fire but by now they had caught their breath. "Let's keep going. One more sprint, okay?" She stooped to pick Tik up with her uninjured arm. "Go!"

They raced back out into the open, toward the ship, more slowly now. Cyann sobbed with relief when she saw Nigel come toward them, a gun in each hand. He veered to the side and fired beyond them. "Go go go!"

They raced past him and Cyann saw the open entrance hatch of the *Scout* invitingly close. But then Tik squealed into her ear and waved her hands. Cyann looked back to see more Jur come over the top of a boulder, their jointless limbs moving effortlessly over the rock. "Nigel, behind you!"

He whirled and fired blindly, backing up as he did. His foot slipped into a fissure and he was thrown back. Although he still fired, a hail of projectiles tore into his body before he had even hit the ground.

"Nigel!" Cyann screamed. "Get up! Get up!"

But it was clear that he would not. Blooms of blood spread over his coveralls and he lay still, surrounded by Jur that now turned their attention to the rest of their quarry. She turned and fled, dragging Kiran with her. At the *Scout*'s gate she tossed Tik into the airlock, then turned and grabbed Kiran to shove him inside as well. She leaped after them and hit the lock, gasping for air through the too-thin valves of her supply when the door shut with a heavy and reassuring thump.

Kiran lay crumpled beside her, also breathing in loud, ragged gulps. Tik huddled in a corner, looking fearfully around the small chamber. Cyann crawled over to him. "Are you all right?" She ran her hands over his fragile arms to check for broken bones.

He nodded, stunned.

She flipped onto her back and tapped her com unit. "Anders," she said. "Can you hear me?" She waited a while. "Anders?"

Finally, a reply. "Cyann! You're back! Did Jovan get off this rock?"

"Yes. I'm in the airlock with Kiran. Can you go into the lab or the cockpit and see what's going on outside?"

"Yes, wait." He groaned and then she could hear him move around. Something fell to the floor.

"Uncle?"

"I'm all right. Just give me a moment."

Cyann dragged herself upright and opened one of the storage units set into the wall. Among the equipment and provision kits she found a portable decon wand and a blade. After enlarging the hole in her suit, she treated the gash on her arm, alternating the program from Human to Delphian to make sure that nothing remained in the wound that didn't belong there. She suspected that all of them were contaminated beyond what could be remedied aboard the *Scout*.

"My God, Cy, what happened out there?" she heard Anders' startled voice.

"They had a long-range weapon. Big enough to take down the ships. Then they got angry. Is... Is Nigel..."

"No life sign," Anders said.

"I have to go get him."

"You will do no such thing! Those creatures are still out there."

Cyann glanced at Tik. "They're not all bad." She snatched up a spool of tape and wrapped some of it around her torn sleeve before drawing her gun. "Scan for Jur at a distance. The slingshots they use have a fairly long range."

"Cyann—"

"I'm doing this, Uncle! We can't leave him on this rock. I

won't." She punched the release for the exit door, her pistol ready. There was no one at the rear of the ship and she moved purposefully to the front where a half dozen of the Jur guides had gathered by the lifeless body on the ground. None of the smaller Jur had come outside their domes.

"Get away from him," she said, aiming the gun gripped in both hands. It shook a little. Aboard the *Scout*, Anders fed the perimeter scans to the screen inside her visor. "Move back!"

They stared at her silently, unmoving. She had expected an attack and hoped for a retreat, but this quiet challenge was puzzling. She moved closer. As one, the colors of the guides flickered purple and then seemed to synchronize their rhythm. It felt like a countdown. She lowered her weapon and fired into the ground.

"To your right," Anders warned of an approaching life form.

One of the guides raised what appeared to be a hoop attached to a handle. Cyann shot through it and his head disappeared in a spray of clear fluid. She turned and fired at the more distant Jur to the right, taking him down in two shots before returning her aim at the guides near Nigel. "Drop those weapons," she hissed.

They backed off, finally, and tossed their slingshots aside. Their colors flashed in less coordinated patterns now. Cyann ducked when the *Scout*'s laser weapon strafed over her head to find some target in the distance. She moved to Nigel and grasped his collar. Even in this gravity she could not carry him in one arm while aiming at the Jur and so she dragged him back toward the ship. When one of them took a step to follow her, Anders' aim dropped him at the feet of his compatriots.

"Hurry," Anders said when she reached the ramp. "Getting all sorts of activity going on in that small dome back there. I think they're all waking up now."

She passed her data unit over the lock to an external compartment beside the entrance to the ship. It was empty, as she knew it would be, and she lifted Nigel into it. Carefully, she straightened his limbs and then removed his hood to deactivate the climate sensors in his suit. She stroked his hair for a moment before setting the freezer controls.

"Behind you!"

She whirled to fire at two Jur that had come around the *Scout*'s landing struts, out of Anders' line of sight. They pulled back but she continued to shoot while she waited for the entrance door to open. It seemed to take an eternity after she slipped inside for it to close again. Ships like the *Scout* were not designed for hasty departures.

"Cyann!"

"I'm here." She struggled for breath as she slid to the floor. Her knees felt suddenly very wobbly. "Made it. We've got him."

Anders' sigh turned into an agonized cough. "Now all we need is a pilot."

"What do you mean?"

"There is no way I can interface with the ship with my head in this state. I... I feel dizzy and I have trouble seeing."

She closed her eyes, willing herself not to scream in frustration. Or slap some sanity into Kiran. Why hadn't she gone to flight school? "Maybe Kiran can manage," she said finally and knelt beside him. He had crawled into a corner where he seemed to be talking to himself. "There must be one or two pilots still floating around in his head."

Kiran turned to her but there was a distant look in his faded blue eyes that she had not seen there before.

"Kiran?"

"Shhh," he said. "Keyhole. Very busy now."

TEN

The pain in his head was unbelievable. Some sort of vise seemed clamped around his skull, tightening with clear intent to shatter bone and then continue on to turn his brain into sludge. Having no one to hear him, Jovan moaned loudly, perhaps he screamed at some point. It was this pod, he was sure of it. Hurtling him through space, toward the damn keyhole that he absolutely no longer wanted to enter.

If any space had existed between his tightly folded arms and legs and the interior of this shell, he would gladly have kicked and clawed his way out of here, never mind that he would spill out into the cold hard nothing of this barren galactic sub-sector.

"Kiran!" he yelled into his oxygen mask. He shivered with cold while sweat poured from his body. Was he seeing the inside of the Tughan's mind? Was this exposure about to destroy his own, as it had destroyed Kiran? He fought against thoughts that weren't his and emotions he did not want. Why was Kiran upset? Why was he angry? What was happening on that damn asteroid?

WhatWhatWhat? Be still be still.

"Stop thinking, you lunatic. You are breaking my brain!"

Busy. Be still. Very busy.

"What's going on?"

Tending the garden, two three. Almost there.

"I'm almost there? To the keyhole?"

Yes. Shantir is going home. Come back soon.

"If you don't stop your ranting I swear I'm going to kick your ass when I see you."

I'm very fragile. Next stop, keyhole. Ready?

"No, wait. What do I do?"

Find exit. You're a spanner. So span. I will calculate. Ready?

Jovan muttered a sting of curses. If this were a jump-capable ship, he would by now be firmly linked to its circuitry, guiding the processors through the required calculation and awaiting their results from which to choose his exit. And now he had no choice but to rely on Kiran's questionable mental processes.

You better not be talking like that around my sister.

"Is she all right?"

Shantir's in love, Kiran giggled into his brain. *Can't concentrate. Keyhole! Keyhole!*

Jovan nodded to himself. He was right. He breathed deeply of the tasteless packaged air, calming himself for the task ahead, blocking out the pain in his head and Kiran's disjointed mental images and all but the keyhole that he now sensed through his link with the Tughan.

"I see it," he said. "How are you going to open it?"

Let the Tughan work. I could tell you how it's done without stuffing the thing full of negative energy until the poor thing shouts for mercy but then where will we be? You'll want to play with it and soon you'll have another war on your hands and more rebels and more people wanting to go places they shouldn't. Trans-Targon is plenty big enough for all of you. So don't be asking me for easy answers because you won't get them.

"It's easy, then?"

No, silly Delphian. Not for you. Let the Tughan work. I might sing.

"It's opening," Jovan said.

Your turn. Touch it. Feel it. Find the door. Go go go. Hurry back.

Jovan cast his thoughts into the vast amount of data that

Kiran showed him. It was not the orderly system he usually felt when linked to a processor, but there was a strange beauty, even logic to the pattern. And then, as always, the talent that made him a Level Three spanner allowed him to recognize his destination as if someone had turned on a light. Before further debating the wisdom of this, he signaled Kiran to launch him into the now-open jumpsite.

Things did not disappear. The disquieting but familiar nothing of sub-space did not envelop him. He saw and felt and most of that was pain and confusion. He wanted to get out of this, desperately, and he clawed at the hood over his face, wanting to tear it off even as he realized that he could not move. Once, long ago, he had stood too close to a broken hangar door that had crashed down onto its metal track, breaking his eardrum as it did. The sound in his head now was a lot like that, accompanied by a strange melody. He was losing his mind, he knew, joining the Tughan like all those other people had to become part of the creature and leave behind only an empty shell. He suspected that he was screaming.

* * *

The sound had changed now. Tapping. Distantly and unevenly. Then humming. Were those voices he heard?

Jovan opened his eyes, seeing nothing, blinking slowly. He became aware of breathing. It felt wonderful. Of stillness. Of gravity. He was alone in his head now. That felt even more wonderful.

He turned his hand and placed it against the inside of the pod as Kiran had shown him and then touched the thread on the other side to complete a circuit. A few moments passed and then he felt the pod dissolve. It took a long while and he was glad for that, needing time to appreciate the fact that he was alive. Eventually, he was able to push his legs outward, stretching the pod's interior skin until it broke. He let himself slump sideways onto the ground.

Someone was there, touching him. Faces behind visors.

Two. Three. A milky fog surrounded everything and he knew that everyone was very busy with decontaminating the thing that had arrived in the pod. He heard the clack-clack of radiation emitters emitting whatever these people thought suitable for the occasion. Someone cut his suit away, then his clothes. More decon gas.

He stretched his cramped limbs out on the floor and let the technicians do their thing. He was shaking but not sure why. There was a glass wall and behind it stood people, watching. They looked worried. Finally, the fog dissipated and the strangers around him removed their protective gear. "He's clean. So's the pod."

The door into the decon chamber opened and Nova rushed through it. "Jovan!" she cried and skidded to the ground to take him into her arms. "We were so scared! Are you all right? Talk to me, please!"

He looked into her frightened face and smiled. "Could I have some clothes, please?"

She reached up and took a sheet from one of the technicians. "Come, to the med service."

He allowed them to load him onto a gurney and transport him to another part of the ship where doctors and his fellow Shantirs waited to examine, prod, scan and question his state of health. Nova hovered anxiously nearby and when Tychon appeared at the door Jovan felt a disquieting sense of guilt.

"How are you doing?" Tychon said. "And you won't hold it against me when my next question is all about my daughter."

"She's safe," Jovan said at once. "For now. But we have a problem." He looked around the assembled medical staff. "Some classified issues here," he added.

Nova gestured for all but the other Shantirs to leave the room. "You found him?"

Jovan nodded. "What happened when I got here?" He sat up on the examination table and waved Nova away when she seemed about to insist that he stay there.

"We were probing the keyhole for your exit when you

came out at just sub-light speed," Tychon said. "Unbelievable. One of the Eagles had to chase after you. They captured the pod and brought you back here."

"When was that?"

"Just an hour ago. We took you to the clean room at once."

"We have to get back there. Now." Jovan put his feet on the ground and reached for a pair of lab coveralls someone had left for him. "That asteroid is about to come through that breach. And it's coming in with a massive energy field that'll take this station apart in a second. We lost both Eagles and crashed the *Scout*. Kiran means to divert the cloud before it gets here. He needs our help to do that."

"Surely, the Tughan Wai is capable of turning aside the asteroid," one of the Shantirs said. "We've heard of him accomplishing greater things before we lost him."

"That's not just an asteroid and right now the Tughan Wai isn't capable of stringing together a clear sentence." Jovan turned to Tychon. "I'm sorry, Shan Tychon. Kiran... he's no longer himself. He's suffering from... I don't know what. It's not any mental illness I've ever heard of. His concentration is badly compromised. He's got moments of lucidity and then it's like he's talking to someone else. His head is like standing inside a wind tunnel trying to catch a piece of paper. I didn't even think he could get me back here."

Nova sighed and rested her forehead against Tychon's arm. His face, however, remained motionless.

"You joined with the Tughan?" one of the Shantir gasped.

"And so will you," Jovan snapped. "I survived. Maybe you can, too. But without us he has no chance at all."

"What is the plan?" Tychon asked.

"One big khamal," Jovan said. "You, me, Shan Evo and Toch, Cyann and Kiran. He thinks it can be done if we keep him focused. He said he needs Cyann for that. I'm guessing there is something about her brain that'll help buffer us from the Tughan. Or slow him down somehow." He looked to Shantir Evo for confirmation.

"Possible," the man replied. "He might be referring to her synapse abnormality. It'd be far more resilient to the sort of overload that the Tughan causes when he..." Evo glanced at Nova. "When he strikes."

"We'll take one of the Eagles back through the breach," Tychon said. He turned to the third Shantir, a nervous individual who had seemed ready to bolt from the room as soon as the Tughan was mentioned. "I think it best if you remain here, Kytra, in case some of us need help when we return."

Nova opened the door. "Lieutenant, would you ask Captain Kimura to get his ship ready for immediate departure? Major Tychon and Shan Jovan will pilot." When she turned back to them Jovan noticed that she had gone very pale. "How will you get through that energy field?"

"We're not," he said. "It's defying our sensors. We'll approach from behind. We'll have to veer wide to get the others off the surface. Another reason to get back there fast."

"Then let's take this ship and hit the cloud from the back. It may dissipate that energy field or shove the asteroid off course."

Jovan shook his head. "Thousands of... people on that thing. Using it as a sort of generational ship to get here. Kiran meant to bring them to Trans-Targon but then he... well, just came apart."

She pressed her lips together and Jovan wondered if some internal dialogue went on between Tychon and Nova that they preferred not to share. The look she gave Tychon before he turned away confirmed that.

They hurried toward the docks where the commandeered Eagle awaited them, two very reluctant Shantirs in tow.

"Thank you, Captain Kimura," Nova said when they had reached the plane. She then spoke into her com band. "Back us away from the keyhole after separation and stand down all weapons. Prepare for immediate departure. I'm heading for the bridge." With another searching look at her husband, she hugged Jovan and then hurried away.

Jovan followed Tychon into the Eagle's cockpit and took the co-pilot's chair. Pre-flight was done; the only thing left to do was to disengage from the Union ship and cruise toward the keyhole. "Get yourselves strapped in," Jovan called over his shoulder into the main cabin of the cruiser where the Shantirs waited. He shrugged at Tychon. "First trip through was kind of rough."

"Trip back didn't look so pleasant, either."

"You have no idea." Jovan engaged the neural interface to the ship. "Guess Nova isn't happy about this."

"No." Tychon's link controls also flashed on the console. "It's always a pleasure to command an Eagle. I think I miss that. The plane, I mean. Not the work."

"You liked being Vanguard."

"I like being alive more. Should have joined Anders' crew long ago." He leaned forward to adjust some manual controls to his liking.

Jovan remained silent for a while. "I'm always amazed how Nova holds it together. We're all she has, really, for family. You, Cyann, Anders, me. She doesn't show it but this must really upset her."

"Yes, it does."

"I think Cyann's a lot like Nova. Maybe not so tough, but she's got a lot of grit."

"I know that." Tychon turned for a moment to regard Jovan thoughtfully. "What's on your mind?"

Another uncomfortable silence followed. Uncomfortable for Jovan, anyway. Tychon seemed to enjoy the dim quiet of the cockpit.

Jovan swallowed hard. "I'm in love with her."

Tychon said nothing. The ship responded to a command from his neocortex and rolled into position facing the keyhole. He did not look at Jovan. "That's a very Human concept," he said finally.

"You should know."

Tychon nodded, just once.

"I respect you as the head of my house," Jovan said, unnerved by Tychon's silence. The older Delphian's sharp profile gave nothing away. "And I have likely overstepped some boundary, I guess. I feel like I took something that isn't mine. I tried to stay away, knowing how she felt about me."

"Is that why you left?" Tychon said.

"Yes."

"You hurt her."

"I thought it was for the best. I have no home. I have no roots. I spend my life floating from one planet to another. I'm your liege and I'm a Shantir."

"What you are is an idiot," Tychon said.

Jovan blinked.

Tychon shook his head, showing a little impatience. "Sorry. Nova told me I shouldn't have said that."

"You're in khamal with her?"

"Of course."

"But—"

"Look, Jovan. Shantir or not, kinsman by oath or not, you were destined to be with her since the day you met."

"She was two years old," Jovan managed.

"Yes. I was there. She took one look at you and it happened, whatever that was." Tychon finally turned his head to look at Jovan. "Long ago, Nova and I worried about what her father might think about us. He was a bit set in his ways and, frankly, not fond of certain species. I guess we all have our prejudices, for one reason or another. It was a long time before he knew about Nova and me. In fact the only reason he found out was because I had to tell him that, despite every bit of scientific fact available to us, she was having a Delphian baby." Tychon gazed into the distance for a moment as if recalling that meeting. "He came around eventually. Cyann has a way of sneaking into people's hearts and she helped to mend things."

"She does," Jovan smiled.

"My point is, don't worry about the old folks. Do what you have to. You have no need to please anybody but yourselves. Cyann has no roots, either. Or so she thinks. Take her away from this backwater we call Delphi. She's every bit the explorer you are. You're a good man, Jovan. Even if you are an idiot."

Jovan fell back into his pilot couch and exhaled a long sigh of relief. "Yes, I'm an idiot."

"Now power this thing up while I say my farewells to Nova. She happens to think we're not going to return."

ELEVEN

"Cyann?" Anders' voice seemed strained. "Are you all right in there? Ready for decon?"

"No!" Cyann said at once. "Wait." She sat quietly, cradling Kiran in her lap while he stared at nothing and occasionally mumbled things that still didn't seem connected to whatever thought preceded or followed.

"Let the Tughan work," he said. "Let the Tughan work."

She looked over to Tik. "Are you all right? Don't worry, they can't get in here."

"They will kill me. For helping you."

"The guides?"

"Yes."

Cyann tapped her com band. "Uncle."

"Yes."

"There is a Jur in here with us. Kiran isn't able to help her right now. What can we do for her?"

"What do you mean?"

"We can't send her back out there. They will murder her."

"We can't take her off this asteroid. You know the rules."

"I'm not asking to take some alien home for a pet, Uncle! It's our fault that she's in trouble. And she's attached to

Kiran."

There was a long silence. Cyann smiled encouragingly at Tik without any idea if the Jur understood the meaning of that.

"All right," Anders said finally. "We've got the composition of the air they breathe inside the dome. I'm going to take some air from outside into the compressor and add a bit more oxygen and a little nitro and water. That should be fairly close. You can fill a few bottles from there. Take the stuff out of the large isolation box in the bay. She should fit in there. It's the best we can do until we figure out how to keep her alive."

"See? This is why you're my favorite uncle!" Cyann winked at Tik. "Did you get what he said?"

"Yes," she said. "You are going to put me in a box."

"She knows our language?"

"Didn't I mention that?"

He mumbled something unintelligible. "Let's get to work. How is Kiran?"

"Coming around," Cyann shook him gently. "We have to get out of here, even if we can just cruise far enough away to get out of range of those guns."

"What guns?" Anders said. "You said you destroyed it."

"I am not convinced that there aren't more."

"Does Jovan know this?"

Cyann sighed. "No. He doesn't. He'll anticipate the energy field but not any directed fire."

"You're right; we have to get out of here."

She gave Kiran another shake. "Kiran? Are you in there?"

He frowned and looked around the airlock. "Where else would I be? Union-built ship. Not Air Command, I think."

"It belongs to Delphi." She helped him sit up. Tik came over to huddle beside him. "Can you fly this ship?"

"I can fly any ship. I used to, anyway. I don't think I can now."

She cursed inwardly. "Why not? Won't you even try?"

He shook his head. "Processors will get all mixed up. Too

much. Too too much!" He flinched when a hissing sound began in a corner of the chamber as Anders transferred the gas. "I break things," he added.

"I think you should try, anyway." She got up to empty the glass-fronted bin set into the wall. "I was looking for this," she said to herself when she pulled out some insect netting. She opened another door and exchanged the net for a tall-size pair of coveralls which she handed to him. "Here, put this on."

"You're scared."

"Yes."

"Go ahead. Ask me."

She bit her lip. "Did he make it?"

"Tughan knows what it's doing. Went through that keyhole and popped out the other side. Not broken even a little. Is there any food?"

Cyann sighed deeply and rested her forehead on the cool surface of the storage units.

"Ugh, gray," Kiran said, inspecting the coveralls. "You know what this place needs? Color. Yellow. Orange! Do you have any purple?" He crouched down beside Tik. "I once had a whole room with blue walls."

Cyann found another suit and used it to pad the isolation container. "Here you go, Tik. Don't worry, it's all very clean. These things get scrubbed more often than we do." She turned to Kiran and nearly cried out in dismay when she saw him without his ragged wraps. He had grown beyond the normal tall and slender build of his people. But there was little muscle left and the poor food available here had left nothing but skin stretched over his brittle bones.

He turned to her, fastening the front of the suit. "I like blue ones," he said. "Oh, and yellow! Do you have a yellow one?" He watched her shift her attention to the tank to fill a few bottles of air for Tik. "The only color here is on their skin. Very pretty, but it comes, it goes."

Cyann picked Tik up and carefully placed her into the glass box. The little creature curled up and did not seem to mind the small space. "Will you be able to help her?" she said to Kiran. "I don't even know if we can take her away from here."

He came to stand beside her and patted Tik's head very gently. "Tughan knows what it's doing." His brow furrowed and the turned to scowl at Cyann. "Take her away?"

"We can't leave her here. They will kill her."

He shook his head. "No. I won't let you take her away. That's just wrong. She won't leave me."

"Leave you? No, Kiran. You're coming with us. If we can get off this rock, you're both coming home."

"Home?" He stared at her, pausing for some train of thought to assemble before shaking his head. "No, can't do that!"

"What? You can't stay here. You have no ship. This place is making you crazy."

"Already crazy." He turned away. "Can't go home. Nova will kill me."

"No, she won't," Cyann said, worried by this new agitation. "She wants you to come home. So does Tychon. You'll be safe."

"You won't be. The Tughan kills. The Tughan breaks things. They know that and they will kill me. Don't believe them." He paced to the exit door and knocked on it as if expecting it to open. "Best if I stay here. Better for everyone."

"You will die here."

"Yes. It's time to go. Time to stop this. Don't want to kill you."

Cyann stepped closer to him and, although he shrank away from her touch, gently stroked his arm. "You won't kill us," she said. "You don't want to kill anybody. You could have killed those Jur out there, but you didn't. You won't."

He nodded and then looked up at the ceiling. His lips moved and he winced as if trying to say something simply too complex to shape into words. At last he just closed his eyes in resignation. "Pain," he said.

She dared to reach up to pull him into her arms. "Can I give you a hug?" she said. "It won't hurt. I won't hurt you."

He said nothing but did not resist when she held him in a loose embrace. "We want you home," she said, aching for him to hug her back. For someone, *anyone*, to hug her and maybe tell her that Nigel wasn't really dead, and Jovan wasn't really flying a rock into nothing, and the most powerful Shantir to ever exist wasn't really relying on her to dry his tears. "Father wants you home. He said so."

Both of them stumbled when something massive struck the side of the ship. Tik peeped fearfully and hid her head in her bin. The lights dimmed.

"Anders," Cyann said. "What's going on?"

"Got hit by something." Anders' voice trembled, as if short of breath. "Projectile."

"Your machine?" she asked Kiran.

He raised an eyebrow. "Of course not. My machine works better than that."

Cyann closed the lid on Tik's tank and ran a decontamination cycle while she stripped out of her coveralls down to her tights and undershirt. "Can you breathe our air?" she said. "If not, grab a tank over there."

He shook his head. "I can breathe. No shields?"

"Anders," she called. "Did Nigel get those shields reset?"

There was no reply.

She exchanged the gas in the chamber and removed her breathing tubes before opening the door into the *Scout*. "Anders!"

"Uncle's over there." Kiran loped ahead of her toward the cockpit.

She followed him down the narrow passage when another hit rocked the ship, slamming both of them into the bulkhead. "Anders!" she cried when she saw him lying on the floor near the forward console.

Kiran looked over the controls. "Uncle isn't feeling well. Maybe we shouldn't disturb him."

"Don't touch anything!" she snapped and knelt beside the

Human. "Anders, come on, let's get you up."

He squinted up at her. "The boy's right. I feel terrible." He looked up at Kiran now sitting in the pilot bench with his knees drawn up to his chin. "You've grown taller," he said.

"You might be bleeding in that thick skull of yours, Uncle," Cyann said and helped him sit up to lean against the com console. "Can you stand?"

"Shields are a necessary constituent of safe aviation," Kiran opined. "They tend to become even more helpful in space." He peered down at Anders. "No pilot, huh?"

Cyann took a long and hitching breath and rubbed her eyes with the heels of her hands. She ached for Jovan's soothing touch to ease the growing sense of dread threatening to overwhelm her. She murmured softly to herself as she shifted into a khamal that would keep her from crawling into some dark corner to await the end of all things. It let her transform the energy wasted on panic into useful concentration.

"All right," she said resolutely. "Enough." She came to her feet and stood by the console to switch the external screens. A few Jur hovered around in the distance. The bubble that Kiran had pointed out earlier now glowed orange, lit from within. She shifted her attention to the ship's control panels. "Shields. Let's hope Nigel got those reset."

"Those are shields," Kiran pointed at the console.

"I know that. Dadda used to take me flying."

He sighed. "Me, too."

She worked with the controls for a while but whatever Nigel had done there had not improved the situation. "Are you sure you can't do this?" she said.

"You can."

"If I could we'd have shields by now. What are they firing at us, anyway?"

He giggled. "Rocks. They're throwing rocks from the pod launch. Clever. Very clever Jur."

"Rocks!"

"Cyann," Anders said weakly. "If they damage the

converter array we've had it."

"Clearly." She bit her lip. "Why isn't this working!" The *Scout* shuddered as another missile impacted nearby.

Kiran reached over to the co-pilot seat and picked up its headset. "You have to do it from the inside, like all the real pilots do. Tell those processors who's in charge, Little Blue."

"What? No, I can't. I told you. Shields are part of tactical and I don't have a program for that. I'm not a pilot, I'm not a navigator and I'm not even a Delphian. So don't ask me to do things I can't do!"

He cocked his head. "Why do you want to be a Delphian?"

"Huh?"

He poked her arm. "You're not a Delphian. I didn't make you to be a Delphian. I gave Tychon and Nova a Cyann. Not a Delphian. You don't need to be Delphian."

She searched his face. His restless eyes had stopped shifting around and he regarded her with something approaching stillness. "What am I?" she whispered.

He smiled, looking fleetingly like Tychon. "You're a Cyann." He held up the headset. "Now be a Cyann. I will help."

She took the gear and connected it to the neural interface. Her device was meant to control intricate lab equipment but the ship's navigational system recognized the link and signaled a ready state. Kiran placed his gaunt hand on her arm and she instantly felt the connection to his mind. She winced. "Slow down, slow down!"

"If I could I'd be doing this," he said with deadpan logic. "The Tughan can't hurt the Cyann. See? Better than Delphian. Kinda. Talk to your plane. Make friends. I'll show you."

She ground her teeth and directed her attention to the controls. Sifting through the blare of words and imagery that he could not control took all of her skill but, gradually, she found her way through it all to touch the plane. He led her to the defensive systems and, after a few stumbles, the lights on the console flashed their approval.

"Forward shields!" she exclaimed. "Aft. Uncle, we have shields!"

He did not reply.

"Anders?" She twisted in her bench.

"Leave him," Kiran snapped. "Go now."

"Go?"

"Yes, go. Leave the Jur." He pointed up at one of the screens that showed nothing but asteroid surface. "They're powering up the aperture and then they won't be throwing rocks any more. Tughan says big flare might soon mess up our pretty shields."

"I can't fly this!"

"Cyann can." He reached across to her and poked her arm. "Are you a Cyann or just a half Delphian?"

She looked over the maze of manual control systems in front of them. "I'm a Cyann." She settled back into the couch and closed her eyes, letting the ship's system show her what she needed to see and accept the commands she sent through her neural link. Kiran's restless mental noise faded into a static blur and she saw only what she needed from him. She felt the *Scout* power up beneath her. One by one, the systems responded. A few power shifts made her a little nervous when the plane adjusted for some of the damaged components.

"Do us a favor, Little Blue?" Kiran said.

"Hmm?" She ran the thruster startup sequence as if she had done it all her life.

"Don't bother with the gravity."

"Oops, sorry!" The *Scout* had automatically engaged the gravitational systems in preparation for takeoff. Both Kiran and Tik would suffer for it. She overrode the setting to match the asteroid's weak pull. "Uncle, I'm going to push off now. Hold on to something."

Kiran looked over her shoulder. "He's out. I'll help." He unfolded his long legs to get up.

"Stay where you are, dammit," she said. "I need you for

this. We're about to launch."

"I know that. I'm not *that* confused." He lowered himself to the floor and wrapped his arms around Anders. "Heavy uncle!" He flapped a hand at her. "Go! I'll hang on to Uncle."

She dropped back into her couch. Kiran was still in her head, guiding her through the steps she needed to take to get the *Scout* airborne. A vibration moved through the ship and then they felt it rock gently as it rose from its landing gear. The ship, like its passengers, ignored a new barrage of missiles launched in their direction, glancing harmlessly off the shields. "It working!" she said. "I'm flying!"

"Little Blue is flying!" Kiran shouted.

She adjusted the thrusters and slowly rotated the plane. It rose higher and soon hovered over the valley. The Jur on the ground either scattered or stared up at them in what was likely surprise. Cyann moved the ship to an open area to give the thrusters the needed space for launch. She shifted her attention to the ship's weapons system.

"Cyann," Kiran said nervously. "Don't break the pod launches. Don't be mean. The Jur need that."

"They'll shoot us down!"

"Go to the other side of the cloud."

"No time for that." The targeting scanners, directed by her mental commands, found the Jur guides' bubble in the distance. She fired. Kiran gasped when the missile she had chosen slammed into the bubble and it exploded into a hail of shards and what she assumed to be Jur body parts. "For Nigel," she said. "Guides gone. So sad."

She engaged the thrusters, whooping in terrified joy when the ship shot away from the asteroid and broke though the thin atmosphere with barely a wobble. She set a course designed to take the *Scout* in a wide arc around the reach of the asteroid's deadly flares and toward the keyhole.

Before breaking her link with the ship, she sent a repeating distress signal and calculated their trajectory and that of the asteroid. "Kiran," she said. "Is the cloud speeding up? Look at those projections."

"Yes, it does that when it gets close to the keyhole. Has to."

She worked with the ship's processors and cursed silently when she had the results. "You could have mentioned that hours ago. No crossdrives, remember? We're not going to reach the keyhole or the others before the asteroid does."

"Not at this speed." He helped her tighten their curving trajectory while still avoiding the energy field's effects. "We don't have to."

"You'll be able to link us all up from here? Without touching them?"

"I found you, didn't I? I can touch them from here. When they get here."

"Shouldn't they be here by now?"

Kiran shrugged. "Probably has a headache. Maybe he's hurt. I don't know."

"Don't say that." She went over her calculations again. "Jovan thinks we still have hours before the cloud hits the keyhole." She climbed out of the pilot couch. "Help me with Uncle Anders." They managed to lift Anders up and maneuver him back into the med service where he dropped gratefully onto the exam table. She engaged the scanners and placed an oxygen mask over his face. Whatever he was fighting was taking its toll on his systems and he seemed barely aware of them.

"Damn. Bleeding, left side of his skull," she said. "Subdural."

Kiran hovered anxiously nearby, holding Anders' hand in both of his. "I'm so sorry I can't help you, Uncle," he said. "I don't dare. I don't dare!"

Cyann stroked Anders' spiky white hair. "Maybe you can."

Kiran shook his head. "No. I'll hurt him. He's Human. I'm too scared to try."

"Then let the Cyann try," she said and placed her hand over Anders' neural interface. "With your help. You changed my mother's genes and you can damn well stop a little bleed. You know what to do. I'll do it for you, just like I launched the ship."

He looked up from Anders pallid face. After a moment a grin formed on his colorless lips. He touched her hand to re-establish their link. She winced, anticipating another jolt of frenzied mental activity but, clearly, something had calmed him.

"You're better now, away from the asteroid?" she said.

"Bad energy. Makes everyone crazy. I'm going to see Tik. She's frightened. She's not been on a plane in twenty years."

"Um, Anders, remember?"

"Tughan knows what it's doing. I keep telling you that. A thousand people in my head. What's one more?" He wandered off down the hall toward the airlock.

Cyann bent over Anders. "Uncle?" She probed carefully, needing at least a spark of recognition before she could join him in the khamal. "Can you hear me?"

He reached for her, well used to the intrusion of the healing khamal after a lifetime spent on Delphi. She followed Kiran's wordless direction to help Anders fight the pain and the damage to his veins and then watched in amazement as her hands seemed to know how to drain the accumulated blood from his skull with tools never intended for this task. They spent time in silent meditation, lending him strength and giving comfort. He accepted it gratefully, aware of Kiran but unafraid. *Should have been a Shantir*, Kiran sent when Anders calmed and the pain had receded.

Cyann grinned as she considered Tychon's reaction to that career choice. *How's Tik?*

Thirsty.

Anders moaned and mumbled something. She reached for a cooler to sponge his face when she realized that her khamal with Kiran no longer felt like a hive of stinging insects loose inside her head.

Any sign of the others? she asked hopefully.

Nothing. Should definitely be here by now.

Cyann secured Anders to the gurney and then returned to the cockpit where she stood, hands on hips, to stare at the display screens that refused to show what she wanted to see. None of the scanners revealed any vessel in range; only the asteroid field remained, gaining speed steadily as it hurtled toward the breach. Even without the Tughan's eyes to show her the whipping flares of energy leading the cloud, the image of the asteroid and its vast field of debris had taken on an oddly malevolent shape that was likely entirely in her mind.

Kiran joined her and curled up on one of the pilot couches where he rocked silently back and forth, uninterested in the data displays that she observed with diminishing hope.

"Maybe he didn't make it," she said finally. "Or they didn't catch him."

"Possible."

"Maybe they just need more time."

"We don't have time."

"So what do we do?"

He lifted his shoulders in an unfinished shrug. "Nothing. Too late now."

"What do you mean?"

"When the flares find the keyhole I won't be able to turn the field. It's just too damn big. Too damn big!"

"Can't we try to do this ourselves? You are the Tughan! This is child's play for you."

He shook his head. "Might have been, once. The Shantirs were right, you know. The Tughan Wai shall destroy the enemies of Delphi. So it's been told. I don't suppose those damn wizards thought I'd destroy Delphi right along with them. This is what happens when you don't leave things alone! You get destroyed, just like Delphi promised. The Tughan will get you in the end."

"No one could have foreseen this!"

His hand whipped out and gripped her wrist. She recoiled instinctively when he blasted her mind with a series of images that buckled her knees and dropped her into the co-pilot bench. "No!" she gasped. Blindly, she saw a battle field on a desert planet. Not planes in the air or missiles dropping from the sky, but thousands of individuals who looked much like the Jur descending upon a fleeing mob. They wielded no guns but she saw devices that spread a yellow fog over the arid landscape. People fell by the dozens to be stepped on by the advancing invaders like the lifeless biomass they had become. In the wake of the attackers came a line of ground vehicles that collected the fallen Jur and loaded them into bins. She turned her mind away from even considering the purpose of this harvest.

"That was my home," Kiran whispered. "I left Trans-Targon to get out of the way. To stop killing. To grow up where I won't harm anybody else. The Jur took the boy into their homes and there was peace in my head for a few years. Didn't have to think about anything, do anything. They are quiet people. Gentle people. But also boring. I left them for a while. To look around; to get parts for the Eagle. And when I got back the others had come. Thousands. My Jur family were dead. Taken for food. All but Tik. The ground was scorched, water poisoned." He released her wrist.

"So you took revenge?"

"Did." He coughed something sounding like laughter. "Killed everybody. Took me minutes. Didn't even take them into the Tughan. Just made them dead."

Cyann closed her eyes, unwilling to imagine the carnage. "And you took their transport and brought the survivors to the asteroid. To find them a new home."

"You'd think I'd get that right, wouldn't you? Wouldn't you! Exiled them on a dreary rock with bad food and bad air and nothing to do but turn on themselves, exposed them to a disease-riddled comet and then gave them a damn weapon! And now I'm visiting all of this on Trans-Targon. Delphi didn't foresee this? They designed me for this!"

"That's what did it," she guessed. "Destroying the Jur like that started to jumble things in your mind. And the radiation on the asteroid made it worse."

"So now you have a demented Tughan," he said. "A botched experiment. Best to stay over here. Best to not *be* at all."

She watched his haunted face for a moment, hovering somewhere between sympathy and fury. He had returned to rocking himself, eyes squeezed shut, mumbling. "So now you're just going to give up?"

He looked up, puzzled. "It's too late. Too late. The keyhole promises sub-space and that's what draws it. Faster and faster. There isn't room to turn it now."

"There has to be something we can do with this thing." She gestured at their screens. "Think!"

He looked from her to the displays.

"Can't you, I don't know, dampen that energy field? Deflect the flares if not the asteroid? Dislodge the anomaly itself? If we can slow the asteroid we can offload the Jur and take them to Trans-Targon."

He shook his head. Then he stared at her for a time but she was certain that he wasn't seeing her at all. He raised a hand and poked his finger into the air like someone working out a mental calculation. His brow furrowed and he flinched as if something unpleasant had crossed his mind. "There is something," he said finally.

"What?"

"Collapse the keyhole."

She blinked. "Collapse it? Is that even possible?"

"Mathematically, yes. Mentally, yes. Physically, no."

"How?"

"Use the anomaly's own energy when it gets there with the cloud." He looked up at the monitor showing the asteroid field's velocity and trajectory. Something like new hope brightened the color of his eyes. "Yes. I can do this. But I need you for this. You're a Cyann. I made you strong. I won't hurt you. It may be enough."

She observed him silently for a moment. "That's going to leave us stuck here. Alone."

"Yes."

"The *Scout* won't make it to the next keyhole at this speed without running out of supplies for us."

"True."

"So we either die out here or go back to the asteroid and hope they don't shoot us. Maybe hide there, like you did, until the next jump."

"I'm used to it. You'll get used to it."

"It drove you mad!"

He shrugged. "Closing the keyhole is more important, isn't it? It'll save your Trans-Targon sector so they can keep having their rebel wars and their solstice parties, and their far-too rich Union Commonwealth. Don't be selfish, Little Blue."

She shut her eyes, once again fighting tears that threatened to overwhelm her. The idea of being lost in space was something all who refused to remain on their home worlds had to grapple with at some point. Equipment failure, hostile species, miscalculated jumps, rebels and pirates all added up to a great deal of hazard. One accepted the risk or stayed at home. She had opted for the risk and had trained for its outcomes. But how fair was this, now that Jovan had finally come to his senses? She had waited all of her life for him and now this?

Kiran patted her arm. "Survival chance is much higher now, seeing how you blew up the Jur's entire ruling class. Very clever of you." He grimaced. "You won't like the food, though. Awful stuff."

"I don't find this the least bit amusing, Elder Brother! How do you know what waits for us on the other side of the next damn keyhole if we ever get there? Could be the next damn galaxy!"

He shrugged. "Maybe a good galaxy. Don't be negative. It's depressing." He pointed a long finger at the com panel beside her.

"What?" she snapped and turned. At that moment, the com system emitted a mild warble. She pounced on it.

"Jovan?"

"It's your father," came Tychon's reply. He sounded exhausted after the long jump through sub-space. "But your beau is with me, as are our Shantirs." There was a slight pause. "You'll need a bit more speed, *Scout*."

"We lost the crossdrives. That's not the only problem. The people on the asteroid have a weapon. They will fire if we get too close. Our shields are useless against them."

"We're coming for you," Jovan entered the transmission.

"There is no time! Check the cloud's acceleration."

"Nigel, is there any way you can kick that engine a bit?"

"Nigel isn't with us," Cyann said. "They... they killed him. Anders is very sick. And Kiran says there is nothing he can do with the engines, either." She swallowed hard. "We're going to close the keyhole before the asteroid gets there. You have to leave. Go back, please."

There was a momentary, stunned silence. Finally Tychon spoke. "That's not going to happen."

"We're all right," she said through gritted teeth. "There is another keyhole. Tughan knows what it's damn well doing." She looked to Kiran. *Make them go back. Open the keyhole and shove them in there. We can do this without them.*

He nodded earnestly. *I'll deal with them.* He reached out and tugged on a loose strand of her hair. "Time's up," he said.

Clearly, they heard a sharp intake of breath through the speakers. "Kiran?" Tychon said. His voice caught when he said the word.

"Hello, Dadda," Kiran said. "Time to close the keyhole now. No time for fainting. No time for crying. Khamal time. All hands on deck!" He took Cyann's hand. "Everyone gather 'round. Bring in the Shantirs."

"How will you..." Jovan said but then interrupted himself. "Never mind, don't say it. Tughan knows what it's doing. The Shantirs are ready. Tychon's a little done in from the jump from Trans-Targon but he will join us. Hold on."

Cyann held Kiran's hand anxiously, idly wondering what

it had taken for Tychon to agree to a khamal with a Shantir other than Jovan. He had not done so for all the years she had known him. Even when he had taken a poisoned dart in the shoulder while working in the wilderness of Phi he had sought out the Union's doctors for a cure rather than turn to the Shantirs, as any Delphian would.

"Ready," Jovan said.

Kiran dropped his head in his hand and almost immediately Cyann felt herself lifted upward and out as he took her along, through the vast empty of space, to reach the joined minds of the Delphians that awaited them like a distant signal in the dark.

One by one, the others were touched by the Tughan. She recognized and accepted Tychon's fatigued but unwavering presence. One of the Shantirs, unknown to her, brought with him some fears that distracted; the other one held firm. She smiled when Jovan met her in what felt like a mental embrace. Minutes passed while their link established and each found their place in this rare conjunction.

All in a row, all in a row, Kiran sent, apparently pleased. *Now we wait.*

For what? Tychon asked.

That. Kiran reminded them of the asteroid field hurtling toward them at ever-increasing velocity, now catching up to the *Scout* limping through space. They saw it on their screens as a wall of floating rock and a long scroll of numbers, and they saw it in the Tughan's mind as preceded by a vast flare of colorful radiation. The energy field began to reach long tongues toward the breach in space that had caught its attention.

Get out of the way! Jovan sent urgently. *It's almost on top of you.*

That's the plan, Shantir. Be still. Help me stay on this. Hold me, hold me.

Help him focus, Cyann translated.

Each of them concentrated on Kiran's chaotic state of mind, using their abilities to help him calm and align his thoughts and myriad moods. It was noisy and quickly drained their resources, soon requiring the Shantirs to support each other as well.

Cyann stared wordlessly at the asteroid cloud looming impossibly large on the *Scout*'s main screen as it barreled past. "Hurry!" she said. Did they even have enough time and speed to catch up to the asteroid? Would it simply careen past to leave them drifting helplessly in its wake?

Would Kiran care if it did? She recalled both Tik and Kiran confiding that he found death preferable to remaining on the asteroid, tortured by the unstable energy field and the people who lived there. "Kiran..."

"Shh," he said. "Hush, little sister. Watch."

She gripped her armrests when a massive plasma surge whipped toward them. Their sensors went blank and strident alarms sounded from all cockpit components. She had no sense of motion but she understood by the alarmed responses from the others aboard the distant *Eagle* that the energy Kiran had drawn from the asteroid enveloped them completely. It took a moment before all of them realized that the Tughan had flung the *Scout* toward the keyhole coordinates just as he had flung Jovan's pod earlier. She heard Kiran laugh.

"Gods!" Tychon said aloud from the speakers in the ceiling. "You're here!"

She blinked and looked over the console. "Life support gone but reserves holding. Got about an hour."

"You have no shields," Jovan reported. "Can you clear the dock? We'll lock on to you."

"Yes, done." She switched the transmitter off and turned to Kiran. "Why did you do this? We can do it without them. Send them back to Trans-Targon now!"

"We'll extend the shields once we got them," they heard Tychon say to Jovan. "Gravity is going to get ugly. Spin us down to—"

Stop!

All of them fell silent, startled.

Quiet. Shut up. Help me and the Cyann, stupid Delphians! Keyhole! Keyhole!

"He's right," Cyann said. "Look! Those flares are going to hit you."

Help the Tughan. Shut up. No more voices! Open the keyhole and go to Nova. Quick!

"What? We're not leaving you," Jovan exclaimed.

You won't. We will close it from there. From the Trans-Targon side. Then everyone is home.

"Is that even possible?"

"Shut up!" Kiran glared at Cyann. *Doesn't anybody just do what they're told anymore?*

"Do it," Cyann said. "Do as he says."

The Shantirs resumed their khamal with Kiran, all of them rattled and slow to return their legendary Delphian focus to the Tughan. Cyann felt a heavy thump against the *Scout's* side when Tychon carefully maneuvered the *Eagle* into its lock.

Shields ready, he sent but all of them felt the uncertainty in his statement. *Going negative.* He began to feed the Eagle's energy into the keyhole, gradually forming the aperture that would allow entrance into sub-space. It responded readily but so, to their dismay, did the asteroid. All of them clearly shared a vision of the towering wall of rubble bearing down on their flea-size bit of technology.

Too fast, Kiran exclaimed. *GoGoGoGo now!*

Not ready, Tychon replied. *Give me time. The exit isn't—*

No! Go now! The Tughan shifted his focus to take control of the joined ships and punched forward, into the breach.

"Too late!" Cyann shouted. "It's here. It's going in with us!"

Collapse it, Kiran said, mostly to himself. *Close it now.*

"With us in it?" Jovan gasped. "Are you—"

They were inside. The total nothing inside the breach removed all sensation and any connection they had to any real dimension. No sound, nothing to touch, nothing to see. Only their minds remained joined, terrified and unable to comprehend something none of them had experienced before. Milliseconds passed like hours. Cyann felt a scream but not certain whose. It might have been her own.

Closed there, Kiran shouted into their minds. *Closed it. Closed it! Cloud's left behind. Now we run. Or get crushed. Crush is a funny word.* Desperate to keep the sub-space breach open long enough for them to escape at its terminus, the Tughan held them in a grip that threatened to push their sanity to its breaking point. Something, somewhere, suddenly went missing and when Kiran roared in anguish she knew that one of the Shantirs had become the Tughan's latest acquisition.

Don't stop now, she sent. *It's all right. Not your fault. Keep going!*

They were free. The *Scout* careened from the keyhole, hampered by the smaller Eagle, and lurched into real-space at a dangerous velocity. Alarm systems screamed. What lights still worked flashed their warnings. Cyann realized, after a moment, that she was still alive. Their khamal had severed. A few of the indicators calmed when Tychon steadied the ships and brought them to a halt.

"Kiran?" She sat up. "Kiran!"

He lay limply on the other bench, eyes shut. She bent over him, her face close to his and her hands on his bony chest, feeling for signs of life. "Kiran! We're home. Please wake up!" A jump of this depth, even under normal conditions, took a tremendous toll on any navigator. But what she had witnessed was beyond what should even be possible. What unfathomable mental power had kept the collapsing sub-space breach open for even the few seconds it took to span it? Tychon had not had time to program their terminus. Had they even exited in the correct place?

"Is anybody there?" she said to the ceiling. "Anybody?"

"We're here!" Jovan's voice reached her, jubilant. "We made it, Cy! We're out! Nova's coming for us."

"Kiran's not waking up! Help me!"

Moments later she heard the door to the *Scout*'s air lock opened by someone not one bit concerned about decontamination protocols. Long strides thundered down the main corridor and then Tychon entered the cockpit. He scooped Cyann up and held her briefly before releasing her to lean over Kiran. Carefully, he gathered the thin body into his arms and turned to lower both of them to the floor.

"Kiran," he said gently. "You're back." He stroked the lank hair from his son's face. "Don't you leave again," he whispered. "We're taking you home. You're safe."

Kiran opened his colorless eyes which, after a few unfocused moments, found Tychon. "Dadda," he smiled. His chest lifted in rapid and shallow breaths. "Can't go home. Just going to sleep now."

"Don't leave," Tychon pleaded. "Stay with us. Please." He held Kiran closely, his face hidden from Cyann.

Jovan rushed into the room and dropped to his knees beside Tychon and Kiran. "Let me help him, Tychon," he said gently. "Let him go."

Gradually, grudgingly, Tychon loosened his hold on Kiran but when Jovan reached for him, Kiran waved him away. "Don't touch me, Shantir. I will kill you, too," he rasped. His eyes shifted to Cyann. "The Tughan isn't coming home. They made me too dangerous, you know that. *They* knew that. I can't stay."

Cyann crouched beside Jovan and took Kiran's hand. "I don't believe that." She brushed her fingers over his cheek. "I think you forgot the other part of the story. The Tughan was designed to protect Delphi, wasn't he? You've done that. You've saved Delphi. And everybody else. That cloud would have destroyed us all. Without the Jur on there, you might never have known in time. We would not even have had any warning."

He frowned as he considered her words.

"Let us help you now. Let the Tughan rest. But let my brother come home. We need Kiran. Tychon needs Kiran."

Kiran's eyes moved to Tychon and then to Jovan.

Jovan raised his hands and, when Kiran said nothing more, dared to touch the Tughan's forehead. He stifled a groan and closed his eyes, looking for whatever it was that allowed the Shantir to reach into an injured mind. His lips moved but words did not appear.

Cyann allowed tears, finally, to stream freely over her face as she watched Tychon hold his son in the bend of his arm like the boy he had once been, both hope and dread clear on the Delphian's face. She moved around Kiran's sprawled limbs to sit next to her father on the floor, grateful when he pulled her close with his free arm. They waited.

Numberless moments ticked by before Jovan nodded. "I think I got him back," he said, his voice a whisper. Kiran still hung limply in Tychon's arm but his breathing was deeper now. Jovan glanced at Cyann, as aware as she that what he got back would not be what Tychon had lost so many years ago. "He needs to rest." He sank back and scrubbed his face tiredly before squinting at Cyann. "You blew up the Jur guides?" he said. "All of them?"

Tychon lifted Kiran from the ground. "I'll take him into Anders' cabin. I'll stay with him." He stopped briefly at the cockpit door without turning. "Thank you, both, for bringing my son home."

Cyann and Jovan struggled to their feet. She had no memory of ever feeling as tired and exhausted. "Can you check on Anders? I'll let the *Repha Zi* know that we're probably contaminated. We need a decon tunnel to the clean room and get Anders and Kiran out of here before we run out of air. That gravity is going to be hard on them. Oh, and Tik. Need to check on her!"

Jovan stopped her from rushing out the door and pulled her into his arms. "She'll be fine. Take a moment. Let the others do their job now. It's over." He kissed her damp face. "You are an extraordinary woman."

She smiled. "I'm a Cyann."

EPILOGUE

The last time Cyann had been permitted into this space seemed like eons ago. No less magnificent, the undisturbed blanket of snow had been replaced by expanses of low growth covered in tiny dots of yellow flowers. Allowed to grow naturally, it resembled waves of green moving in the breeze. Curling wands of night fern edged flagstone pathways shaded by the fronds of purple sentinel palms undulating over their heads.

Jovan walked beside her, respectfully garbed in his Shantir's robe. He, too, took a moment to admire the pleasing arrangements of verdant growth, stone and wood all around them. Both of them slowed their steps when they passed a basin of water on which floated large, colorful leaves. She glanced around and quickly nipped off a seed pod from one of the spent flowers among them.

He laughed. "We used to sneak out here when I was a boy to pilfer these." He bent to take one for himself. "I think all of the novices dare each other at least once. Of course, these days I'm allowed." He tasted the sweet treat. "Although I think they taste better when you steal them."

They continued onward through a blooming arbor to a shaded rest stop in the gardens of the Shantir enclave. A few benches were placed here and Cyann's steps quickened when she saw that one of the people waiting for them was her brother.

Seeing that Kiran was about to get up, she rushed to sit beside him before embracing him carefully. "I'm so happy to see you out here!" she said.

Jovan also took a seat but remembered to greet his elders. "Shan Moghen," he said to his mentor. "Shan Regin, thank you for allowing us to visit today."

Cyann blushed. "Yes, thank you." She turned to Kiran. "Thank you for letting us come see you."

He nodded. "I'm glad you came. I was not well, earlier."

She hooked her arm around his, pleased to note that some of the wasted muscle was restoring itself and his emaciated frame had begun to fill out. When they had arrived on Delphi he had spent weeks in reduced gravity with Shantir healers who worked with him to repair his body and begin to repair his mind. Moghen himself had been the first to dare to touch the Tughan via khamal, setting an example for the Shantirs selected to help Kiran restore some order to his tormented brain.

Kiran had responded well, eager to escape the pain and, once free of the effects of the asteroid that had held him captive, able to reach out to the healers. Through this, Tychon had remained at the enclave and rarely left his side. Cyann suspected that Tychon had finally made some sort of peace with the Shantirs but did not trust them entirely with his fragile firstborn. Finally, Kiran had sent word that he wanted to see Cyann and so she and Jovan immediately returned to Delphi.

"You look so well now!" she said. He was no longer as pale as he had been and his hair was neatly braided. More importantly, the glassy stare of his eyes had been replaced by a deep Delphian blue and his voice had lost that rapid cadence of his rants. He had chosen to wear the simple robe of the novices but his feet were still bare.

"I'm getting better," he said. "And stronger. I don't have to rest as much."

She reached up and stroked his forehead. "And in there? How are you feeling?"

He smiled and nodded toward Moghen. "I am in good hands. Things are quieter now and I can speak my own words. At least that's what it feels like. What I mean to say is actually what leaves my lips. Most of the time."

Cyann tried to peer through Moghen and Regin's non-committal expressions. "And... I mean... Are you still the Tughan?"

"Very much so," Moghen answered for Kiran. "But we hope that Shan Kiran will be able to take control of it."

Jovan raised an eyebrow. "He could lose it again. I can't help thinking that this could get very dangerous."

"It already is. Kiran is here because he wants to be here. Certainly, none of us have the means to stop him if he decides to leave, in case you're wondering why he's not locked up in chains somewhere."

Jovan grinned. "Yes, I supposed I was."

"For now, we join with him to subdue some of the processes, to help him slow down and determine priority functions. Some of us are constantly linked to him." He acknowledged Cyann with a small movement of his hand when she looked up, concerned. "So is his wish, don't worry. He is not captive, with or without chains. He has the ability to break our khamal as he wishes."

"But he doesn't," Kiran said. "This is as it must be right now. Maybe I'll never be able to leave here."

"I hope you will," Cyann said. "Although the peace of this place is glorious."

"And so much color!" he said. "There are vines over there of such red as you've never seen. I have some of them in my room."

"Speaking of red," she laughed when Tik toddled into the arbor. Her flat shape was dressed in a sumptuous wrap in brilliant shades of red fitted with a stiff hood to protect her translucent skin from Delphi's sun. The long-toed feet were also still bare and her mouth was smudged with berry juice. She climbed up on the bench to sit beside Kiran who handed her a corner of his robe to wipe her face. Cyann noticed a tight-fitting suit under her clothes, likely some sort of external support to keep her upright in this gravity. "You look very pretty, Tik."

Tik's edges flashed green with pleasure.

"She seems to be doing well," Jovan said. "You were able to adjust her to life here on Delphi, I see."

Kiran nodded. "A Tughan's prerogative, I think," he said with a glance at Moghen. "Although it is not my intent to enter into the GenMod business."

"With one exception," Moghen said. He turned to Cyann. "Shan Kiran has agreed to work with our geneticists on the issues we face with our dwindling population."

"How so?"

"We know that choice of mate, libido and reproductive cycles aren't the problem. But Kiran may have some thoughts similar to what made your birth possible, Cyann."

"You're talking about Delphians," Jovan said. "Our people balk at cutting their hair, never mind having their DNA rearranged."

"I'm not so sure," the Shantir replied. "We already have inquiries from some of our childless Shantirs here to meet this Tughan Wai. If we increase the family size of even a fraction of our population, our future is safe."

Kiran nudged Tik with his elbow. "Tughan isn't done saving Delphi."

She gurgled something in reply that was probably not meant to be understood by the others.

"Only the Shantirs know that Kiran has returned?" Cyann asked.

"Lord Phera knows, along with a few others on Kiran's side of the clan. Some Air Command agents and officers know what you brought back from the Badlands. We assured them that he remains in seclusion, unable to communicate." He paused a moment. "It may be necessary to inform them that we've had to terminate the Tughan, for everyone's safety. They don't have the authority to demand access to him, but we don't believe they will stop trying to reach him.

Neither, I'm afraid, will the Union's enemies."

"So you'll stay here, then," Cyann said to Kiran.

"It's safe here," Kiran said after some thought. "But I can't hide forever." He looked down at his little companion. "Tik's been my only family for years. My other little sister. I survived because of her. But she is lonely and misses her people. Someday I may try to find them for her. Perhaps they will have found their home."

"We'll keep an eye out," Cyann promised.

"Yes! I heard. Tychon told me you were going to travel. Tell me more."

Jovan smiled. "Cy signed up to join the specialist team on the next outbound I'm navigating. Big research vessel. She's going to run the exobiology lab."

"We have a huge cabin to ourselves. They treat their spanners well," Cyann added. "We'll be gone two years but we'll be in range fairly often. I'll send message packets. You make sure to answer them."

"I will. What did Uncle Anders have to say about that?"

"He blustered a while, complaining about losing his crew. But I think he and Tychon are planning a few trips into the Badlands by themselves. Something they've been planning to do since Anders got his stripes."

Kiran nodded. "I hope someone is willing to lend them a ship. So when are you leaving?"

"Before Winter. I want to spend some time with you, if you'd like."

"I'd love!"

She winked at Jovan. "And finish basic flight school. You never know when you might be stuck on an asteroid without a pilot."

* * *

*

ABOUT THE AUTHOR

Chris Reher is a first generation Canadian currently and out of necessity residing on planet Earth (which, in the general and interplanetary scheme of things, could *really* use a catchier name. Imagine heading past Proxima Centauri and someone asks you whence you came and you tell them "dirt". All theological implications aside, that just won't do.)

When not finding ways to defy the laws of physics or torture her subjects or entice them with inter-species hanky-panky, she designs web sites or writes about designing web sites. She enjoys long walks on the beach or, given the local beach shortage, writes about beaches far beyond Proxima Centauri.

www.chrisreher.com

Sky Hunter
The Catalyst
Only Human
Rebel Alliances
Delphi Promised

Quantum Tangle
Terminus Shift
Entropy's End